DAMAGED & DANGEROUS

THE SACRED HEARTS MC BOOK 6

A.J. DOWNEY

COPYRIGHT

~

ISBN: 978-0692527634

Edited by Barbara J. Bailey

Book design by Maggie Kern

Cover art by Dar Albert at Wicked Smart Designs

DEDICATION

To Jennifer Mitsada, Bethany Stonebraker, Jennifer Wolf, Melanie Beswick, Sherelle Ross, Christina McCormick-Franco, Deanna Bewley-Davis, Gabrielle Prendergast, and all the folks in NaNoRotica for all your support. Seriously. Y'all are my favorite bitches to bitch about bitches with. You've kept me sane, propped me up, pushed me to keep going and have just generally cheered me on through a lot of things going sideways over this last summer. This is for you.

PROLOGUE

Four months ago…

Dani…
I hated this. I hated what I'd become and I wished that Jared had never brought me here. Life wasn't a fairy tale, though. It never would be. There wouldn't be any Prince Charming to come to save the day. And I wasn't some fairy tale princess, either. I was just an idiot girl who had loved an idiot boy. And now here I was, sprawled naked and open on the pool table, the felt rubbing my back raw as my Ol' Man pounded his cock mercilessly inside of me.

The big problem was: I didn't want him. I had never wanted him, had never felt anything close to desire for the giant ass, and I never would. I had loved Jared, believed in him and our teenage dreams, but that had all turned to shit the minute he decided to prospect for the Suicide Kings Motorcycle Club.

I winced as Pig-Pen grunted above me. I turned my head to the side, away from having to look at him. I'd become good at disassociating over the years, at finding a place inside my own head where I could pretend that I wasn't here, that I was some other girl, in some other place, a girl who was happy and carefree, who had never been idealistic, who had never believed that Jared would protect me and that I was his special girl. He had been so stupid! And me? I had been stupid right along with him. I had been so incredibly naïve to believe that this was just a club, or that these men actually looked out for one another.

I. Was. So. Stupid.

I felt eyes on me, which was nothing new, and I let my gaze focus for a moment, sliding along the wall, over the couches and low coffee tables.

There.

He sat on the end of one couch with a foot propped nonchalantly on the edge of the table in front of him, the beer in his hand resting casually on his knee. I knew they watched; they always watched. Some even took their dicks in hand and jerked off while they watched. I hated it. I always had, I always would, and this was no exception.

Pig did it just to punish me, the public sex. Honestly, the rough public fucks were always worse than the beatings were. Those only happened when I really pissed him off. At the same time, the public sex didn't always hurt the next day. That, at least, was something to be grateful for, right? Well, they didn't hurt, unless Pig-Pen was in a sharing mood. Then they hurt. They hurt a lot, and for a long time.

My thoughts drifted back to this particular man and his staring. I had to admit there was something different about him. His cool green eyes slid over me as he watched my tits bounce, his expression distant. He looked at me stoically, appraising, but with a detached interest. It was almost as if he was watching one of the other guys fix a bike.

Finally, it struck me what was different. Unlike the others, he was not amused by my plight. A deep, hidden sorrow filled his eyes for a fraction of a second when they met mine. I swallowed hard. I didn't cry anymore when Pig-Pen did this to me, but there was something about the way this unknown, new prospect looked at me. It caused my hidden shame to rush to the surface, pricking the backs of my eyes with hot tears.

I tore my eyes away from the man and turned my head to the empty wall on my other side. Pig-Pen grunted and thrust into me one last time before letting out a gusty, satisfied sigh. He slapped my tits together and pulled out, tucking himself back into his pants, and all I wanted was to fucking shower.

"You want a piece, Prospect?"

I was horrified at the question. I mean, I knew I'd pissed him off. But he'd never offered me up to one of the prospects before. I clamped my mouth shut on my bitterness and covered my chest with my arms as I blushed furiously.

"No thanks, man. I'm good," the unknown man called from the couch.

"Suit yourself. Get gone, Coon, I'm fuckin' sick of looking at you." He gave my outer thigh a rough, stinging slap. I sat up immediately, then jumped down from the pool table and snatched my dress off the floor. He didn't need to tell me twice.

I hated that nickname 'Coon' hated it to the very bottom of my soul. I wasn't Dani Broussard anymore, I was Raccoon. Rac, if they were feeling charitable, but still. The nickname was a result of just about always sporting two black eyes from Pig-Pen, whom no one fucked with. Forget about standing up for his bitch, his property. The name reduced me to a nothing, a non-person like the rest of the strung-out meth- and heroin-junkie whores who hung around Pig and the Suicide Kings. I had never truly been one of them, though, and never would be. No matter how bad it'd gotten over the last three years, I had never touched that shit voluntarily. I'd die first.

I bolted for the nearest bathroom, taking advantage of Pig-Pen's order to get fucking gone. He didn't have to add the 'or else' anymore. Still, I felt the prospect's sympathetic gaze slide down my nude back as I clipped along the narrow hall out of the game room. The back of my neck stung with heat. Whether I was feeling a blush of humiliation or a burn from the friction of the pool table's felt, I had no clue. All I knew was that I had been dismissed, and I wanted gone. I wanted gone so badly it was a sharp ache in the center of my chest. I slammed the door to the bathroom behind me and leaned heavily against it, jumping when Pig-Pen's booming voice filtered through the red-painted wood.

"Bitch!" he bellowed, "what the fuck did I tell you about slamming doors?" I held my breath until my chest burned and waited for him to start hammering on the other side. Long moments ticked by, and I slowly let the breath out.

Just yelling this time. No banging, no pounding, no fists... I was so relieved, the tears that had started earlier on the pool table came back again. I sniffed and forced them down. There was no sense in crying. If Pig saw it, he would just flip his lid. And I didn't need that.

1

Present day…

R ed-XIII
The wind was cold, a blade made out of pure ice that cut across my exposed skin. That is, what little skin showed between my face mask and the ski goggles I used in the wintertime. I was a full-time rider: no cage, no fair-weather bullshit. I was on the back of my bike, rain or shine, and that's just how it was. It had its disadvantages, like moving to a climate that actually had snow and freezing temperatures, but I adapted. That's why I got the assignments I did.

My main objective: to feed information to my real club. The secondary one? Running across state lines with a couple of Suicide King douchebags called Bandit and Flyer. This was the eighth time in the last six months I'd gone out on a run, and the first time still fucking got me. That first run had been just in time for me to miss a raid on the SHMC's clubhouse – a raid that'd gotten one of our officers killed, along with another officer's Ol' Lady.

We were all, and by 'all', I meant both Sacred Hearts and Suicide Kings, stepping lightly for now. The clubhouse invasion was a cluster-fuck on both sides from the word 'Go'. The Suicide Kings were a fucking joke as far as clubs went, just as much at war on the inside as they were on the outside. Griz wasn't holding shit down for shit as Pres. And to top it off, there was Pig-Pen, his VP, who had a habit of getting some really fucking great ideas when he was high. Pig had enough guys terrified of his fucking psycho ass that they'd go along with whatever he said, as long as it kept them off his fucking radar.

Only reason Pig's reign of terror worked was because the club was mostly made up of new kids who didn't know any better, or dudes who were just that fuckin' dumb.

I about shit a brick sideways when D had called and told me what went down. As a prospect, I wasn't entirely up on what was what. Any club worth their salt kept it that way until a prospect proved himself. At least the Suicide Kings had *that* half right.

I'd moved up from hang-around to prospect inside a month, which was un-fucking-real and, honestly, just a stroke of good luck. There had been a barroom brawl and I'd had Pig-Pen's back, busting a bottle over some dude's head who'd been about to waylay the SK's VP with a chair. Griz had seen it and told Pig-Pen to make a note of it. But Pig, ever on his Own Fucking Program, took that to mean he should move me up a rank. I could tell it didn't sit well with Griz, but at the same time, what had been done couldn't be undone, not without losing face, so I'd graduated a couple months ahead of my class. Some serious fucking half-assed bullshit if I ever saw any. Especially considering that I knew where everything and everyone was inside the first month.

Inside those first few weeks, I was able to tell D and the guys exactly where the Suicide Kings' meth operation was. I gave 'em Griz's home address, too. They'd gotten the drop on Danimal and Joker at the meth lab. Joker thought he was hot shit, slashing Blue like he did, but Blue was fucking fine. The meth lab was another story, blown to hell and gone. If that hadn't left Griz and Pig frothing-at-the-mouth pissed! Especially Pig, now that his steady supply of crank was all dried up. Poor baby.

I'd told D he should have killed those two rotten fucks, but he'd disagreed. Maybe he was going soft in his old age. Who the fuck knew? But after Chandra and Reaver ... shit, man. I could feel it through the line, how much he was kicking himself for not listening to me. The thing I liked and respected most about D was that he didn't make the same mistake twice.

I rolled to a stop with Bandit and Flyer and sighed. We were almost back to the SKMC's house, which was just a badass retrofitted garage building in an industrial area. No real sleeping quarters, not that that stopped them from crashing out there, but it had the main club staples of any house: booze, drugs, bitches, and some game tables.

I fully intended to call dibs on their hockey table once we had all these sons of bitches in the ground. It was the one thing the SHMC's house, which did have all the comforts of home, was lacking. Not to mention, my real club had way classier Ol' Ladies and club sluts. I wouldn't stick my cock into any of these bitches, even after wrapping it twice.

Coon.

The name came unbidden to my mind and conjured up the image of long black hair, silkier than a crow's wing, and cornflower-blue eyes that were un-fucking-real. Those eyes were surrounded by long, dark lashes and pale, perfect skin that just begged to be touched. She was the only looker out of all the club's washed-out, drugged-up bitches, and she was completely different from them all at the same time. She didn't use. Her eyes were too sharp, too clear, and all it took was one look to know that she was fucking smart. So I didn't have any fucking idea of A) why she was hanging around here, and B) how the hell she was hooked up with Pig-Pen, the worst of all of the fucking guys.

"Hey! Pretty-boy! Stop yer fuckin' dreamin', get yer shit, and let's go!" I looked over to Flyer. He had his nose so far up Gordy's ass it was a wonder he didn't have a white film over his eyes like some god-damned cave fish.

Gordy was another real winner. Loyal as all get-out to Griz, and a mean motherfucker. He was the new SAA for the Suicide Kings, since the old one, a dude by the name of Snake, who had served under Sparks and then Griz, had gone down in the attack at the SHMC.

I got off my baby, a fully resto'ed 1963 Harley Davidson panhead. Her skin was a glossy sleek black, and silky smooth to boot. Her chrome gleamed softly under the overcast early March sky. I unfastened my saddlebags and threw them over my arm. With my boots thudding and crunching against the half gravel, half packed-dirt surface of the lot, I made for the club's back steps and Flyer's glowering mug.

"What the fuck you daydreaming about, Prospect?" he demanded as I went to slide past him.

"What do you think, after a long-ass ride like that?" I demanded. He frowned, perplexed, and I threw the dumb fucker a bone. "Pussy!" I exclaimed, and he barked a laugh and slapped me on the back.

"Well, the pussy is inside, boy."

I scowled. "Sure as fuck ain't doing any of these busted-ass hoes," I griped.

"You ain't lyin'," Flyer snorted. "It does in a pinch, and some of 'em suck cock real good."

I felt bad for any of these bitches that were required to put Flyer in their mouth. Not that he was a bad dude to look at, trim but not cut like me, certainly not fat, or old, although he had some liberal doses of white to his short beard and greasy shoulder-length hair. No, the way I heard it, Flyer had partied a little too fucking hard for a dude in his early forties and wasn't entirely careful about who he partied with. He didn't always keep his shit clean, and as a result, he had, on more than one occasion, given a girl some VD or another. Nothing he'd passed around the club had been lethal or incurable yet. But that was the operative word – 'yet'. So far, it was just a case of the clap and something else easily fixed by antibiotics. Not sure of the name, but yeah. I had to shudder inwardly. There was no fucking way I was going to touch any of these bitches with the way these nasty fuckers shared. Except Coon. I might make an exception for her... You know, if she were checked out... and I'd still fucking wrap it up.

Pig didn't share her much. But when he did put her through that particular slice of hell, he insisted that the other brothers wear a rain-coat. I knew Pig fucked around on her, but when it came to any of these other nasty whores, he wore a condom. Even if they were just sucking him off. He may be a drugged-out, crazy, psycho mother-fucker, but at least he had his shit straight on that one thing.

I ruminated on all of this shit as we traipsed through the club. Lo and behold! There was the girl of the hour. Last I'd seen her had been a week-and-a-half ago, after I'd gotten back from the last run. One of the first times I'd ever laid eyes on her, she'd been laid out on the pool table, her eyes vacant and staring as Pig had ravaged her body, plowing into her like he was gonna come out the other side. It was disgusting, and at the same time, fuckin' tragic. I could tell she'd gone someplace else, someplace deep inside her own head, and I couldn't help but study the perfection that was her face.

She'd felt me staring, I think, because her eyes had suddenly focused on me. Whatever she saw on my face, in my eyes, no matter how carefully I'd schooled myself neutral, had hurt her. Her bright eyes were suddenly so much brighter, illuminated by the tears she just barely managed to hold back. She'd turned away then, and I'd felt frozen and heartless down to my very core. Never in my life had I felt more like a depraved douche, and I'd done some pretty spectacu-larly shitty things in my time. That was why I was here, in an effort to balance my Karmic scales some. So far, I felt like I was doing a bang-up fucking job.

"You look like a tool," Pig said, from where he sat at the bar. Rac put another beer down in front of him, a cold one, and whisked away his empty. She turned and continued stocking the bar.

"Good to see you too, man," I said with a smile. He chuckled. I set my bags on the unfinished concrete floor, unfastened my helmet, and ripped the grinning-skull facemask off the bottom of my face. The Velcro gave way with an angry, grating sound. I whisked the amber ski goggles off my face and stretched my jaw, squeezing my eyes shut and opening them wide.

I stuffed the headgear into my overturned brain bucket and set it on the bar before cutting to the fucking chase. I brought the two bricks of speed out of my saddlebags and set them on the bar by Pig's elbow.

"You got a brass pair to go along with that mile-long cock of yours, buddy," he said, taking a toke off the joint he had grasped between his fingers. He held it out to me and I took a hit off it. Weed had never done much for me but mellow me out and give me the munchies, but if I wanted to keep up appearances, this was the way to go. I really wanted no part in any of the other shit these guys did on the regular.

I handed the joint back and exhaled. "Tell me something I don't know," I said.

Pig chuckled. "Get Whitezilla here a beer," he ordered, and I put up my hand in Rac's direction.

"No thanks, darlin'. If it's all the same, and you ain't got nothin' else for me to be doin', I'd like to take a ride out to the ol' homestead and sleep for, like, a week." I racked my neck from side to side, and felt a satisfying pop.

"Yeah, sure thing, man. Good job out there." He held out a hand and I grasped it and let him pull me in and slap me on the back. I returned the favor, then snatched my helmet off the bar. Hoisting my bags up, I made for the door.

I was hooking the bags back up to my bike when the back door swung wide with a bang. I looked up; Rac had run full-tilt into the crash bar and she looked down at me from the top step. She skipped lightly down the back stairs and strode across the lot towards me.

"You dropped this." She held out my face mask and I crooked a smile at her.

"Thanks." I took it from her. "Been meaning to ask you something."

"Oh?" Her tone was cool, but her voice was thick, like she had some kind of a cold or something coming on. I swept my gaze over her porcelain-doll features.

"How'd you end up here?" I asked softly.

"Same way you did," she said.

I had to laugh.

"I doubt that, Sweetheart," I said dryly.

She tilted her head to the side, considering, and started walking backwards towards the steps.

"You're a prospect, aren't you?" she asked.

"Yeah."

"So was Jared. That's how I got here."

I frowned, but she was up the stairs and back inside in a flash. I geared back up and drove home, an hour from here, on a lake. It was a small fishing cabin my granddad had owned, and no one else in my family had wanted. It didn't have electricity, but it served its purpose when I needed a fucking break from these assholes. The woodstove worked, and despite the place being a summer cabin, there were enough permanent residences nearby that it got cell reception.

As soon as I got there, got a fire started and the shit sorted in my bags, I sat down, put my feet up, and pulled out the burner I talked to D on. He picked up on the fourth ring.

"Was wondering when you was gonna check in. I was starting to get worried. How the hell are ya, Thirteen?"

"I'm good, D. They had me go all the way out to fucking Colorado, but the amount of shit I brought back... That should fucking hold off any more runs for a while. You guys about ready to start playin' ball?"

"Girls are good in Florida. I forgot to tell you, there's a bit of a change in plans concerning Rev. His woman is pregnant."

"Is that what that picture was?" I asked.

"How the hell you get that?" he demanded.

"Came through on my personal cell, someone mass-texted it. I have so many goddamned contacts, I didn't realize I still had anybody from the club in it. No worries, my cover is secure. No one saw shit. I don't leave things like that lyin' around."

D grunted into the phone, "Cops're still sittin' on us. They still watching you?"

"If by 'you,' you mean the Suicide Kings, then, yeah. Unmarked tan cargo van when we pulled in from the run. It's a good thing Gordy's a paranoid fucker and sweeps for listening devices on the regular. Pretty sure they only got visual. They'll get tired soon enough and fuck off onto something bigger and better."

"Yeah. With our history, they ain't investigatin', or cryin', too hard about our plight." Dragon sounded both tired and downright pissed-off at that. I didn't blame him. Chandra deserved a lot better. Reave, too! Don't get me wrong, but as a brother, you expect this shit to happen. 'No women and no children' had been the SHMC motto from the beginning, even before our reformed ways. We did some gnarly and seriously rancid shit back in the day. Guns, drugs, gambling – you name it. But we always left the women and children out of it.

No prostituting, no hitting. Rape was liable to get your dick chopped off – which is why, no matter how fucking hard, no matter how often, the Suicide Kings tried to get me to join in on one of their trains, it was no fucking dice. Because, very rarely, if ever, were the chicks they were fucking at all clear-headed or into it.

It bothered me, a whole fuck of a lot, the way these animals treated their women and I found myself spilling it all. I told D everything I'd seen going on, everything I had garnered about their operation, unburdening my soul from all the awful shit I'd been a party to in the name of the greater good, in the name of spying out our enemy. He was quiet for a long time on the other end and finally let out a sigh that made him sound like he felt every single year and every single mile.

It'd been weeks since I last talked to him, beyond a short text. The deeper I got in with these fuckers, the more I was around them, the less opportunity there was for full-on communication.

"Do you need out?" he asked.

My thoughts drifted to Raccoon, to her sharp and calculating stare as she'd passed me my face mask.

"No, man, I'm good. My work ain't over yet. Not by a long, flat, mile. It'll be done when every one of these fuckers is in the ground and the Suicide Kings ain't nothin' but the dust of fuckin' memory."

"Poetic," he said. "What about our little rodent problem?"

"Ain't heard much, on account of bein' out on the road. Just know it's female, and from what I *have* heard, it ain't pillow talk. They're strong-arming her, somehow. I just don't have enough to say who, or how they're doing it. Curse of being a prospect and it being straight-up Gordy and Pipes' show. Those fuckers are paranoid as all get-out, and play things super–close to the vest. I'll let you know when I got something. What about on your end?"

"Narrowing the field of suspects. Been a lot easier since the girls' been stayin' in Florida. If you're sayin' they've been in contact with the rat recent, then it eliminates all of our women in the club." He gave a gusty sigh. "Not that I figured it was any of them in the first place."

"Dray's heading down to the girls this weekend; he's taking Open Road Garage's books down with him for Shelly to go over. She's already been over Open Road Ink's and, as suspected, come up empty. ORG's got employees who aren't strictly club, but it's a club business so we're digging deeper. 'Sides that, the fucker we caught during the raid had some interesting things to say about what our people were up to the day we got hit, and damn few people knew what was up with that. Just keep doing what you're doing and give us a heads up when you can. Stay sharp and straight, Brother; you need out, we can go at this another way."

I sighed, "I'm oh-for-two, but not about to give up yet." I said determinedly.

"Hey! Grinder ain't your fault, boy. Neither is what happened to the club. It was just shitty luck they had you on that run when the club went down. No one knew a goddamned thing about Grinder until the deed was already done. Those fuckers were smart about it and kept their mouths shut until they was sure he was dead. You don't get to take those on."

"Yeah, about that... Rush, Archer, and Nox still in town?" I asked.

"Patched over. They're in it to win it until they got blood for blood on Grinder. They all came up in the system together, under the same roof. May not be blood, but whatever they got is sure as fuck thicker."

"You tell 'em it was a couple of twins that did it. Go by the name of Ace and Deuce. Fucking tweakers and I'm not sure how the fuck they pulled it off, keeping quiet about it for days. I know you guys buried Grinder in a cut, but his cut is hanging nailed to a wall in the Suicide

King's clubhouse like some kind of trophy." Me, I wouldn't give those three any of this until D was ready to turn 'em loose to go hunting. I'd worked with 'em before, and knowing them, they'd go OFP – sorry, that's 'Own Fucking Program' – and settle that particular beef on their own. Still, it wasn't my place to tell the Pres how to run his club.

I tuned back in to what Dragon was saying, "...wheels are turning slower than I'd like but it's a necessary evil. Too many of my guys have been netting themselves Ol' Ladies. I want to see 'em have a better go of it than me 'n' Tilly. Got some damned fine women attached to this club, and I wanna see them and my brothers thrive. Maybe I'm getting maudlin in my old age, who the fuck knows? I just know we were doin' fine until these cocksuckers showed up, and I wanna get back to that as soon as possible. No more dying, no one going to prison, so we gotta do this careful. Not above seizing the moment, though, if you catch my drift."

"I get you."

We were finally getting to that stage. Cops stopped investigating if you behaved like pious little angels long enough. I was surprised they'd hung on this long. Six months was a long time to devote manpower and resources when, by all rights, they should be pleased that the two MC's were taking each other out. I was well aware of the rep my true MC had. It had been well-deserved back in the day.

"Good," Dragon grunted in my ear, pulling me from my walk down memory lane. "Thank you for doing this, Brother. You keep the dirty side down," he finished.

"You too." It was an old saying among bikers, 'keep the dirty side down', and as I hung up I sighed. Unfortunately, I wasn't doing what I was doing to keep the dirty side down. Nope. It was my job to pry up all sorts of rocks to find these fuckers crawling underneath. That way we could crush their sorry asses under our bootheels.

We'd given them every opportunity to leave us be. It was too fucking late for them now. Let God have mercy on their souls, and here was to hoping that this little adventure didn't tip my scales even further out of whack, but rather did something to right them.

2

Dani...
    I didn't know what to make of the prospect. There was something strange and different about him. I returned to the bar after giving him his facemask and finished restocking the booze.

"Coon, go on and get the fuck out of here," Pig ordered.

"Do you want me to stick around the club, or should I go home?" I asked.

"Ain't you got shit to do at home?" he asked. I nodded rapidly and held my breath.

"Well, shit, get you gone, bitch! What'd I just fucking tell you?" he yelled. I flinched, snatched my purse off the shelf under the bar, and skirted around its edge.

"Fucking bitches, man! You have to tell 'em every fucking detail under the goddamned sun. Swear to fucking Christ, they're born with less than half a brain," Pig griped at my back as I made for the back exit. I said nothing. I knew better.

The only time I opened my mouth and put myself in the line of fire was for a new girl. But only until they learned, and only in hopes of them getting away from these animals before it was too late, like it was for me. I did it less and less as time went by, once I realized it was pretty much just wishful thinking on my part. The girls, they never left, and some weren't as innocent as they looked or portrayed themselves to be.

I went back out into the parking lot and coughed. I had this damned cold coming on and I was pretty grateful I was headed home. I was starting to really feel like shit, and just wanted to be alone, to try and create something beautiful. It was both my blessing and my curse.

I'd grown up with my grandfather. My grandmother had died before I was born. My mom had ditched me with my dad, who couldn't take care of me for anything. So, it was his dad who had taken me in, bless his heart. Philip Broussard was French, and a master jeweler. He had taught me everything he knew, and had given me the best childhood a girl could ask for. When I was seventeen, he'd gotten too sick with the cancer to keep his custom jewelry store open. We lived in an apartment above it. The storefront sat vacant now, but his workshop space in our living room and in the shed outside – I'd hung on to those.

My granddad had died when I was eighteen, just after I graduated high school. Jared, my high school sweetheart, had moved in with me and things were good. We lived off my inheritance from my granddad for a while. Then, Jared fell in with this guy named Rabbit, who introduced him to another guy he hung out with. The next thing I knew, I was seeing less and less of Jared. Then one night, he came home in a leather vest and told me he was a prospect in a motorcycle club, and I had to come with him to meet the guys.

That had been a mistake, and it would be the last one he ever made. Pig-Pen declared that I was his, the moment he saw me. He said that prospects didn't get to have girlfriends or Ol' Ladies, that whatever a prospect had, belonged to the club. I didn't understand anything that was going on.

Jared had tried to argue, to fight for me. But Pig-Pen had ordered him beaten to death, and then forced himself on me, turning my life upside-down and inside-out. I didn't dare run. I'd tried it once, and Pig had almost killed me. Then he saw my workbench, found out what I could do with a little bit of metal and a few stones, and suddenly I had value again.

Instead of killing me, he let the whole MC pull a train on me as punishment. He said it was to remind me that if I didn't want to belong to him, there were other arrangements that could be made.

It wasn't long after that, he started bringing me jewelry. *Stolen* jewelry.

I'd done the only thing I could. With what I knew and the skills I'd learned from my grandfather, I kept myself alive. I melted down and re-tooled the stolen shit into new, different, unidentifiable pieces that the Suicide Kings could easily pawn off without any blow-back for the club.

It was my idea, but Pig-Pen had pulled it off so that Griz and Sparks thought he'd come up with the whole thing. It was one of the things that got Pig the VP seat after Sparks was murdered.

I was Pig's dirty little secret, his whore, and his golden meal ticket rolled into one, and he was mean enough and frightening enough that I stayed silent. I never tried to run again.

I let myself into my apartment with a soft, tired sigh, closing the door behind me. I still lived in the sad, shabby, lonely little apartment above the shop. But the workbench - littered with tools, gems, and bits of settings and scrap metal - was a comfort to me. It was a piece of my grandfather and the person I used to be. All the melting and other heat work was done in a little stone shed out back where, if anything happened, there was no risk to the incredibly old building. Up here, in the apartment, I did all my finishing work and polishing.

I took a shower, as I always did after coming back from the club. I hated smelling like weed, cigarettes, and – depending on the night – spilled booze, beer, or Pig. My clothes immediately went into the wash and I made some hot tea. I sat at my worktable and stared at an unfinished piece, hugging my knees.

I never imagined that at age twenty-three, this is what I would be. Or that this is what I would be doing. I closed my eyes and tried not to let the hopelessness, the despair, overwhelm me. I was well aware that I was riding that razor's edge again, like I'd been before Pig discovered what I could do, that I could be an asset to the club. He was doing more drugs than ever, quicker to anger, and even quicker to hit lately. I just tried like hell to stay out of his way, and out of the way of the other brothers with nasty temperaments.

They weren't all bad, at least not to me. Skid, an older man – and by older, I just mean older than me – saw me as the little sister he never had. He was in his late thirties, early forties, and had warm, kind brown eyes. When things got real bad, he turned away and couldn't watch. He kept his distance until I healed up again and didn't make fun. He'd stepped in only once. But if ever there had been a time I'd needed someone to step in, then the time that Pig-Pen tried to brand me was surely it.

Pig-Pen had whooped Skid's ass that night. But I would never, and I mean never, forget what he tried to do to me.

Thankfully, Skid's interference kept me from getting branded with an iron that night, but then Pig dragged me to a tattoo parlor owned by a buddy of his. He'd held me down while the tattooist inked Pig's name under my skin. The ugly mark was on my lower back in big, nasty, spiky script. I suppose I should have been grateful for what Pig-Pen called his 'tramp stamp of approval'. With it being where it was, I didn't have to look at it every day. I could pretend it wasn't there, and only rarely did I catch sight of it in the bathroom mirror.

I scrubbed my face with my hands and sniffed. I hated it when I made a slide on the downward spiral of self-pity, but that was harder and harder not to do, the more time dragged on. The more brothers that disappeared or got themselves killed, the harsher and angrier the guys that were left became.

I think most of that was from fear.

The Sacred Hearts didn't play around. I'd seen that for myself when they'd come out of the woods at their Lake Run, Sparks' bloody vest in the maniac's hands.

He'd looked like some crazed avenging angel, bloody to the elbow, his white shorts spattered and smeared with blood. His cut hung loose over his bare chest. His eyes were hollow and empty, a barren, frozen wasteland, desolate, devoid of anything human.

I banished the image, for fear it would haunt my dreams, like it had, on several other nights since then. That beautiful man with the empty eyes and savage look scared the ever-living shit out of me.

No one knew what had happened, but the rumors and whispers started pretty quick. The one that had turned out to be true was that Sparks had taken one of their women by force, and not anyone's Old Lady, just a club slut, some random girl. I'd been floored. The concept that there were clubs out there that actually valued anything female simply blew my mind. I didn't think such a thing could actually exist. Of course, it didn't exist for me. It never would.

I hung my head with a gusty sigh that ended in a fit of coughing, and picked up my latest project, a heavy gold ring shaped like a crown the whole way around. I was setting rubies into the gold at even intervals, alternating them with diamonds. The piece was something Pig could present to Griz, to make Pig look good, but Pig was a damned idiot. Griz didn't go for a bunch of flashy bling. Still, Pig had told me to make something he could give Griz and I picked this as a lesser evil. It wasn't super flashy. Gold? Yes. Real stones? Yes. But still, the ring was understated and tasteful, and fit within the club's theme.

I managed to carefully set one stone before the jeweler's glasses began to give me a splitting headache, the pressure in my sinuses becoming too much to bear. I set the project aside and got up, going to my room. I plucked a bottle of nighttime cold medicine from my nightstand and took two big swallows of the foul green liquid. I recapped it and laid down in my full-sized bed. The bed was somewhat of a blessing. Pig-Pen hated to sleep over because the bed was too small, so he rarely ever did. I switched out the light, though it was still early. I didn't care. I felt like hell.

I woke to the shrill ring of my phone. I found it on the nightstand and dragged it under the quilt with me.

"Hello?" I answered and winced. I was so stuffy, and I sounded just plain awful.

"Coon, get your ass to the club."

I tried to suck in some air through my nose, but it so wasn't happening. I struggled to sit up, and opened my mouth to speak, but that touched off a fit of coughing.

"Let me take a shower and I'll be right there," I moaned. There was no telling Pig-Pen no, so I didn't try.

"Jesus, what the fuck is the matter with you?" he asked, disgusted.

"Just a cold coming on, I'll be fine as soon as I get moving." That was true. He grunted.

"Hurry the fuck up," he demanded, and the call ended. I dragged myself to my feet and trudged into the bathroom.

3

R ed-XIII...

I leaned back in an old, tired recliner, and watched Raccoon move behind the bar. Girl was getting sick. She looked wrung-out, just exhausted. She was deathly pale, and she had a dry cough coming on. I got up, went to the very end of the bar, and took a seat there. She drifted over after the patched members were all served, and her so-blue eyes lifted slowly from the bar-top up to meet mine.

"What can I get you?" she asked. I tilted my head, considering her. She had on a tight, long-sleeved black top that accentuated her curves. The material was cut in front, over her chest, to create an asymmetrical window pattern, giving glimpses of the pale skin beneath. It was sexy as hell, not because of what it showed, but more for what it didn't. Small peeks, the illusion of mystery. I liked her style.

My eyes fixed on a necklace below the hollow of her throat. It was a crown. White gold –or maybe silver? – nope, gold, by the way the dim light of the club was reflecting off it, I was pretty sure. The piece was wide, the necklace chain attaching to points at either end of the crown. It was made to look like the real deal, set with diamonds in a marquis cut at regular intervals. Between each set of diamonds was a blue stone – something super-light, maybe sapphire, in round cuts. The crown sat on the flat of her chest, beneath her graceful throat. But the *piece de resistance* was a sword, thrust up through the circle of the crown, at an angle, just like the Suicide King on the playing card.

"Hey, Prospect! My eyes are up here." She snapped her fingers in front of her chest and my eyes jumped to them. She brought her hand up and, of course, I followed her fingers, up to her equally-snapping blue eyes.

"What's your name?" I asked. She frowned, her dark brows crushing downward.

"You know my name," she said thickly. "They call me Rac on a good day, Coon the rest of the time." She shrugged. "Now, what do you want?" It was one of the things that impressed me about Coon. She still stood up for herself. Even to Pig-Pen, on occasion. But, looking into those blue eyes of hers, I could see it was pretty much all bravado. The glint of fear was always there, just beneath the surface.

"Now, we both know that ain't your name, Gorgeous." I gave her my best smile, which made her frown more.

"What does it matter? It's who I am now. You drinking or not?" Her irritation was clear, but I wasn't easily deterred.

"Jack and Coke. And that's what they call you, not who you are."

"Okay." She leaned forward with a quick, spidery glance around us to take in who was there. Satisfied that no-one was paying attention to us, she spoke just loud enough for me to hear. "What's your real name, then?"

Interesting. So she'd been around the MC life long enough to know that you just didn't ask that, but she was still brave enough to do it anyways. I smiled genuinely. I liked her moxie. The girl had a fire inside – or a death wish. I couldn't help my mind drifting back to her sprawled on the fucking pool table while Pig-Pen rutted away, back to the glazed, faraway look in her eyes, to the shame and pain in those eyes when she'd caught me looking at her, before she'd turned away.

I looked around and leaned forward. This was dangerous. Names were powerful things. Names led to records, records to histories best left buried. Especially in my case. But I wanted her to trust me and in order to earn trust, you had to give a little, right?

"Chris," I told her. It was true, but it was also pretty generic. She rolled her eyes and I smiled. I knew she was smart. "You gonna tell on me?" I asked.

Her expression cooled considerably, and she looked up the bar toward Pig-Pen. He was deep in conversation with Spade and Dredd, the club's Treasurer and Secretary. She turned back to me, her china-doll face so solemn.

"Don't tell me your last name," she said quietly.

I raised an eyebrow.

"Now, why would you say a thing like that?" I asked.

Her cornflower-blue eyes flicked to my own and, with another careful glance to see who was nearby and who might be listening, she resolutely shut her mouth and poured my Jack & Coke, shaking her head just a little. I leaned over the bar, reaching out a finger. She flinched backward, but in the end she stood her ground.

"Nice piece," I said. I brushed the crown where it rested against her chest, the metal warm from her skin.

"Thanks," she said with a tremble, visibly nervous.

"Pretty-boy!" Pig-Pen slapped the back of my cut and I sat back. Coon slid my drink across the bar to my hand. I smiled at her as I took it. "Got a thing for my bitch?" he asked me.

"Nope, just got a thing for her taste in jewelry; that's a nice piece she's got there."

Pig-Pen looked at the crown and sword necklace. She took it off and handed it to him.

"I was waiting for you to finish talking, I didn't want to interrupt you," she said.

Pig took the necklace from her hand and stared her down. She licked her lips and rushed out, "I finished it last night and that other thing you wanted done? It should be done in a day or two. I just need to cast a couple more settings for it, find the right size and shape stones." She smiled bravely and Pig-Pen pocketed the necklace, nodding.

"You just keep being useful," he said quietly, menacingly. Coon nodded rapidly. Pig pointed down the bar, away from us. "Now go be useful over there."

I raised an eyebrow and watched her as she ghosted, her shoulders hunched and head bowed, down the bar to the other end. Skid was there, and he smiled at her, engaging her in conversation.

"Got somethin' for you to do," Pig-Pen commented dryly.

I turned my attention back to the man. "I'm listening."

"The bitch Gordy has in his pocket came through. Found out where one of those holier-than-thou fucks is layin' his head at night, and it ain't at their clubhouse like a lot of the rest of them scared-ass pussies." Pig-Pen eyed me carefully. "Go with Axe and Corbin while they take care of business," he grated.

I nodded slowly.

"When we doin' this?"

"Now! Jesus Christ, man!" He gave me a little shove with his shoulder.

"Like Jack & Coke?" I asked with an impetuous grin.

"Yeah, why?"

"Had one made, just for you." I handed him my drink, and he boomed out a laugh that sounded like fucking cannon-fire. I walked down the bar and caught sight of Corbin and Axe by the door to the parking lot. They each nodded at me before slipping out. I moved that direction, pausing when something caught my sleeve as I passed the hall to the bathrooms. I turned and looked over my shoulder.

"Dani." She swallowed hard and let the sleeve of my jacket go. "My name is Dani," she said nervously, melting back into the shadows of the corridor, where she was less likely to be seen by Pig.

I made like I was going through my pockets looking for something.

"Thanks for telling me, it's a pretty name," I uttered and continued to search my pockets. "Why don't you want my last name?"

I was genuinely curious. I caught her sad, one-sided smile out of the corner of my eye before she drifted back further into the shadows.

I shook my head and, making like I had found what I was looking for, slipped into the cold, dark night. The final glimpse I caught of her face was a startled expression mixed with relief that I hadn't pressed. Yeah, it was a dangerous game I played, expressing any kind of interest in the VP's Ol' Lady. But the gnawing impression that shit just wasn't right wouldn't let me go.

Dani was smart, pretty, and didn't use. The cherry on top? She was clearly unhappy about being with that dirty, nasty fuck. It was an interesting mystery wrapped in an enigma, why she was with him. But it also wasn't why I was here. Still, the damned girl tugged at my heartstrings; that could be bad news, but only if I let it. Only if I wasn't smart about it.

I put on my facemask and goggles, fixed my helmet, and pulled on my gloves after zipping my jacket. Axe and Corbin were similarly suited up and sitting astride their bikes. We had the machines warming up while I fiddled with my wardrobe and they smoked. I furiously tried to think about where we could be headed, who it was they had in their crosshairs, and more importantly, how the hell I could tip off D before we got there.

"Where we headed?" I called above the chugging bikes, trying to make it sound like an idle question.

"You'll see!" Corbin replied.

"We sure this fucker's alone?" I asked.

"No, you dumb cunt! Which is why we're just watching for the first bit. When we're sure, we'll move," Axe yelled. He kicked his stand out from under his bike, righting it, and I nodded once.

"You scared, Prospect?" That was Corbin, and I could see the outline of his grin through the bandana that covered the lower half of his face.

No, but you should be, I thought to myself.

"Lead the way, man!" I called, and we pulled out. The ride was cold, the night clear, and the moon hung about half-full in the sky. It may have only been half, but the moon's light was still bright enough to illuminate the surrounding countryside by a fair bit. When we pulled off at a cheap station to make sure the bikes were gassed up and I knew where we were, whose place we were close to, I made an excuse to take a piss and shot D a warning text.

Close to Lucky's – Rat gave up his 20. 2 SK's & me.

I pissed into the urinal and the burner pinged back.

Watch yourself. Place Trapped. Lucky warned.

I texted back I was burning the burner, snapped the old-school flip-phone in half, and ditched it in the trashcan, which was one of those metal domed affairs, just as Axe came through the door.

"Ready?" he demanded. I hadn't washed my damned hands but he'd seen me throw something in the trash, so it was best to let him think it was paper towels. There were worse things in life than not washing your hands once after you'd pissed.

"Yeah, let's go," I grumbled.

"Fuck, man, you take forever to piss," Axe griped.

"I got a thirteen-inch cock, it's got a long way to fucking travel," I shot back over my shoulder as he followed me out. I put my helmet on to the sound of their laughter after he shared what I'd said with Corbin, and started up my bike. They probably wouldn't be laughing in a couple of hours. They'd probably be dead. I almost felt bad about it. Corbin and Axe weren't half-bad when they weren't high, although I couldn't shake the image of them double-teaming a girl who was clearly fucking out of it and unable to consent. Still, not going to lie to myself about it, that was pretty much the worst sin I'd seen 'em commit, compared to a lot of the others. That really just told you how fucked-up and depraved these assholes were.

From what I'd gathered, under Sparks they had at least tried to maintain some kind of mask of humanity. But Griz? Griz was so hell-bent on revenge he didn't bother with such pleasantries. I had a sudden stroke of inspiration... but it had to wait until we were stopped up the block from Lucky's run-down, tired old house.

It was a little two-bedroom in a rough part of town, built back in the 1910's, maybe the early 20's, and looked like it had just about fucking had it. His bike, an old but fully resto'ed Indian, was parked in a carport that had been a ramshackle add-on in the 60's or 70's and didn't fit the rest of the house at all.

"Griz know we're doing this? I mean, six guys went down raiding these asshats' club and he was fucking pissed!"

Corbin snorted, "Griz knows everything that's going on. Pig-Pen is just a fucking scapegoat. So busy kissing Griz's ass, he doesn't realize Griz is having him hand out the orders."

Axe put his two cents in. "Griz is ready to burn the whole fucking world down around him - the club, and everyone who gets in his way - for revenge. Pig-Pen is just a fuckin' patsy in case the club revolts. We're out of dumb fuckers." He eyed me. "I can tell you ain't one of 'em, which is why I'm telling you this. He doesn't care who gets dead in the process just so long as they're taking Sacred Hearts with 'em. Only reason we're out here now is it's one dude." He shook his head, "I mean, how fuckin' hard can it be?"

"No shit, three against one, what could possibly go wrong with odds like that?" Corbin grinned through a five o'clock shadow that looked like someone had packed coffee grounds on his face. I nodded.

"Gotta like odds like that," I agreed and brought out my piece, a tried-and-true Beretta. I pulled back the slide and checked the chamber to be sure it was ready to go, and Corbin and Axe did the same with their guns.

Lucky's property sat between two vacant lots overgrown with blackberry vines. The house was on a raised foundation, so there were three narrow cement steps with thin, rusted-out rails to either side. The front stoop was just big enough for one guy to either side of the door while the third kicked it in, and apparently Axe and Corbin seemed to think this was the ideal way to do it.

I didn't know much about Lucky, other than he came by his road-name honestly. To hear it told, he was a crazy motherfucker with a penchant for explosives and explosive devices. A cool hobby for sure, but fuckin' crazy as hell, if you wanted to keep breathing and didn't feel like raining from the sky in nasty, wet chunks as your way of going out.

I took the left side of the door, while Corbin took right. I glanced across the street to the house there and, satisfied that it was totally abandoned, with the way the roof sagged in the center and how the windows were either busted out or boarded, I gave Axe a nod. He heaved up a leg and smashed his booted foot into the door by the lock and knob, and the whole thing gave with a crash – and a 'Boom!' much louder than a dude in motorcycle boots kicking in a door would cause.

Gunsmoke filtered through my facemask and burned my nose as Axe fell backwards and slid head-first down the stairs, a hole bigger than my fist in the center of his chest.

"Son of a bitch!" Corbin yelled and went in first, which was good, because it put me right behind him. I raised my gun and double-tapped him right in the back of his fucking head.

"Clear!" I called, and Lucky rounded the kitchen doorway.

I looked up at the shotgun hanging from brackets bolted to the ceiling.

"Really?" I asked, pointing up to it.

Lucky dropped the cord in his hand leading to the pulley and trigger mechanism.

"Worked, didn't it?" he grunted.

"Thirteen," I said.

"Lucky," he came forward and we grasped hands. "Thanks for the warning." He sniffed and looked down at Corbin, whose blood and brains were leaking out onto the hardwood.

"This get you the rat?" I asked.

"All but a done deal now. Soon as Shelly gets back to us, we'll have proof in the puddin' and the bitch will be all kinds of hosed."

I nodded gravely. "You got neighbors we gotta worry about?" I asked.

"Nope, that's why I live out here, or I did, before I went up to help my folks. I been pretty much living at the club." He wiped some sweat off his upper lip. I nodded.

"Got some brothers coming to help with the mess?" I asked.

"Right here," we heard from outside the front door. Lucky and I went to it. Trigger stared down at Axe, who was still breathing, or trying to. His breath was coming in short, hurried gasps, sawing in and out of his ruined lung. Trigger leveled his handgun right between Axe's eyes and pulled the trigger. The big man's light-colored eyes had gone cold and distant, the way a lot of guys got when they killed. I'm sure mine had held the same look more than a time or two.

"How the fuck you gonna spin this?" Revelator asked from behind our SAA.

"You're gonna hit me," I said. "Make it look good. Then you're gonna send me back to 'em with a message." I knew I sounded grim; that was because of the ass-whoopin' I was about to get.

"Oh, yeah, and what would that be?" Rev raised a dark eyebrow over his equally-dark eyes. Of course, we were only operating by moonlight right now, which now that some clouds had scudded over it, was barely enough to see by. Couldn't really tell you what his eye color was, other than brown. Wasn't no way I were switching on lights, even in a run-down, half-empty 'hood, for me to check for sure.

I explained what Axe and Corbin had told me when we'd got here. About how Griz was out for revenge and fuck anyone who got in his way. How he was taking his club's name a little too literal and for real, at least the 'Suicide' part of it, except that it wasn't his life he was playing with. The club was dividing on it, apparently. And Pig-Pen, who was Griz's mouthpiece, was too stupid to realize he was putting his ass on the line with every order he issued.

Trig listened thoughtfully while Rev and Lucky started to clean up. Finally, he nodded.

"You understand we have to make this look good?" he asked.

I nodded. "Just don't hit me in the balls. I fucking hate that." They chuckled dryly and we all uncomfortably cast looks in the direction of the dead.

"Where you gonna bury 'em?" I asked.

"Were they decent guys?" he asked. I shook my head.

"No, man, no, they weren't. But they weren't as bad as the rest of 'em," I said.

Trig nodded.

"Does it really matter, then?" he asked.

He had a point. I shook my head – and didn't really have a whole lot of time to think about it, because Revelator's fist crashed into my face. I went down on Lucky's dry, dead lawn.

"Motherfucker!" I bitched.

"Sorry, man, thought it might be better if you didn't see it coming." Revelator lifted one of his hulking shoulders in a half-assed shrug.

"Well, you got my attention now!" I spit blood and tried a couple of teeth in the back with my tongue. Nope, not loose, still solid. "Make it look real. But I lose any fucking teeth, I'm kicking your ass when this is up!"

Rev grinned, flashing his chipped tooth in the front, and his fist crashed into my cheekbone. It fucking hurt, but I struggled back to my knees and heaved a few breaths and stood my ground for probably the second-worst ass kicking of my life.

4

Dani...

I heaved the bag of trash from behind the bar up over my head and, with a little jump, got it up and over the lip of the dumpster. I turned at the sound of a lone bike turning into the lot and wondered what'd happened. I'd seen the prospect leave with Axe and Corbin, but he was returning alone and he was clearly holding himself all wrong. After three years around men riding motorcycles, you recognized the cocky confidence with which they held themselves when they rode. It was still present even when they were relaxed and riding; this aura of *I'm a badass and I know it* surrounded them at just about all times.

The exception to this rule? Pain. Which is exactly what Pretty-boy, Thirteen, Chris was holding himself with.

"Thirteen, what's wrong? Where's Axe? Where's Corbin? What happened?" I called, dashing in his direction. He shut off his bike with a groan and lowered the kickstand. He didn't have his mask or goggles on, and his face was red and purple and swelling. He bled freely from a cut on his cheek, and the corner of his mouth was crusted with dried blood as well.

I scooted under his arm, and he leaned on me as he dismounted his bike. He kept his left arm snapped in tight against his body, which told me clearly that his ribs hurt. He was heavy, and as we staggered for the door, I opened my mouth and screamed, "Pen! Pen, help! Help me!" As much as I loathed the man, it was the only thing I could do.

It was Skid who popped out the back door. "Jesus Christ! What the fuck happened?" He clattered down the steel steps and took Thirteen from me. My shoulders sighed with relief as I let the bigger, stronger man take over.

"What the fuck is going on out here?" Griz bellowed. "You!" He pointed at me. "Answer me!"

I hated being the center of attention, but I stepped up.

"I don't know, I was taking out the trash and he rode in alone. I saw him go out with Axe and Corbin a few hours ago, and here he comes back alone and I could see he was hurting. I don't know what happened. I didn't know what else to do."

"Stop your fucking babbling, woman, that's enough. You've patched guys up before, yeah?" he demanded. I nodded mutely, biting my lips together. "Then get your ass in here and go to work, bitch!" More club members had come outside and they were helping get Pretty-boy to one of the couches. I dashed back into the clubhouse and got the first-aid kit, which was really a big black-and-yellow plastic toolbox, from the office.

Skid blocked my way briefly in the hall. "You did good, kid. Give 'em a minute to talk to the prospect and find out what went down before you show your face," he suggested and gave me a worried sweep of his eyes. I nodded and followed him to the edge of the common room. I kept back in the shadows of the hall, near the bathroom doors, and waited until it was okay for me to show myself. I listened to the men talk.

"What happened, Pretty-boy?" Pig-Pen growled.

"The place was one big fucking trap!" Thirteen gasped. "Fucker had a shotgun rigged, pointing at the door, Axe kicked it in and it blew a hole clean through his chest! Corbin, he didn't wait, he went right in and the Bleeding Heart got the drop on him. I pointed my gun, but he had one pointed at me and it was a standoff."

I could hear him panting through the pain for a few moments while he tried to fight it back down so he could keep talking.

"I think he got a call or a text off while he was hiding in the kitchen, 'cause the next thing I know, I got a gun barrel pressed to the back of my skull and what was supposed to be three of us on one of them became three of them on me. I thought I was a fuckin' dead man for sure," he groaned.

"Why the fuck they let you live?" Pig-Pen demanded, and it was a good question. I tucked myself against the wall and continued to listen.

"They wanted me to deliver a message. Told me to say that the shit stops here and now. That they didn't start this, but they damn sure were gonna end it. Then they told me that once I'd delivered the message that they'd better never see me in a Suicide Kings prospect's cut or wearin' your colors, because they'd fuckin' kill me."

"You sayin' you want out?" Griz asked.

"Fuck no! Fuck those fucking fucks, man!" He made a pained sound and that was my cue.

"Where the fuck is Coon?" Pig-Pen demanded and I materialized at his elbow.

"Here, I was just waiting for permission," I murmured.

"Fuckin' stupid-ass cunt," he grated. He and the council, or what there was of it here, moved off into the corner.

"Here, take these." Skid handed Thirteen two round tablets.

"What are they?" He winced, reaching for them. I knew Skid's drug of choice and answered for him.

"Oxy, it'll help with the pain," I said and poured hydrogen peroxide on some gauze. I dabbed at the cut on his cheek and he hissed out between his teeth, but didn't move or flinch from me.

"You did good, Prospect," Griz called from across the room.

They believed him. The knot of anxiety in my chest eased. I frowned, and hoped they would mistake it for concentration on my part as I cleaned Thirteen up. I was trying to decipher why I'd feel concern for a club prospect. I mean, most of them didn't survive to patch in and when they were patched, it seemed to give them an even shorter life expectancy. At least lately, with the war going on. I was a little horrified to realize that secretly pleased me. *Maybe the Sacred Hearts weren't such a bad lot after all?* I caught myself thinking.

I was an absolute study in concentration as I worked to patch Thirteen up, carefully washing the blood away, closing the wound in his cheekbone with steri-strips. Skid helped me wrap his bruised and battered ribs with an ACE bandage and I had to admit, Thirteen had a spectacular physique. His body was sculpted to perfection beneath his plain tee. He laid back without putting his shirt back on and I honestly think I must have been blushing, because when he noticed we were free and clear of being overheard, he asked me, "Like what you see, Rocket?"

I searched his face, which I would never describe as 'pretty', but certainly was handsome. He was a true strawberry-blonde, the short-ness of his haircut barely kissed with the reddish tint of a newly-minted copper penny. His jaw was dusted with the same burnished color in his few days' worth of beard growth.

"Who's Rocket?" I asked softly, and met his eyes with mine. His pupils were the size of saucers, which was a shame. I liked the green-blue of his eyes. There wasn't a single gemstone, either precious or semi-precious, I could think of to compare it to and it seemed to change with his mood. What I could see right now of his eyes, they were more of a stormy grey-blue, but it was hard to tell, and I wondered if he was in much pain.

"You are." He tweaked my nose with a blunt fingertip and I jerked back, wrinkling it. He was high, alright, and I don't think he was feeling much of anything.

I sighed, "I'm Raccoon, Coon... not Rocket."

He chuckled deeply.

"You're Rocket now, babe." He murmured and closed his eyes. I think he was asleep in a matter of seconds.

"Coon! Bring me a bottle of Hennessey for Griz!" Pig-Pen bellowed from the main area of the club. I went, fetching the bottle from behind the bar, and took it out to the main area. The men were all gathered around a battered metal table that was half rusted out. I set the bottle and a glass at Griz's elbow. He slapped me on the ass, hard, and gestured that I should piss off, which I did, gladly. They were discussing a plan of action, and I think most were agreed that the plan now included a full club meeting with everyone involved.

As I went back down the hall to the back, I found myself hoping against hope that they all ran afoul of the other MC, that all of them were killed off, except maybe Skid and Thirteen. I knew the odds of that happening were slim to none, though. God hadn't exactly been kind to me thus far. Why should he start now?

Once I was sure that the prospect would be all right sleeping it off where he was, I tucked two more Oxy from the stash that Skid had slid me - for when Pig beat on me - into a square of receipt paper from my purse. I'd written "For when you wake up. –Coon" on it, and folded it carefully around the two pills, before, with a guilty look to make sure I wasn't caught, tucking them deep down into his pants pocket. Whoops, and oh my god! If what my hand brushed against was real, then there might be some truth to some of the rumors I'd heard about the new prospect's size!

I wrote on the underside of his wrist 'Check your front pocket' so he knew to look there, before laying his hand against his stomach, the writing hidden from view to the casual observer. When he woke up, hopefully he would see it and find the pills. Then, hopefully, he would wash it off and keep me out of it. I had to hope he wouldn't tell on me. The last thing I needed was one of the brothers accusing me of stealing drugs from the club supply. I doubted Skid would step up in my defense again. I could still see the last time he had, the beating he'd gotten from Pig, and how it haunted him every time he looked at me.

I knew how he felt. I was haunted by Pig every waking moment of my life, and sometimes during the sleeping ones, too. I gathered my purse, slipped out of the club, and went home, certain that with two more dead brothers, I wouldn't be missed.

5

Red-XIII...

The fucking Oxy that Skid had given me had knocked me for a motherfucking loop, but not so much that I couldn't remember. Sound traveled real well in the metal warehouse building, and I'd lain there, pretending to sleep, as I listened to the Suicide Kings little war council while Rocket Raccoon took care of me.

Just like the furry little badass comic book character, Dani was proving to be a crafty and brave badass of her own. She'd stuck around after I'd decided on her new nickname, and when she thought I was out, had gone fishing in my pocket. At first I thought I'd misjudged her, that she was trying to rip me off. Even so, her small gasp of surprise when she'd brushed against my dong almost blew my possum act. I'd almost smiled, almost laughed at her reaction. I hadn't, though.

My confusion went up a couple notches when I felt her writing on the inside of my arm.

As soon as I heard the door shut and was sure I was alone, I'd taken a peek at my arm. 'Check your front pocket' had been scrawled in a short line of her feminine loopy script. So she hadn't been ripping me off, but rather, had left something behind. When I was sure no-one was coming to the back from the front room, I checked. I found two white tablets, wrapped in a receipt with another note: 'For when you wake up –Coon'. I'd thought to myself, *Well I'll be damned.* It looked like I had made a friend and ally in Dani, which was a small bright spot under this deep, dark mountain of bullshit.

The Suicide Kings gave me a few days of peace at home to heal up, which, honestly, in a cabin with no electricity, wasn't that great, but at least I had a bed and a working woodstove. I cooked up canned stew and soup on its top, and would run into town once every couple of days to charge my phones and the battery sticks I used the rest of the time to keep 'em going.

It took a couple of weeks, pushing three after my cover story beat-down, for the final vestiges of stiffness to go away. In the meantime, I communicated everything I overheard to D and the boys after I bought a few new burners, which I charged up and activated as needed. They, like me, were just satisfied my cover wasn't blown.

Pig-Pen, Spade, and Neo went out on a run for guns in those weeks. I'd been just doing the general scut-work doled out to prospects, which, for the last three or four nights, included playing bartender. Rocket had been conspicuously absent.

"Hey, Prospect!"

"Yeah, Boss?" I turned away from the back of the bar towards Pig-Pen, who tossed a Crown Royal cloth bag at me. I caught it, the contents inside grating together, clinking gently with a metallic sound.

"Ain't heard from my bitch for a few days, she was whining she was sick. Take this over to her and check on her. Tell her she better get her lazy ass back to being useful before I ain't got no use for her. You get me?" he asked, and gave me a pointed look.

"Sure thing, where's her place?"

"Over on Tullamore Street. She's got an apartment up over an abandoned storefront, the one with the green awning, old jewelry store. You can get to her place by a stair out back."

"Got it." I tossed down the rag I'd been using and stuffed the Crown Royal bag into my jacket pocket.

"Tell her she better not be fucking avoiding me. I hate that shit!" he called at my back and I gave a wave over my shoulder. Somehow I doubted Rocket would be that stupid.

After the whole 'pills in my pocket' thing, she'd pretty much avoided me like the plague. Wasn't a hundred percent on why, but I thought she was afraid I'd sell her out? Thank her or something and get her in trouble, maybe? Who knows? All I know is that she was extra-careful not to get left alone with me, and that she wouldn't look me in the eye or engage in conversation.

I was half-afraid Pig had said something to her or gotten a hold of her. For a guy who didn't give a fuck about his property, treating her like shit, smacking her around, and berating her constantly, he sure as fuck didn't want anyone else taking an interest.

I'd gone so far as to tell him I had me a girl outside the hoes that hung with us, to get him off my back about her the second time he informed me that I had my chance to fuck her and I'd taken a pass.

He got real interested all of a sudden, and told me I should bring my mythical girl around for the brothers to meet. The look on Rocket's face, behind his back, boy – she looked like she was about to puke! It was such a gut-wrenching and visceral reaction to the notion, I realized I'd probably just stumbled onto how she'd gotten in with a crowd like this. Fuck me swinging! That would be a hell of a thing, if it were true.

I was thinking about it again as I mounted my bike. I put on my new facemask and shades. My brothers had thought it would look better, more convincing, if I came back without my last set. They were waiting for me back in my SHMC club room. Replacing the ski goggles would have to be an online thing, and since I didn't technically have an address where shit could be mailed and I hadn't gotten around to opening up a PO Box, I just dealt without for now. Wasn't like I really needed them. Spring had sprung and then some, even though winter had hung on like a motherfucker this year. It was really only cold enough to need the mask and eyewear riding at night, but I think that was more because I was a pansy. I still hadn't acclimated to the cold after coming from a warmer climate.

I pulled out of the lot and headed for the nearby town, where I knew there was a street by the name Pig gave me. If I recalled correctly, it had been a nice part of town once, before developers had bought up all the retail shops, etc., with dreams of erecting a new and modern shopping center. The plans were stalled by historical preservation societies filing suit to protect some of the buildings from demolition. They were in the process of trying to prove that they were deserving of being on the national registration of historic places.

How the fuck did I know all this? By shamelessly eavesdropping on Rocket talking to one of the new girls to the club who was looking for a cheap place to flop out. Rocket had told her that her 'hood was a shitty place to live, but if you found an apartment above the abandoned retail outfits, the rent was generally real cheap. You just had to be ready for an eviction notice any day, depending on if the developer won their way.

I thought about her probably way more than I should. She was a pretty little thing, for one, but that wasn't it. There was a keen intelligence underneath those wide blue eyes and under all that long dark hair. She was infuriatingly closed-mouthed about her history and where she'd come from, and that just made me want to get to the bottom of her damage even more.

It was a relatively short ride from the club to her place and when I pulled onto her street, it was kind of incredible. It looked like something out of that zombie series or that Stephen King movie about the world after a deadly virus wiped everything out. The whole street had that middle-America, small town Main Street-type feel, but the buildings were falling into serious disrepair. The sidewalks were cracked and weed-choked, windows were boarded and busted out, and the cars that were parked here and there were old, rusted-out pieces of shit.

The building with the green awning that Pig-Pen had described was midway up the block. It wasn't as bad off as some of the rest. Its front window was mostly intact, except for one long crack in it, faded gold leaf lettering spelling out *Broussard's Custom Jewelry* on its front. There was a recessed metal gate, that wasn't locked, between it and the building next door. I parked my bike and took off my helmet, shoving my mask - which was just a bandanna now - and glasses into its overturned bowl.

Rocket's sad, tired, old green Honda was parked at the curb, so she was home. I pulled out the Crown Royal bag and opened it up, now that there was no one to see me being fuckin' nosy. It was filled with jewelry. Real shit – necklaces and rings and bracelets, likely all of it fucking stolen. I shook my head and drew the strings taut, closing up the bag.

"Just what the fuck you into, Rocket?" I asked the empty air. Only one way to find out; I let myself through the gate and went down the small brick alleyway. It emptied out into a courtyard, which surprised me. A small, bricked-in shed sat in the corner of it, the windows dark and a shiny padlock in good repair keeping folk out of it. An iron stair led to the open-air second floor landing. There was only one door above the jewelry store, so I mounted the steps two at a time and went to it.

I pounded on the door, "Rocket! It's Red-Thirteen!" I called. There was no answer. I pounded on the door three more times with my closed fist.

I was suddenly gripped by a creeping dread.

I knew she was safe from my club, my *real* club. 'No women, no children'. But I wouldn't put it passed the sick fucks that were the Suicide Kings to have done something to her, to blame the Sacred Hearts.

I gripped the doorknob and it turned easily in my hand. I expected resistance when I pushed on the door, but there was none; it swung inward on well-oiled hinges. I set my helmet down carefully on the floor just inside the door and swept the dimly-lit interior with my gaze.

Small, two bedrooms, maybe. The kitchen was just to the left of the front door, a hall leading to what looked like a laundry area and one bedroom on the left, living room space directly ahead, and a dining area directly through the front door and to the right. Another hall past the dining area. A darkened bathroom door; I could see the sink from here. Past that, I think, was a second bedroom. I slid my gun out from underneath my prospect's cut and held it at the ready.

It was quiet, and still. So very still.

"Rocket?" I called, and there was a weak cough and a moan from the direction of the bathroom, past it, off to the right. My heart squeezed in my chest and a hot rage started to burn in my belly. *If those sons of bitches sent me out here to bear witness to her dying...* I didn't want to finish the thought. I swept the apartment and, satisfied that there was no one there to jump out and take me down, I went for the last door, the one that held that weak feminine groaning.

I opened the door flush against the wall and what I saw– *Fuck me.* I knew she'd been fighting a cold, but this was fucking ridiculous! She lay in bed, the blankets and quilts piled high. Her hair was matted and used Kleenex overflowed the small trashcan by her bedside, piling against the hardwood like a drift of snow. Her nose was bright red and her breathing was off, way off. It wheezed and rattled in her chest; I could hear it from all the way across the room.

I didn't think anyone had been out here to look in on her until I'd shown up today. I'd seen people at Death's door, dropped more than a few in a heap there myself. And Rocket, she was fucking *there*.

"Oh, Jesus Christ," I heard myself swear.

I put my gun back in my waistband and pulled my cell out of my cut. I dialed Pig-Pen.

"What?" he demanded, by way of greeting.

"Did you know she was sick?" I asked, and my voice was edged with disbelief.

"What? Yeah, some cold or something, I told her to take care of it and stop comin' around 'til she did. None of us want that shit." Pig-Pen sounded irritated, *irritated!*

"Sorry to piss on your parade, Boss, but it's blown up into something much worse than that! I'm lookin' at her right now, and your Ol' Lady is knocking on Death's front door. I don't know, man, it looks bad." I sat down on the bed next to her and smoothed back some of her hair, which was lank with sweat. She was burning the fuck up.

"Fuckin' deal with it," he growled into my ear. "My bitch dies, I'm holding you responsible." *Was he fucking kidding me?*

"I gotta get her to a hospital then, man..."

"No hospital! I ain't paying for that shit. Fucking figure it out, man, but no fuckin' hospital," he yelled.

"All right! No hospital, I know a dude does house calls. Fuck me, man... I got this. Might be a few days before I'll know if she's gonna make it."

"She fuckin' better or it's your ass, Pretty-boy. She's valuable to the club, it needs her."

"Got it. I gotta hang up." He did me a favor and ended the call for me.

I pulled the burner out of my other pocket and hit 'Send' twice. I murmured to her while it rang through.

"Come on, baby girl, hang on for me; just hang on." I pried up her eyelids, but her eyes were rolled back in her head, nothing but white.

"Hello?"

"D! D, I need Doc. I need Doc, right fuckin' now, man!" I said into the line and there was a half-second of silence.

"You hurt?" he demanded, and I heard him snapping his fingers in the background.

"Not me, Dani... Coon. She's real sick, man."

"She OD?"

"Naw, she doesn't do that shit, this is something else. She had some kind of a cold." I put my other ear to her chest and listened.

"Jesus Christ, is that her breathing?" I heard Dragon cry.

"Yeah. It's bad, D, it's real bad and she's fuckin' important to these assholes. She does something - I dunno what yet - but their VP said it'd be my fucking ass if she died, so whatever it is, it's big." The phone switched hands.

"R.T., it's Doc, tell me what's happening and describe her symptoms, I'm throwing some shit together now."

"Uhhh... she's burning up. Her breathing sucks, man, it's like she's not getting enough air. She was fighting some kind of cold the last few weeks and I think it snuck up on her and laid her out."

"Is she conscious?"

"Hell to the motherfuckin' no, man, and I can't get her to wake up! It's freaking me out!"

"How long she been like that?"

"I don't know, I don't know, man! Uh, Pig said he hasn't seen her in a few days, she could have been like this that long, or longer for all I know."

"All right, I'm on my way. You gotta get her cleaned up. Strip the bed and get some fresh sheets on it. Can you do that?"

"Yeah, yeah, I can do that!" I said.

"Where you at?" he demanded. I rattled off the address and description of where we were at, and dropped the phone on the bedside table.

"Come on, Dani. We gotta get you cleaned up, babe." I threw back the blankets and winced. Most definitely, she'd been here a couple of days. The girl was ripe. She moaned and her brow furrowed, but she was so far fucking out of it, it was unreal. I strode into the bathroom and hit the taps, waited for the water to heat up, and started the tub to filling. This was going to be messy and graceless, but I didn't give a fuck. I stripped my shirt over my head and tossed it over the top of the door. I'd need something dry to put her in, and I didn't know where any of her shit was. Doc would be here inside an hour, so I didn't really have time to go fish for anything other than bed linens.

I went back to the bedroom and stripped her out of the oversized tee and the panties she'd been sleeping in. I kept talking to her, hoping it would somehow make what I was doing better. I doubted it very much, though. The girl had been violated six ways to Sunday by the SKMC, and I was just another set of male hands taking liberty at this point.

"I'm so sorry, Rocket. I'm so sorry, baby, I didn't know. If I'd known, I would have been here before it got to this. Hang in there for me, girl. Just hang on," was mostly what I said, or some variation thereof. I got her into the tub as it slowly filled with water, shutting it off when it got to a certain level. I made sure there was no way she could slip under, and went to the next thing on Doc's list.

I stripped the bed fast and bundled the dirty linens up, flinging them down the hall towards the washer and dryer. They could live there for the time being, in a heap in front of the two machines. I tried the closet and – Jackpot! Some fresh ones were folded on the top shelf. I pulled them down and made the bed. I took a couple of the top blankets, that hadn't been against her body, and put 'em back on the bed. The bottom two joined the pile in front of the washer and dryer. I pulled a couple of old quilts out of the closet and finished up the bed quick, and returned to the bathroom. She hadn't moved. Her breathing sucked just so damned bad that her lips were almost blue.

I went to the kitchen and grabbed a clean, empty saucepot off the top of the stove. It'd have to do.

I washed her carefully and used the pot to wet her long hair. I washed that, too, carefully shampooing and rinsing.

She moaned and coughed, and weakly tried to struggle throughout my ministrations, but what really threw me was when she started speaking French in a quiet, broken, pleading voice.

"*Se il vous plaît pas, se il vous plaît laissez-moi mourir.*" She repeated it over and over, and I didn't have a fuckin' clue what she was trying to tell me.

"Man, Rocket, I don't understand, babe. English. Please, baby, tell me in English..." but it was just more of the same thing over and over again. '*Se il vous plaît pas, se il vous plaît laissez-moi mourir*', over and over again.

I pulled the plug and the water siphoned down the drain on the tired old, but clean, tub. I started the tap and, an arm curved around her back and shoulders, held her up and used the pot to give her a final rinse. I shut off the water and snatched a large towel from the bar, wrapping her in it awkwardly. I got her back up and into my tee shirt by propping her on the couch out in the living room.

"Okay, babe. Almost there."

She was so fucking out of it, so weak she couldn't even hold her head up. She'd stopped speaking and that death rattle in her chest got worse and worse the more time that ticked by. I tipped her against my shoulder so I could pull my shirt down in back and that's when I saw the tattoo. Rage, hot and immediate, surged in the center of my chest. 'Pig-Pen' was scrawled across her lower back in black, spikey script reminiscent of the anarchy 'A'. The son of a bitch had claimed her, but he wouldn't fucking take care of her.

I was just pulling the blankets on her freshly-made bed up over her shoulders when Doc shoved through the apartment's open front door. I pointed my weapon out of habit and he raised his hands, his medical bag over his shoulder.

"Just me," he said, then frowned. "Where's your shirt?"

"On her. Hurry the fuck up." He came into the bedroom and I moved aside, shoving my weapon away. He stuck a thermometer in her ear, one of the kind they use on kids, and made a growling noise.

"103.2." He took her pulse and shook his head, jerking his stethoscope out of his bag and sticking it in his ears. He pulled the blankets down and put his hand up my shirt and listened to her chest. I was about to get twitchy about him leaving it there too long when he pulled it back out and covered her up to her armpits, leaving her arms out from under the blankets.

"Without x-rays to confirm, I have to guess pneumonia. I brought IV fluids and a broad-spectrum antibiotic. You're right, she's in miserable fucking shape. I'm gonna get an IV started. You might as well settle in, boy. You're gonna be here a while, and so am I."

I nodded and let Doc do his thing. I started the washer with her sheets and the shit I'd stripped off the bed. It was gonna be a couple of loads.

"R.T.!" he called.

"Yeah?"

"Bring me that coat rack I saw in the dining room, need somethin' for an IV stand."

I brought the rack, which held only one coat, and set it up by the bed. It was one of those old-fashioned ones made out of a thick and rich wood.

"Grab me a coat hanger from the closet there," he said. I did as I was told. I could tell he'd done this back-alley medicine shit a time or two before. It didn't seem like he was improvising so much as using some tried-and-true methods. He hung the IV bag on the hanger, and the hanger on the coat rack, and messed with the tubing leading into Dani's inner arm. She was so fucking pale. Her skin was translucent, the veins standing out almost neon on the inside of her forearm... the same place where she'd written on me where I could find the pain medicine she'd left me.

"This the way they treat their women?" he asked me.

"Just the ones that're valuable to them. Swear to Christ, they treat the sluts better though, 'cause those bitches can leave if they don't.'"

He smoothed some of her hair back from her face and looked her over.

"She's a knock-out," he observed.

"Yeah. Different, too. She's smart, doesn't use. I don't know what she does for them, but whatever it is, it's important."

He nodded. "You been protecting her?" he asked.

"No. Not as much as I want to. It'd blow my cover, but I'm beginning to not care so much about that right now."

Doc turned cold, hard eyes on me.

"You better care," he said and I nodded, catching his meaning. I wasn't any good to her or my club dead, and we still had work to do. There was a long pause in conversation as we both retreated inside our own heads.

"Rev really kicked your ass," Doc said flatly, breaking me out of my thoughts. I turned and saw his tired blue eyes roaming across my fading yellow bruises and the flat, shiny pink scar on my cheekbone.

"Dude doesn't know any other way to do it," I said, with a shrug.

"Ain't that the ever-loving truth of it?" he asked.

Indeed.

"How much longer until we can start really being the hunters versus the prey?" I asked.

"Sure we should be talking about any of this in front of her?" he countered.

"She isn't out?" I asked, surprised because she looked like she was out fucking cold.

"Were you?" he shot back, and I palmed the back of my neck, chagrined.

"Fair enough, old man."

"Who the fuck you callin' 'old', boy?" he smiled, but it was still weighted by his loss and his grief over his Ol' Lady. I stared down at Dani. If she died I was going to own Pig and the lot of them into next week. She had taken care of me at risk to herself; it was more than time I manned up and returned the favor.

6

D ani...
   I had woken up to two problems and two discoveries.

The first problem was that I had to pee, and the second... well, the second was that I woke up at all.

The first discovery was that I was warm, too warm, and when I opened my eyes, it was to look down the length of my forearm to see the white swatch of tape holding the plastic of an IV in place against my skin.

The second one? I wasn't alone in my bed. A strong, muscled arm curved over the top of my waist, the back of my body snug against a hard body that was putting off an amazing amount of heat.

I searched my memory for who it could be and came up empty. All I knew was that I'd been so close to being free of the nightmare I'd been living and someone had pulled me back from the brink of that beautiful oblivion. I choked and bit down on a sob, and whoever it was that had a hold of me jolted.

"Shhhh, s'okay, Dani." The voice was warm and gentle and not Pig's. Warm, soft lips pressed to my skin on the back of my shoulder, where the neckline of the tee I was wearing didn't quite cover. I sucked in a breath and a broken cry of crushing defeat escaped my mouth, and I doubled in on myself.

Why? Why do you hate me so much? I silently asked God, but as always, there was no answer.

"Oh, baby, I'm so sorry." The arm around me drew me back and held me close and I cried, broken and bitter at still being alive. I couldn't cry forever, though, and my bladder was screaming for relief. I still didn't know who held me fast but I'd learned a long time ago that 'who' didn't matter so much, especially when it came to the Suicide Kings. Though, truthfully, whoever had me was being both kind and gentle, and it was a mark of how damaged I'd become that it was that which was scaring me, more than being in a stranger's arms.

"I'm going to let you go. You have to promise me you won't rip out your IV. You promise?" The voice was familiar but the face that went along with it was eluding me. The arm locked around my middle eased off and I sat up abruptly, swinging my legs over the edge of the bed, my feet making contact with the old, worn hardwood of my bedroom floor.

"Easy, Rocket." The voice soothed and I stiffened, turning my head slowly.

"Thirteen?" I asked, not quite believing. But sure enough, there he was, shirtless, with his head propped in his hand, smiling that roguish smile at me.

"How's my patient?" a grizzled voice asked from my bedroom door and I whipped my head so fast in that direction to face the new possible threat that the ends of my hair lashed the half-naked prospect behind me.

"Who the fuck are you?" I asked. The man harrumphed.

"I'm yer doctor," he said. He looked like one, sort of. Soft brown shoes, khaki Dockers, blue button-down shirt... except his head was shaved and he had a gray-and-white handlebar mustache. "Why, thank you, Doc, for saving my life!" he mocked, and I smoothed my long hair behind my ears, pulling it tight with my distress.

"I didn't ask you to do that!" I snapped. He leaned a shoulder against the doorjamb and raised an eyebrow at Thirteen behind me. I stood up abruptly and swayed on my feet, black spots and weird color-bursts flashing in my vision. I felt extremely light-headed and Thirteen was just suddenly there, standing behind me, a solid wall of man at my back, his hands on my waist gently supporting me.

"Easy, girl," the doctor intoned. "You were so dehydrated we almost lost you, you got pneumonia, you're weak; who the fuck knows when you last ate... You need to take it slow." He sounded genuinely concerned and when I looked, his blue eyes had lost their hard edge.

"I really have to pee," I said hollowly.

"'K, c'mon, I'll help you," Thirteen murmured just above my shoulder. I looked up at him.

"How'd you know where I live?" I asked.

"Bathroom first, then there will be plenty of time for conversation. Doc?" The doctor came forward and gently grasped my wrist, turning my arm out.

"Keep it straight for me?" he asked and I nodded. He unhooked the line and capped the thing in my arm, with quick and sure precision. They'd brought my granddad's old coat rack in here and my bedside trashcan had three of the empty saline bags in it. And the fourth one, hanging, was almost empty. No wonder I had to pee so bad!

I looked down at myself and frowned, I didn't recognize the tee shirt I was in, but that was a puzzle for later. Thirteen was walking me out into the hall and I went with it, a little afraid of what would happen if he let me go. I felt so strange! He turned me loose just inside the bathroom door and shut it behind him, closing me into the small space by myself. I did what needed doing and washed my hands, grateful for the counter to hold me up.

I opened the door and the two men were waiting on the other side. I let Thirteen help me back to bed.

"You hungry?" the doctor asked.

"Starving, actually."

"You two talk. I'll fix you some soup, then I gotta get out of here."

I frowned, "How long have you been here?" I asked.

"Found you two days ago," Thirteen said softly. The doctor went out into my kitchen.

"Pig?" I asked fearfully.

"I been keeping him updated but he hasn't felt the need to stop by." His green eyes cooled and turned more stormy blue and I nodded carefully.

"Who is he?" I asked quietly.

"A friend," he answered simply. I gave him a look and he laughed softly, but then his face grew solemn. "I know you're a smart girl, Rocket. Which is why I can't figure how you got here."

"Don't change the subject," I said softly and stared at my hands, which were folded in my lap. He tipped a finger beneath my chin and lifted my gaze to his.

"It's really better if you don't know. Sometimes ignorance is bliss, same reason why you told me not to tell you my last name."

I nodded. If I didn't know, then Pig couldn't beat it out of me. He would be safe. Still, I had my suspicions, which could be just as dangerous in some ways.

We were silent for a time and he gave me my space, sitting near me but not too close. I didn't quite understand why that bothered me. Usually I didn't want anyone anywhere near me, but there was something different about Thirteen.

"How about you answer my question?" he said, but his voice was kind, soothing, even.

"What question? I didn't hear a question." It was his turn to give me a look that screamed 'don't patronize me' and I gave a weak smile.

"It was around three years ago. I was nineteen, about twenty, and my granddad had died. I was alone except for my boyfriend, Jared. He got mixed up with some guys and a friend of his introduced him to a friend of *his* who was a Suicide King, and he started hanging around them." I took as deep a breath as I could, which admittedly wasn't much. I coughed, and it hurt, and I grimaced. Thirteen handed me a glass of water from the bedside table but he was waiting me out, patiently.

"One night he comes home wearing a prospect's cut and tells me

I have to come out with him; that the guys wanted to meet me." Thirteen's brows drew down into a scowl, and I rushed through the whole horrible ordeal. By the time I was through, he'd had to take the glass of water from me, my hands were shaking so badly. He sighed and I could see the struggle on his face. Finally one side won out and he pulled me against him, tucking my head beneath his chin. I stiffened.

"What are you doing?" I asked.

"I'm holding you, babe. You look like you need it," he murmured. I tugged back from him and he immediately let me go. I couldn't remember a time that ever happened. I stared at my hands for a long time and he stood with a sigh.

"Here we go," the doctor said from the doorway. He brought in a tray with a bowl of soup and some crackers on it. Chicken noodle.

I smiled a bittersweet little smile.

"You're a doctor... any scientific proof to the whole chicken soup thing?" I asked and coughed.

He smiled and set the tray in my lap.

"Empirical data suggests that it is indeed good for the soul," he said and I laughed a little. He took out my IV after giving me a final dose of antibiotics through it, then set out an orange bottle of pills on the table beside me.

"What's that?" I asked.

"More antibiotics. Three times a day. Morning, mid, and night. You should be fine in seven to ten days. If you're not all better, have R.T. here call me."

I frowned. "R.T.?" I asked.

Thirteen, who had taken up the doctor's place at my bedroom door, smiled, "Red-Thirteen. It's what I been called since I was a kid. People usually shorten it somehow. Red, usually, but if there's another 'Red' around I get tagged with 'Thirteen' or just 'R.T.'"

"Oh, I guess I'm just used to the guys calling you Thirteen or Pretty-boy."

The doctor arched a brow.

"Pretty-boy, huh? I'm gonna have to remember that one," he

chuckled. "Time for me to get going. You take care of yourself, Rocket," he said.

"Dani. My name is Dani," I said and the doctor smiled.

"Dani," he repeated, nodded, and slipped out the bedroom door. Thirteen saw him out of my apartment and came back to sit on the foot of my bed while I ate.

"Hope you don't mind, I used your washer and dryer while you were out cold." I shook my head and took the spoon out of my mouth, swallowing the soup, which was perfect. It was the good kind you got in the plastic tubs at the grocery store, full of big noodles, carrots, and celery.

"Why did you come here, anyways?" I asked, before taking another bite. He smoothed a hand over the blankets covering my foot and shin, massaging my foot through the covers absently.

"Pig-Pen sent me over here."

He got up and came back with a Crown Royal bag and I held out my hand for it excitedly. I knew it was wrong, that these things had been stolen from their rightful owners, but still, my ability to create, to make things the way my grandfather had taught me, that was mine and the only small source of joy I really had left.

"What is all this stuff?" he asked me, holding the bag out of reach. I tried to set the tray and soup aside and he held the bag up and said, "Ah, ah, ah. Eat your soup and then you get the goods." His green-blue eyes held a sparkle of mischief and I settled back, nodding, and ate the rest of my soup and the crackers, which was good. The salt sort of burned my lips where they were cracked and I took a drink of water from the glass on the bedside table. He set the stolen jewelry pieces on the nightstand and took the bowl and spoon to the kitchen, knowingly leaving the tray behind. When he came back, I was already sorting through pieces.

"There's a workbench in the living room, I know you've seen it. If you bring me the jeweler's loupe from it, I'll tell you what this is about. But you have to swear to me, Thirteen! You have to promise you won't tell Pig I told you anything!" He studied my face with troubled eyes and nodded.

When he came back with the loupe in his hand, he wore a heather gray tee shirt. I was surprised to find that his putting on a shirt actually disappointed me a little. I was even more surprised to find that I had rather been enjoying the view of his body. I pushed those thoughts away and held out my hand for the loupe. He went to hand it to me, but pulled it back at the last second.

"Explain." He raised his red-gold eyebrows and retook his seat at the foot of my bed. I set the ring in my fingers down on the tray.

"The club runs and sells drugs," I said, and I could see that he already knew that; there was no surprise on his face. "My grandfather was Philip Broussard." That did raise his eyebrows. I frowned, "You know the name?"

"I'm not blind, Rocket. It's the name on the jewelry storefront downstairs."

I blushed. "Um, right... anyways, my dad couldn't take care of me. My mom, either. Drugs, apparently, and so when I was two I ended up in the care of my *grand-père*." He smiled at the French pronunciation. "He was a custom jeweler from France; it was a family thing, his father's father taught his father and so on down the line. My *grand-père* wanted to teach my father, but my father... I don't really know what happened there." Which wasn't exactly true; I did know, but it was just something I really didn't want to go into, and wasn't part of this story.

"Anyways, my *grand-père* taught me everything he knew and when he died, I inherited all of his tools and his workshop and everything in it. A few months after Pig-Pen claimed me it became apparent that I was only going to be kept around until he got bored with me, and that I had better be of some sort of other value after that point came or I was going to die or be passed around. I didn't want either of those things so I sold a piece of my soul. " I bit my lips together.

"No judgments here, baby. You did what you had to do," he said, and that reassuring touch was back. His hand gripped the top of my foot with a gentle, even pressure, stroking up my shin halfway to the knee and back down. Up and down, up and down... I closed my eyes and just let myself enjoy it for a fraction of a second before letting my breath out slowly.

"The club had most of East County hooked on their shit, and the more people become addicted, the less reliable they are with the cash flow... Pretty soon people were stealing shit to pay for their drugs and were trying to barter with everything from electronics to jewelry. Sparks was livid when some of the younger club members and dealers started showing up with the jewels. Said that he couldn't pawn this shit without it being traced back to the club and it was worthless, and by then Pig was getting restless with me, so I told him about what I could do." I looked at him a little hopelessly.

"I knew people were being hurt, that some of the pieces that were showing up were priceless or family heirlooms... But I was scared, and I didn't want to die or to disappear, and I thought it was 'better the devil you know'. You know?" I sniffed and he nodded. "So I told Pig-Pen that if they gave me the jewelry, that I could take it and melt it down, make new pieces and reset stones so that it could be sold on the internet, or pawned, and no one would be the wiser that it was stolen.

"Pig told Griz, made it sound like it was all his idea. Griz told Sparks, and Sparks liked it, so the jewelry started coming to me.

"It became more than a means of survival though. It became mine. They didn't care what I made as long as it sold, and made the club money. So I could design my own stuff and it became a way to escape this bullshit for a little while – something that they couldn't touch, that they couldn't spoil or take away from me.

"I've been doing it ever since. They don't really care what Pig does to me as long as I keep producing. I threatened to stop once." I shuddered. "I'll never do that again." That had been the one and only time that Pig-Pen had let the brothers have their turn at me, after I'd said I would stop, tried to run. I'd made sure to behave ever since; there were no more brave proclamations. I never wanted to pull a train ever again. It had been a nightmare and taken me a long time to recover.

Truthfully, I couldn't say if I were really fully recovered. Some damage couldn't be repaired.

Thirteen looked me over and picked up my hand where it rested on my tray. He pressed the jeweler's loupe into my hand and said softly, "I'm sorry all of this has happened to you. I never would have kept it from you, not even teasing, if I'd known." He sighed a broken-down and weary sigh, and I knew just how he felt. "You're a beautiful woman, Dani, and you deserve so much better than any of this."

I looked at him sharply. "Don't you ever let any of them hear you talk like that!" I held my breath and willed him with all the strength that I had left, to promise me.

He stared at me, his blue-green eyes, more blue right now, searching my face. He'd gone very still, his expression unreadable, and finally he straightened; he'd made a decision.

"You don't gotta worry about that," he said. "It's just you and me here, for now. I think I can buy you a couple of days more to recover, then I just need you to keep doing what you're doing for a little while longer." He pursed his lips and nodded with finality, before getting to his feet. He bent at the waist, and before I knew what he was going to do, he pressed his lips to the top of my head.

"Just hang in there, Rocket," he murmured into my hair. I closed my eyes, his breath was warm against my scalp as he spoke and it sent a rolling rush of pleasant tingling down the back of my neck and shoulders.

I nodded, confused. It was like something had flipped the prospect's switch and I didn't know if that was a good or bad thing.

I knew with absolute certainty, though, that there was more to Thirteen than met the eye. I'd been watching men scheme and play each other against one another for a really long time, and Thirteen had that feel to him. He had another feel too, though. Thirteen was dangerous. I could see it in the way he moved around the apartment and in the way he took everything in.

I just couldn't decide if he was going to be dangerous to me or not, and so for now, I simply and wisely kept my mouth shut.

7

R ed-XIII...
      I didn't know exactly what it was about Rocket, but the girl
flipped just about every switch into the 'on' position where my protective instincts were concerned. The more I learned about her, the
more I simply just liked her.

She was as smart as I thought she was from the beginning, maybe
even more so. The girl, for all the fear she held inside, was incredibly
brave. Another thing that got me about her was just how fucking self-
less she was, even in the face of all she'd been through. For her to
fucking warn me about not being overheard saying anything kind?
Damn. She was incredible.

She adapted pretty quickly. And speaking of adapting, I needed to
do some of my own, because my mission of destruction had suddenly
become a mission of mercy too. I had to figure out a way to not only
take out the Suicide Kings, but to do it in such a way that there would
be minimal blowback on Rocket while I was at it. I wasn't sure how I
was going to do that.

Losing Axe and Corbin had lit a rather substantial fire under the
Suicide Kings' asses and the more their members dropped like flies,
the more unglued the council was going to become. Pig-Pen had

already proven that he wasn't above using Dani as his whipping boy – er – girl, as an outlet for his anger and frustrations. The problem was, she and Doc were both right: I couldn't care, I couldn't put myself in front of her and act as a meat-shield without drawing suspicion onto myself and exposing my ulterior motives.

I was sitting with Rocket as she ate another bowl of soup when Pig finally decided to show up to check on his woman. The front door to her place just opened and he walked in like he owned the place which, seeing as he thought he owned her, shouldn't have come as a surprise. It shouldn't have surprised me either, that he had a fucking key, but I'd been so absorbed in keeping her alive it'd slipped past me. So, when I heard the door open, I automatically went for my gun and had it pointed when Pig-Pen appeared in the door.

"The fuck you doin'?" he demanded.

"Sorry, man." I pointed the Beretta skyward. "Didn't expect you; after Axe and Corbin, can you blame me for being jumpy?" I raised my eyebrows and put up my gun, tucking it into the back of my waistband. His expression crushed down into a scowl.

"I don't check in with you, you check in with me. Don't you forget it, either." He turned to Dani, who was still pale and wan and looked like ever-loving shit.

"You finish it yet?" he demanded. She nodded her head rapidly, flinching back from his looming presence.

"Yeah, man, it's out here." I got up and put myself between them, subtle enough to keep Pig's hackles from going up, but enough to cause some of the fear and tension to ease from the set of Dani's shoulders. "You done?" I asked her. She nodded and lifted the tray from her lap feebly. I looked to Pig and jerked my head toward the door.

"Might not want to get too close, my guy said she could still be contagious through the end of the week." That was total fucking bullshit and anyone with half a brain would know that, but I was betting the only person in the club that would tell Pig to his face that he'd been had, let alone laugh at him, was Griz. All the rest of them were either afraid of his temper or would keep their laughter to themselves so they could get off on it behind his back later.

Dani's eyes went real wide and Pig made a disgusted noise and ducked back out into the hallway. I dropped the tray in the kitchen and went to the workbench. I picked up the ring she had finished that day, a gold band in the shape of a crown. She'd needed one last diamond for it and had found the perfect-sized one with the right cut in amongst the latest lot of jewelry I'd brought her.

I hadn't wanted her working, but she promised all she needed to do was set the one stone and polish the ring and she'd be done, and she'd done exactly that. It still had taken her some time though. The girl was absolutely precise and the result of her effort sat, stunning, gleaming softly in the palm of my hand as I held it out to Pig. He picked it up and held it up in front of his face, squinting at it. He smiled and gave a nod, then fixed me with a hard look.

"You sleeping with her?" he demanded, narrowing his eyes. *Yes.* But I was only sleeping, and I sure as hell wasn't going to tell him that.

I blinked, put my thumbs through my belt loops in the front of my pants, and gave the Suicide Kings' VP a hard look. The thing about most MCs, when they got a prospect, they look for certain traits. Loyalty, an ability to keep their fucking mouths shut, a willingness to learn, and a certain level of badass are all looked upon favorably. When it came to the Suicide Kings, if there was one thing I'd picked up on quickly, was that they also prized a certain level of servitude. The guys they brought in tended to be followers, easily-cowed to an extent. They were looking for non-threats to the upper echelon of the club's hierarchy, which was total bullshit and made for a weak-ass club.

I could see that I was being tested here, but I wasn't one-hundred-percent on what exactly Pig was looking for. It was always hard to tell, especially when you were dealing with a dude who was using as much as him. I postured myself with a level of badass, nonchalantly, like I didn't give two fucks, my body language screaming *Sure, all right, you wanna throw down? I'll throw down.* But I schooled my expression into lines of worry and picked my words carefully.

"Naw, man! I been out here the whole time." I gestured to the couch, which was still made up from when Doc was sleeping on it. I'd been lucky. I had all kinds of excuses as to why Pig should have stayed away while Doc was here but I hadn't had to use a single one of them. Pig really didn't give two fucks about Dani, except for her ability to generate him cash, make him look good to his club and his Pres., and for when he felt like fucking her. My reasons for wanting to bury this son of a bitch were growing exponentially by the hour, never mind by the fucking day.

He inspected the couch, which was made up like a bed with the sheets and blankets I'd washed, after I'd arrived and while Doc had treated Dani, and finally he nodded and sniffed.

"You can have a taste if you want," he said. I felt my brows crush down into a frown. *Was he for fucking real?*

"Naw, man, that's yer Ol' Lady," I stated and crossed my arms over my chest, tucking my hands flat under my arms to resist the urge to punch him in his smug, smiling face. His mood turned on a dime and he scowled at me, leaning in, menacing. I wanted to stand my ground but I didn't know what he was playing at, so I leaned away from him.

"You saying my woman's pussy ain't good enough, Prospect?" he demanded.

"No, man! I'm not saying that either! Your woman is damn fine, she's just *your* woman! I got mad respect, Dude! No disrespect here!" I put my hands out, as if to ward off any offense I may have caused, and his laughter boomed through the tired old apartment.

"I'm just fucking with you, Prospect! You did good here, keeping my bitch alive. When we going to see you back at the club? Tonight?" he asked.

I tried to look relieved and really only had to half-fake it. Fucking Pig-Pen, man, with as much shit as he did and as squirrely as his moods were, you never really could tell. I shook my head, and answered him with a total fucking lie that I hoped sounded remotely believable, "Naw, man, not tonight, maybe tomorrow night. My guy said someone should be here to make sure she took her pills at least through tomorrow night, that after that she should be good. I know she's pretty valuable to you and the club, so it's better that I do what the doctor ordered and protect your investment. You dig?"

He eyed me with some suspicion and I found myself praying silently, *Please buy it, please buy it, please buy it...* Finally he nodded and pounded me on the back as we turned for the door.

"I knew I did right by you, letting you hang around. You're smart and loyal and I like that." We got to the door. "Coon! I'll deal with your ass later! You'd better have some shit done and ready for me to sell by the end of next week, you hear me?" he called down the hall in the direction of the bedroom.

"Absolutely! I will, I promise. Don't you worry," her voice called back and then dissolved into a fit of coughing from trying to project it that far.

"Tomorrow night," Pig said and I nodded.

"I'll be there."

He ducked out the front door into the evening and I shut it behind him. Once I heard his bike start up, I threw the locks and let my shoulders sag. Fucking-A, I hated that cocksucker. I drifted up the hall and leaned silently against the doorframe to her bedroom. She sat up in bed, still looking so small and frail, staring at her hands. Her eyes drifted shut and tears slipped silently down her face. She sniffed and took a wretched breath and let it out slowly. I knew she'd heard everything and I knew it bothered her; it hurt, and filled her heart with resentment and anger and such a feeling of hopelessness. It was plain to see in the way she held herself.

"You okay?" I asked. She took a breath and nodded, and I pushed off the frame of the door.

"You didn't get sick on purpose, but you damned sure let it spiral out of control, didn't you?" I asked softly. She looked at me, her blue eyes sparking and flashing with anger and resentment, which slid away just as quickly as they had appeared, as if the emotions had been thrown at her wall and instead of sticking, had just slid to the floor, regret and resignation revealed underneath.

"Oh, baby, you can't give up," I said. I sighed and sat down by her feet.

"Why?" she asked, her lips parted. Her chin trembled and fresh tears welled in her bright and intelligent eyes, and slipped free, down her porcelain skin. The whole effect, surrounded by her raven-dark hair, was breathtaking. She jerked back and her expression turned confused. I reached out and thumbed a tear from her chin.

"What is it, baby?" I asked her, ignoring her question.

"Why are you looking at me like that?" she asked.

"Pig's an asshole."

She gasped but I pressed on. She'd told me some of her secrets, things that could get her in trouble; I owed it to her to say a thing or two that could land my ass in the fire, to even the score between us once more. "He's got this smart, beautiful, fiery woman right in front of him. A treasure that should be treated like the jewels she flips for him to line his fucking pockets, and look what he does to you." I felt my mouth set into a line of resignation. If anyone from the club heard what had just come out of my mouth, I would have my teeth knocked out by one vicious curb-stomping. If I was lucky, it would stop there, but I didn't think luck had much to do with anything when it came to the Suicide Kings.

Dani raised her cornflower-blue eyes from her hands to meet mine and I could see the keen intelligence there. She knew what I'd just done by saying that. She sniffed and her tears started to dry on her face. She nodded carefully.

"Thank you," she whispered, and I gave her a smile.

"Sure thing, Rocket," I murmured.

"This moment, right here, right now, this stays just between me and you, right?" she asked carefully. I considered her.

"Yeah. Yeah it does." I didn't know what she had in mind but I was willing to give her that.

"Come here?" she whispered barely loud enough for me to hear. I edged closer to her, shifting from sitting by her feet to sitting up by her hip.

"What is it?" I asked. My heart was squeezing down tight in my chest. *Was she gonna do what I think she was gonna do?* She leaned forward, oh-so-carefully, her eyes holding an intoxicating mixture of bravery and fear with an undercurrent of determination. I held stock-still and didn't do anything. Oh man. This was some heavy shit.

She brushed my lips with hers, oh-so-lightly, in a chaste kiss, her breath warm against my skin. I felt my eyes slip shut and my world went dark for a heartbeat so I could capture and hold this feeling forever; secrete it away for when the whole fucking world was on fire and I needed a small hope to cling to. Dani Broussard had been trashed six ways to Sunday by the Suicide Kings MC, yet she still held inside her this pure and innocent... just... fire, and she shared a little bit of that with me just then.

"Thank you," she murmured against my lips before withdrawing completely. Her lips left mine and my eyes snapped open to meet her somber, yet beautiful, stare. I sucked in a breath, remembering finally that I was supposed to breathe.

She'd kissed me. Knowing what it could cost her, knowing what it could do to me, she pulled out an incredible moment of badass and fucking kissed me even after everything she'd been through. Years of Hell, years of abuse at the hands of that psycho, drugged-out fuck. She'd bravely given of herself to me after so long and so many men just taking whatever the fuck they wanted from her, and she sat there and thanked me! I blinked at her. I just couldn't comprehend how incredible she was, and she had no fucking idea what she'd just done.

Dani had just sealed her fate with that kiss, because she was going to be mine. Oh yes, she would be mine, and I would be doing it the right way. I wasn't about to go all caveman on her sweet ass, no. No, no, no, and NO. I was going to take this damaged girl and do everything in my power to restore her. The only problem was, I still had to do what needed doing for my club, my real club, the Sacred Hearts. I was fortunate that the two paths I was on ran parallel to each other, that there was no conflict. I didn't know what the fuck I was going to do if those paths ever crossed, but I guess I would just have to cross that particular bridge when I came to it.

"I... I'm sorry." Her hands started shaking when I'd been quiet too long, my thoughts caught up in a hurricane of machination. I took her hands between mine. They were slightly cool and I did what I could to warm them.

"Don't be sorry," I told her sharply and she flinched. I raised her hands to my lips and gently kissed her fingertips.

"You're fine," I soothed. She nodded, and I was acutely aware that I couldn't make this last beyond tonight and tomorrow, that her reprieve was finite and coming to an end. I swallowed hard, and even though I didn't want to, I stood up.

"Come on, let's get you some sleep." She scooted down in her bed and I tucked her in, pulling the blankets to her chin.

"I'll be right out in the living room." It pained me to say it but I needed some distance from her if I was going to manage to keep a clear head. "You call me if you need anything." She nodded and I switched out the light on her side table and went out, mostly-shutting the bedroom door behind me, leaving it open just enough so that if she called I would hear her.

I checked all my phones and there was a text that I'd missed by only a couple of minutes on my SHMC burner.

How's my patient?

I smiled a little to myself. Seemed Dani might have made an impression on more than just me.

8

D ani...
   I didn't know what was going on and I wasn't sure how
he'd done it, but Thirteen, the prospect, had bought me an additional
week of peace with which to recover.

I'd spent it getting better, along with taking apart and melting
down the pieces he'd brought me, refashioning them into something
saleable, and taking the odd stones I had nothing to make with and
spiriting them into my secret stash, which was the bottle of 'Sensual
Amber' perfume that I carried in my purse. The bottle was, as the
name of the perfume implied, a rich, deep amber color, almost as
dark as a beer bottle. It only held smaller gems, which was just fine;
take something too big, or more than just one or two at a time, it was
bound to be noticed.

I know it was damned foolish stealing from the MC, spiriting
these odd little bits away, but I had to do something. The money I had
from my grandfather was dwindling little by little on rent, food, you
name it – just the general cost of living. Pig-Pen and the MC sure as
hell didn't provide for me to keep a roof over my head and clothes on
my back. I still marveled that it had never occurred to any of them
how I managed to pay rent, or keep gas in my car or food in my

pantry or fridge. The odd crumpled twenty or two that Pig-Pen tossed at me certainly didn't cover any of it.

I had also spent my week of blessed solitude thinking about my curious exchanges with Thirteen. I didn't know what I'd been thinking, kissing him like that. I don't really think I had been thinking, I had simply been feeling when I'd done it. A multitude of emotions really, gratitude paramount among them, but also, upon reflection, maybe a little desire. I was a woman, after all and he was a damned fine specimen of a man, and not just in a physical sense, either. There had been nothing but gentle kindness in his eyes in the time he cared for me in my apartment.

He'd been there later, on the night that Pig-Pen had come, gently shaking me awake and snapping the nightmare I'd been trapped in. It'd been another bad one. The blankets and sheets had twisted around my legs, the tee shirt I'd been in was stuck to my skin with sweat. I'd showered and by the time I'd returned to my room, wrapped in a great big towel, my bed had been freshly-made with clean sheets, the others were running through the wash, and he'd lain a fresh tee out for me. It had not gone unnoticed by me that he didn't go through my things; that the tee he laid out for me was one of his.

We didn't speak. We didn't need to, both of us simply moved around each other, instinctively knowing what the other needed or wanted. He didn't go back to the couch right away. Rather, he stretched out on top of the covers beside me. Not touching, just lying on his side, facing me, one arm tucked under his head. I lay on my side mirroring him, my hands tucked beneath my cheek, simply watching him across the short expanse of mattress between us.

"When I first showed up, you were really out of it," he'd said gently, sometime later.

"Yeah?"

"You were speaking French. I didn't know you could, your English is perfect."

I'd frowned. "What did I say?"

Thirteen had smiled and laughed a little and said, "Hell if I know,

I don't speak anything other than English!" which had elicited a tiny smile from me.

"Sound it out?" I implored.

He tried, and the words had broken my heart. I knew I'd been delirious; I mean, I was running a high fever and I had pneumonia, the doctor had told me so. But still... Tears had sprung to my eyes and I felt as if I'd been cut, deeply, on an emotional level, except instead of blood, despair had welled up.

Thirteen had asked me what I'd said, his free hand moving long strands of my hair gently behind my ear and out of my face. I didn't tell him. How could I? It was just so weak and pathetic. He let me cry, and didn't push, didn't pry at all, for which I was incredibly grateful. I just didn't have it in me to tell him I'd been begging him to let me die in the tongue I had learned as a child from my grandfather, that I'd been begging him to let me go and be with the man who'd raised me.

A hand closed around my upper arm with bruising force and jerked me right out of the memory. I looked up, startled, into Pig-Pen's face. He'd said something to me but I'd completely missed what it was. His hand came down across my face in a brutal backhanded slap and he shook me. Tears sprang to my eyes with the stinging pain.

"I said get me a fucking beer! Jesus Christ! You aren't here to stand around fucking daydreaming all goddamned day!" He shook me by my arm savagely one last time and thrust me away from him. I stumbled into the bar, my hip checking painfully in to it.

"I'm sorry!" I cried, swallowing hard. I got him one of his favorites out of the cooler, and popped the top off of it with the bottle opener mounted into the wood under the bar top. I handed it to him and he snatched it out of my hand so violently that foam boiled out of the long, narrow neck and ran over the backs of his fingers.

"Awww fuck! Look what you made me do, you stupid –" he raised his hand to strike me again and I cowered back, but he was behind the bar with me and there was nowhere for me to go. I closed my eyes and braced for the blow to land, but he was stopped by Griz's angry bark.

"Pen! Knock it off. We got problems bigger 'n this right now."

I panted, my chest heaving, and opened my eyes to stare straight into Thirteen's. He was seated in his usual spot on the couch, his face shut down, his eyes the color of a storm-swept Atlantic ocean. I'd seen it once, when I was a girl, off the South Carolina coast when my grandfather and I had travelled there for a gem show. His face gave nothing away but his posture was tense and I begged him with my eyes: *No, just stay there, be safe; please don't intercede.*

His posture lost none of its rigidity but he blinked once, slowly. Message received. Pig-Pen's looming presence backed away, his shadow leaving me, and I slowly eased back to standing from my cowering. He stalked off after Griz and Pipes. Gordy gave me a dirty look before falling in behind them. Skid sighed from where he was seated at the opposite end of the bar from where I stood.

"Girl, why do you do this to yourself?" Skid asked me, leveling a pitying gaze at me. I smoothed my sweating palms over the thighs of my jeans.

"Glutton for punishment, I guess," I said, my voice low and shaky with fading adrenaline. He huffed a sardonic laugh.

"Yeah. Can't argue with you there," he returned.

"Everybody good on drinks?" I asked and Skid nodded; so did Thirteen, and Flyer, who was playing around on his phone in one of the recliners.

I gathered the trash from behind the bar, even though it was only half-full. I wanted out of there, to get some air for a moment, and taking out the trash was the perfect excuse. I slipped out the fire exit and down the metal steps of the back lot, to the dumpster up against the building, and heaved the sack into it.

"I think about you, too. But you gotta stay sharp in there, Rocket." His voice came gentle and low from behind me, but I hadn't heard him follow me. I jumped and startled hard, my heart leaping clean out of my chest before slamming back in painfully. I pressed a hand to my breast and his hands fell on my shoulders, a firm, even pressure that held me together.

"I'm sorry," I uttered and he turned me around to face him.

"Don't, not with me, not ever," he whispered.

"Someone might see us," I hissed. He dropped his hands from my shoulders and started to take a step back, but at the last second, he held his ground.

"Some things are worth the risk," he muttered harshly and before I knew it I was in his arms, his lips pressed, warm and inviting, against my own. I faltered for a moment, melting against his chest, his heart thudding solidly through his soft tee beneath my fingertips. I moaned softly and opened to him and he deepened the kiss, his tongue, hot and velvet-soft, sweeping past my lips.

He tasted so much better than I imagined he would, masculine and crisp with an overlay of hops from the beer he'd drunk inside. I pushed back suddenly and pressed my fingertips to my lips where the feel of his kiss still lingered. He let me go immediately, didn't force anything, simply let me go, standing a pace away, arms loose at his sides, chest heaving, a match for my own.

"Go inside," he said gently. I nodded and, with shaking legs, climbed the stairs. I took a second, my breath fogging in the cool spring night, and tried to regain my composure before opening the door. Sticking to the shadows, I resumed my place behind the bar, my back to the club and my hair hiding my face, which felt flushed.

The door opened behind me a few minutes later and I heard Skid turn on his stool before he said, "You find it?"

Thirteen answered him. "Naw, man, it was a sweet ride though; the picture must be back in my stuff at the cabin. If I find it, I'll bring it in. I thought for sure it was in my saddlebag..." The two men launched into a continuation of a conversation on restoration projects and classic bikes, and I continued doing what I was doing as more guys arrived. Still, I kept my head down and my eyes resolutely off of Thirteen, even though I could feel his eyes on me.

Not for the first time, I thought to myself that he was a dangerous man. This time, though, it was for a whole different reason.

9

Red-XIII...

I had to watch myself around her at the club. She'd been absolutely right. Someone could have seen us, and that could have been bad. Really bad.

Shit was seriously starting to fall apart for the Suicide Kings that week, the week after my stolen kiss with Dani. I got a text on the SHMC burner that, once deciphered, meant only one thing. They'd caught their rat. I had to wait a day or two before I could dial in and get the 411.

I was at my cabin and Dragon picked up on the second ring. "I figured you'd be calling in any day now," he said by way of greeting.

"Yeah, I figured something was going down when their council started having more closed-door meetings. With everyone present and accounted for, I figured you must have caught the mole."

Dragon grunted. "Shelly did, actually. She found some inconsistencies in ORG's books. Darlene, the office girl, was skimming off the top. She's got a sick kid; somehow the Suicide Cunts found out about it and offered her enough green to keep her kid breathing. Stupid bitch should have just come to me or Dray, we woulda kept her straight and flyin' right." He sighed and it was a sound that held the weight of the whole damned world in it.

"Shit, a woman and her kid?"

"Yep."

"Do I even want to know how we handled this one?" I asked. I knew how it would be handled in the old days; it wasn't a situation that I wanted to think about too much. Didn't matter your gender in the old days, you ratted and got caught, the end result was the same. You got yourself perished.

"We brainstormed, took a vote... Lucky, Zeb, and Doc took her and the kid; they're relocating them as we speak. Doc will be back middle of the week, next week. Lucky and Zeb are gonna stay with her 'til we see this thing through."

"After that?" I asked.

"She's on her own. Far away from here. She darkens our door again, we got a spot all picked out for her with a nice view from Cicada Woods. Up to her on which way it goes," he said. I nodded, more to myself than anything. Not like he could see me.

"We can spare Luck and Zeb?"

"Yeah, no problem. Duracell has Lucky's special capabilities with a lot less of the 'luck' part factored into it, so we should be good."

"Good."

"You still got eyes on you?"

"Nope. Ain't seen the van since Tuesday two weeks back," I said, speaking of the cops who'd been surveilling the Kings since the attack on my club. "You?" I asked.

"Nope. Moving into phase two the end of next week," he said, then, "How's that girl? You ever figure out what's doin' with her?"

I explained about Dani's special skill-set, how she'd gotten in with the Kings in the first place, and that she was most certainly not aligned with their way of thinking. I felt guilty as sin spilling all her closely-guarded secrets to my Pres., but at the same time, I had to if I had any hope of getting her out of there.

"Sounds like one of the most fucked-up situations I've ever heard of," Dragon said disgustedly, "You think she's got a clue about you or Doc?"

I answered him truthfully. "D, she's fucking smart as hell. I don't think she knows *where* we come from but she definitely knows something ain't right about me. She's keeping her mouth shut, though."

"You think she'll sell you out to save her own skin?" he asked. I hoped so, but I wasn't about to tell him that.

"Honestly? I don't know. I'm hoping it doesn't come to that."

"You see it headed that way, you gotta choose between her and maintaining your cover? You make the right choice, Thirteen. I do not wanna lose another brother to these assclowns. You get me?"

I nodded, realized he couldn't see it, and answered him, "I hear you loud and clear." I answered.

"Good. When do you think you can get me names and locations of these guys?" he asked.

"Thought you was never gonna fuckin' ask!" I felt a grim sort of satisfaction knowing that we were finally going on the offensive with this. I was getting tired of the game and I wanted to get Dani out of the life she was stuck in with these animals. Out from under Pig-Pen. Unfortunately, I knew how these kinds of things played out. The more members my club shaved off the Suicide Kings' roster, the more riled and hungry these guys were going to become, the angrier and more savage, and the trickier the game would become to play. I hung up with Dragon feeling a mixture of marginally better and marginally worse. Better because things were finally in motion, worse because I was beginning to realize I was developing some serious feelings for Dani, and that those feelings could compromise me.

I thrust those worries aside. There was no sense in wondering and worrying about shit that hadn't happened yet. Focusing on what-if's was a good way to get distracted from what was right in front of your face, which was a good way to get dead. I had no intentions of doing either of those things.

None whatsoever.

D ani...
Things went from bad to worse over the next week. Neo, a young member of the club, around my age, who was so-named for his resemblance to Keanu Reeves, got himself arrested dealing and had enough drugs on him that he would be spending a really long time in prison if he was convicted, which he would be, because the club was flat broke. Neo would be stuck with a public defender and this was absolutely not his first offense.

So not only was the club out yet another member, they were out most all of their drugs as well. Griz ordered Ace and Deuce to go on a run to the supplier, after shaking down just about all of the club members for enough money to make another purchase. The Sacred Hearts blowing up the local meth lab had hurt Griz's operation badly. I couldn't help it... that thought made me smile every time.

What *didn't* make me smile was when Griz and Pig-Pen got into it over how much of the profits from the club's drug trade Pig had smoked. He was officially cut off, and he was hurting, which made him extremely temperamental and dangerous, a level of crazy I'd never before seen. I did what Thirteen told me to do. I stayed sharp, but staying sharp was only half the equation where Pig-Pen was concerned. In order to deal with him you had to have your crystal ball in perfect working order and unfortunately, I wasn't a mind reader. Not at all.

The twins, Ace and Deuce, were leaving on their run and both were intense and nervous. They were both tall and lanky, with brightly-colored mohawks. They always did their hair in two or more tones and opposite each other so you could tell them apart; this time around Ace's mohawk was red toward his scalp and yellow at its spikey end, while Deuce's was red at its ends and yellow towards his closely-shaven scalp. I never understood how anyone mixed the two up when they had their cuts on nearly constantly, with their name flashes prominently displayed, but I guess it was a testament to the level of some of these biker's intelligence that it still happened all the time.

"Okay, we're out of here. See you, Rac," Deuce said. I forced a smile and nodded.

"Ride safe," I told them quietly, but silently I cursed them to death by roadrash.

Ace winked at me and I forced my smile just a little bit more. I turned back to mopping the floor, biting my lips together, trying to forget.

Ace and Deuce were unbelievably cruel. Unlike Pig-Pen, they were quiet about it. Well, not exactly quiet. They just seemed to be more selective about it, didn't indulge in a constant trickle of small acts of cruelty like Pig, but rather saved it up, and when they finally tapped it... I was grateful I had never been on the receiving end. There had once been this girl, Marissa, a club slut who was pretty much into anything, once you got her high enough. She'd gotten high with the twins and they'd raped her half to death. Cut her face up so bad that no one would ever be able to call her pretty anymore.

I wrung out the string mop and dropped it with a wet splat to the floor, swiping it across the dried beer spills that had gone tacky on the clubroom floor, and tried not to look at the Sacred Hearts cut nailed to the wall above the air hockey table.

Those two had had their heads together for days, talking in

murmured and low, reserved tones, stopping their conversation cold anytime anyone drew near. Finally, a couple of nights later, they'd come in laughing and boasting, and had presented Griz with their trophy, which reeked of their urine. Pig-Pen had praised them, Griz had nodded and quietly rewarded them with a new girl, who'd spent the rest of the night screaming.

I closed my eyes, bile rising in a stinging acid-wash in my throat.

It had been Pig's idea to nail the cut up on the wall. His idea too, to take a can of black spray paint and add three hash marks down and to the right of it. One for every dead Sacred Heart. I'd heard one of those hashtags was for an Ol' Lady of theirs that had died when Joker, Rowdy, Snake, Danimal, Nord, and Reefer had gone to the Sacred Hearts clubhouse, guns blazing, expecting to find just one or two men and all of their women.

I'd been frightened after I'd heard Gordy and Pipes talking about it, fearful that the Sacred Hearts would come looking for an eye for an eye.

Griz had seen the look on my face and had started howling with laughter and told me I didn't have shit to worry about from the Sacred Hearts, then called them pussy-whipped and a myriad of other names, implying that it was their women who really ran the show over there. I didn't know what to make of that then, and I still didn't know what to make of it now. I'd pretty much kept to myself at the lake run, hadn't strayed far from Pig, for fear of what he'd do to me if I did.

I finished cleaning the clubhouse, all the while trapped in memory. I didn't realize that I'd had company as I'd worked. As usual, he was there, parked on the end of the couch, boots propped on the old, scarred garage-sale coffee table, only this early in the day he'd forgone the beer in favor of a bottle of water. That was another thing that set him apart as 'other'; to the rest of the guys, beer *was* bottled water.

I sent a small, secret smile in his direction and he returned it, but we didn't speak, we didn't need to. Soon, Skid came around and our little private moment was in the wind, but that was okay. I knew that I never could or would be with Thirteen, but having him around had become a little ray of light in an otherwise dark room. Maybe it was foolish to hope or to dream at this stage, but I couldn't help but believe that with a guy like Thirteen around the club, maybe, just maybe, things could get better.

"What you smiling about?" Skid asked me as he bellied up to the bar. I startled, *had I been smiling?*

I glanced at the older biker and he raised an eyebrow under his faded black do-rag. "I don't know…" I frowned and flailed helplessly inside my head for a convincing lie. "I was just thinking about a piece I was going to try and create. I think I have all the parts now."

Skid chuckled. "It's good to see you smile, Rac. How 'bout you get me a beer? One of them ones with the orange dude on the label." He turned on his stool and started talking to Thirteen, who had come up to join him, grinning like an idiot behind his back, but who quickly schooled his features into neutrality before Skid turned.

I rolled my eyes at Thirteen behind Skid's back and got him the bottle he asked for, popping the top. I set it on the bar by his hand and he picked it up and drank, never breaking his stride as the two of them spoke bike. I was simply nothing more than furniture again, which I didn't like, but at the same time it was definitely the lesser of two evils.

Pretty soon Gordy, Pipes, and Cooter came in from the front of the club, and I was serving them up drinks when Pig-Pen and Griz made their arrival. The rest of the guys started to trickle in from the front or the back lot and girls started coming, intermixed with the guy's arrival. The party was in full swing, the sky dark outside, when Gordy swore and pounded his fist on the bar.

"Goddamn, fucking son of a bitch!" he bellowed, looking at the lighted screen on his phone.

Griz shoved down on the head of the strung-out broad sucking him off, and she choked, struggling.

"What is it now?" he demanded and let her up. She stood up, disgusted, and stumbled towards the bathrooms.

"Trouble!" Gordy declared. "But if we all go now we might make it. Ace and Deuce are holed up at the northwest safe house, says Sacred Hearts have 'em pinned down, four of 'em."

Griz stood up and tucked himself back in his pants, doing up his jeans. "Boys! We're goin' huntin'!" he yelled. A cheer went up and I swallowed hard. Thirteen stood.

"Not you!" Gordy stabbed a finger at him. "Take Coon to your place and keep her locked down. She's our last bet on making any goddamned money."

Thirteen raised an eyebrow. "I live in a cabin with no electricity!" he declared.

"So fucking what?" Pig-Pen called, "Don't care if she's comfortable so long as she can produce, you goddamned pussy!"

Thirteen gave a shrug and I gathered my purse. The guys were all going out the back door to the parking lot where they kept their bikes; I could already hear some of them firing up. Dredd and Flyer were chasing out the club sluts, truthfully, there weren't many left hanging around since the club's drug supply started drying up. I came around the bar and Pig grabbed me by the elbow, hard.

"You're my bitch, so don't be getting any ideas about spreading those whore legs of yers for Pretty-boy over there," he muttered savagely in my ear, his breath washing over me, a fetid mixture of whiskey and cigarettes with an overlay of just plain rot.

"I wouldn't dream of it." I plastered on a fake-as-hell sincere smile. "I know who takes care of me," I said.

"Damn right." And as if to prove his point, he shoved his mouth against mine and his tongue in my mouth, all the while looking daggers at Thirteen. I gave little resistance. I didn't want or need any more bruises beyond the ones that were likely already imprinted on my arm where he gripped me. Besides that, I'd learned a long, long time ago that resistance was futile and only hurt more in the end. Pig-Pen finally broke the kiss and thrust me in Thirteen's direction before going out the door.

"You good to ride?" he asked. I nodded grimly. I just wanted to get outside so I could spit. Thirteen grabbed my coat off the hook in the wall behind the bar and handed it to me, and I shrugged into it.

"C'mon." He put a hand on my shoulder and made like he was shoving me in front of him out the door, though his grip on my shoulder was light, not painful. He put on his helmet and glasses sitting astride his bike. I put on the spare, and with one final brave smile at Pig, who was glaring at me and standing with Griz and Gordy, I got on behind Thirteen.

I actually loved to ride. It didn't matter who I was behind, the wind whipping my hair, the fresh air, the thrum of the bike up my spine, and the feeling like I was just flying was the only thing that made me feel free anymore, the last illusion, as delicate as a soap bubble but full of vibrancy, until the ride stopped and the bubble popped and it was as if those rainbow colors had never existed.

I spit out the taste of Pig-Pen's mouth as soon as we were clear of the club, and I felt the vibration of Thirteen's laugh through his back, which I was quite snug against. As we went through town, he pulled off into a fast-food place's parking lot as soon, I think, as he was sure we wouldn't be seen. He tapped my hands, which were firmly on his stomach, in the classic signal for *Get off*, and I did. He got up and dug in one of his saddlebags and, with a wink, handed me a bottle of mouthwash.

I bit my lower lip and grinned and, laughing, took it from him. The burn and bite of the minty alcohol mixture was welcome and efficiently scrubbed the lingering bitterness of sour whiskey and ashtray off my tongue.

I think I more than liked Thirteen in that moment for knowing exactly what was in my heart and mind, but mostly for not judging me for it. For seeing me, the real me, and understanding. There was no pity from him, no derision, nothing to make me feel two inches tall. If anything, I got the impression of silent admiration from him. Thirteen, the prospect, made me feel human again.

"Ready to go?" he asked.

"Yeah, thanks." I handed back the mouthwash and we resumed our journey, only this time when I got back on his bike, he gently tucked my hands in his pockets to keep them warm. It was still cold at night, the wind crisp and biting.

I was surprised at how long the ride was, at least forty-five minutes to an hour, if not more. We were winding along a lakeside road when he slowed and turned on to a pitted gravel track that led towards the water. I tipped my head and peered into the dark over his shoulder.

"Your people, they welcome you!" he joked and I laughed lightly; two raccoons sat up on their haunches in the sweep of Thirteen's headlight before dropping to all fours and trundling into the under-brush at the side of the narrow lane. I pulled my hand from his pocket and playfully slapped his shoulder. He laughed and hit the throttle just enough to throw me back a bit, I 'Eep'ed and hung onto him. He laughed again and I found myself laughing, too.

The narrow gravel lane spilled out into a drive in front of a small cabin that was built out over the water. The little front wrap-around porch clung to the land and a dock stretched out further over the water past the building from the back.

"You live here?" I asked.

He shut off the bike and tapped my arm. I jumped down, careful of the hot pipes even though I wore jeans. I immediately went for the catch beneath my chin, unbuckling the helmet from my head. Truth-fully, I sort of swam in it, so it was really more for appearances than any actual useful protection.

"Yeah, I like the quiet. Wait here a minute, I'll get some lights on and make sure it's not a total sty."

I hung the spare helmet from his sissy bar.

"You don't have to do all that for me," I said softly.

"I want to, just hang tight."

He unlocked the front door and disappeared inside and I stood patiently, gripping the strap of my purse beneath my coat. A few seconds later the golden glow of firelight, warm and inviting, filled the dirty windowpanes on either side of the door.

A few minutes later, the door swung in and Thirteen waved me forward, "Come on. I got a fire going, it'll warm up in a minute or two."

I went forward, curious more than anything about what the little cabin would look like on the inside.

It was cozy, and small, all right. The interior was as rustic as could be, the walls on the inside the same as the outside, simply stacked logs. Oil lamps bolted to those walls provided the light needed to see by. There was a bed just inside the front door, and past it a big, black, stocky beast of a woodstove. There was a sink in the back left corner and a bit of a kitchen-like counter. Behind the wood-burning stove, which was in the center-right of the room, there was a little four-seater rustic wood table with matching wood chairs. I didn't see a bathroom at all and I bit my lip.

"I think I can guess what you're thinking," Thirteen said with a smart-assed grin. I raised an eyebrow. "Bathroom is an outhouse. Out the front door and that way, in the corner of the yard." I nodded and pursed my lips. He chuckled.

I went back out the front door to take care of business and when I returned, Thirteen was kneeling in front of the wood stove, stoking the fire and adding a bit more wood, coaxing it into a cheery blaze. It was warmer in here already, though admittedly, there wasn't a whole lot of space to warm up.

"That's better," he remarked and stood. "Can I take your coat?"

I slipped it from my shoulders and handed it to him. I wore a fitted long-sleeved shirt with a neckline that left my neck and shoulders bare. His eyes, more green than anything at the moment, slipped from my face and traced the curve of my neck and out and down over my shoulder. It was one of those looks so full of weight and substance that you felt it like a caress, but instead of leaving me feeling dirty like it would have if it had come from Pig or any of the other guys, the look Thirteen gave me left me feeling like I was beautiful, a fine piece of art to be admired from afar. Except I really, really wanted him to touch me.

There was a small dresser behind the cabin's front door and I took off my purse and set it on its top. He hung my coat to the right of the bed, off a hook beneath one of the oil lamp sconces there. There were two fixtures, one to either side of the bed, and he'd lit them both, along with the two behind the front door.

He turned back to me and I wish I could say that things suddenly became awkward, but they didn't.

Desire shimmered the short distance between us, a palpable thing like heat from a summer sidewalk. I swallowed hard and he did, too. I wanted so badly for him to touch me, maybe even kiss me. I mean, we were alone and Pig... Pig would never know, would never have to know. I kept him in the dark on so many things. But if we did, Thirteen stood to lose so much more than I did. I mean, they couldn't kill me. They could hurt me but they couldn't kill me, and I had become rather adept at accepting their pain, cruelty, and humiliation.

"What do you want to do, Rocket?" he asked me, softly.

I raised my eyes to his and asked him, "If some things are worth the risk... is this one of them?"

His eyes went feral and dark and in three long strides he closed the gap between us.

"Hell, yes," he growled and I was in his arms.

His mouth crashed into mine and I opened for him and drew him to me. I wanted so badly to remember what it was to feel good when a man touched me, and Thirteen promised me that – and so much more with the way his mouth moved against mine, the way his hands traveled over my curves in a warm and gentle press of skin on skin, after he'd delved beneath my shirt.

I shoved his leather jacket off his well-formed shoulders and it crashed to the floor in a heap of leather and rattling buckles, snaps, and zips. His hands immediately returned to my shirt, which he gathered in his fists.

"Off," he growled into my mouth and it was an intense passion-filled command that left heat pooling in my womb and started a deep, throbbing ache of wanting in my vagina. I wanted him, I wanted this, and it was more about how Thirteen made me feel alive and how life was worth living than anything else. I obediently lifted my arms above my head and he whisked my shirt away, his hands returning to my jean-clad hips, curving around my back and drawing me closer to him.

I cupped his face with my hands; his short, three days' growth of beard was surprisingly soft beneath my palms as I held his face to mine. His kiss was hot, warm, and sweet, and despite the urgency of it, patient. I could feel him holding back and like so many things I just knew about him, I knew it was for my benefit. His palms, rough with callouses but so warm and so incredibly gentle, smoothed up my back to the catch on my bra.. My body broke out in a wash of gooseflesh and tingles, a pleasurable euphoria ghosting across every inch of my skin.

My bra disappeared and I wanted so badly for there to be more skin contact between us. I gathered the hem of his soft cotton tee in my hands and tugged.

"Off," I whispered against his lips, and he smiled against mine, obediently lifting his arms as I had done. As soon as his shirt was off, we both came together, pressing against each other's bodies like he was just as starved for a gentle physical touch as I was.

I don't know how long we stood there, fingertips tracing along muscle definition and along curves, exploring one another's bodies as we made out like teenagers. But finally Thirteen turned me in his arms and laid me down on the bed, his eyes never leaving mine, beseeching me to trust him.

I was surprised that even though I'd been hurt by any number of men since Jared, that I really did trust Thirteen, that there was something about him. Was he dangerous? Yes, but it was a controlled danger, and that's when it struck me. *Thirteen was in control.* None of the men of the Suicide Kings had even a tenth of the measure of control that Thirteen had over himself and his surroundings.

"You okay, baby?" he whispered.

"Yes," I answered and I was – I knew I was okay with him. He would never tell. I just knew, deep down in my gut, that Thirteen was different than anyone I had ever met before in my life, and that I was safe with him.

Safe. It was such an alien concept. But right here, right now, while I had it, I was going to revel in it, because I knew, beyond any doubt, that come the pure light of morning, I would have to go back, and who knew if I was ever going to be able to steal a moment like this ever again? This might be my only chance and I was going to seize it!

I lifted my hips and let him peel my jeans and panties down my legs. He paused just long enough to pull off my shoes, and whisked my clothes off the rest of the way. Then there he was, looking at me like that again. Like I was a particularly beautiful bike, or a fine piece of art.

"God, you are so fuckin' beautiful," he breathed and my eyes drifted shut as I savored his words, turning them over and over in my mind, committing the sound of awe in his voice to deepest memory, engraving it in stone so I would never, ever lose it.

"Kiss me," I begged, and his lips found my neck and my chest, traveling lower and lower to take one of my nipples into his hot mouth. I gasped, my fingers threading through his hair, cradling his head against my chest in open invitation to stay as long as he'd like. He chuckled and the vibration of it thrummed through his body and into mine, striking a chord deep inside of me, resonating sweetly. I know I probably shouldn't have, but I let him into my heart and what's more, I let him make himself right at home there.

He awkwardly kicked off his boots as he kissed down my body, ending up kneeling on the floor as he kissed lower and lower. He kissed along my stomach, his hands smoothing out the trail of fire left behind by his lips. It was like he was worshiping my body and I was falling in love with the sensations he wrought by the second.

He kissed my shaven mound and I gasped, and his lips spread into a smile there. He was between my thighs, nothing hidden to his sight, and I didn't mind it. I didn't mind it at all, which surprised me. I'd never been sexually brazen with anyone; I'd even been shy with Jared. Apparently Pig-Pen and the guys had broken me of it and I hadn't noticed.

No. I would not think about them right now. They would not spoil this for me.

"Rocket, you okay?" Thirteen asked softly, pausing. I looked down the length of my body at him and nodded.

He met my eyes and tipped his chin downward, a clear indication that he was checking with me, giving me the chance to speak up to tell him anything. He waited patiently and I gave in.

"Ask me again, only say my name?" I pleaded and his lips curved into a beautiful, if sad, smile.

"Dani, are you okay?"

I closed my eyes and couldn't help but smile.

"Yes," I answered.

And he licked me, his tongue traveling from my opening to my clit, his hands warm and gently holding me just above my hips, splaying across my ribs to keep me from moving too far when I arched and cried out.

He made love to me with his mouth, gently kissing, licking, and sucking until I was crying out and writhing beneath him. He held me on that pinnacle for a long, long time before finally, eyes gazing up the length of my body to meet mine, he sent me plummeting back to earth, my body splintering beneath his mouth and hands, coming apart to be remade better than before.

He stood up and I heard, rather than saw, him unfasten and drop his jeans. I stared at the ceiling, catching my breath a moment more before looking and when I looked? My God, it stole what little breath I'd gotten back right away again. The rumors were all true.

Thirteen chuckled. "Relax, Dani, I don't need you to take it all for it to feel good. This, tonight, is less about me and more about you anyways." I frowned at that and he laughed again, settling between my thighs.

"Relax," he repeated, "I want it that way."

I stared for a long time into his green-blue eyes and he smiled, tearing open a gold foil package. *Where had that come from?*

He rolled the condom down his length and, oh my God, he went on forever! He settled between my thighs and huddled over me, kissing the tip of my nose, my lips, and as he deepened the kiss I began to relax underneath him. He probed gently with the head of his long, thick cock at my opening and I tensed just a bit, which was when he soothed me, talking to me.

"Shhhh, you want me to stop? Is it too much?" he asked.

I shook my head.

"Don't stop, please? I really do want you," I whispered back.

He nodded and pressed into me, slowly, gently, all the while searching my face for any signs of discomfort. Just when he reached a point that I was sure I couldn't take any more of him, he stopped.

"There?" he asked me and I bit my lower lip between my teeth and nodded. He smiled at me and it was so beautiful and so sweet. "God, you feel good," he breathed and then began to move. He started with slow and gentle, almost minuscule, thrusts back and forth that woke something deep inside of me that I'd almost forgotten existed. I held him to me and he kissed me, hot and hungry, a slightly more-insistent kiss than any we'd shared to date, and his thrusts became longer as he drew himself further from my body and eased back in with slightly more vigor as time went on.

It drove me wild. *He* drove me wild. Thirteen felt incredible, slowly building me back up all over again, holding me gently on that precipice, his breath panting, our bodies lightly dewed with sweat. He moaned, a deep and dark and primal thing, full of lust and something deeper that I didn't dare put a name to.

"Oh my God," he moaned, "Oh my God, Dani you feel so good, so hot and tight and wet. Oh God, I'm not gonna last, I need you to come for me, babe, I want to feel you come all over my cock, can you do that? Can you come for me?" His voice was so strained with how he held himself back, and so incredibly sexy and passionate, I found myself readily agreeing to his demands, readily agreeing to do whatever he could possibly want from me.

He held me close but still held himself off of me in such a way it was intimate without being in the slightest overbearing. He slid a hand between our pelvises, his eyes locked tightly with mine, and his thumb found my clit. I jerked when he touched it, I know I did, I felt myself tighten around him where he rode inside of me, it felt so good! It made him smile and he encouraged me one more time.

"Come on, Dani. Come for me, baby girl..." and it was all I needed and I was falling all over again, tumbling into a pleasure, a pure bliss beyond anything I had ever experienced before. I think I screamed – I'm pretty sure I screamed – I couldn't be sure. But if I did, I can tell you one thing: if you could make ecstasy into a sound, whatever poured from my throat would be it. Thirteen cried out above me, his eyes squeezing shut as I felt him throb in counterpoint to the uncontrolled muscle spasms my orgasm created.

Too soon, he collapsed on top of me, his weight a solid and comforting thing as he pressed me into the quilt on his bed. I kissed his shoulder, which was conveniently near my lips as we lay panting, both climbing metaphorically from the craters that we found ourselves in from crashing back to earth.

"Is that what that's supposed to be like?" I heard myself ask through my gasping.

Thirteen laughed through his, the sound broken by his attempts to draw breath.

"Yeah," he gasped out. "Yeah, that's exactly what that's supposed to be like."

I giggled into his shoulder and he pulled back enough to look at me.

"You're incredible," he said and kissed me, long and sweet and slow. I didn't know how he figured but I didn't want to argue the point. Not with his lips moving against mine like they were. I put absolutely no thought into how this all would end. I simply accepted the gift I was given and appreciated that God might be taking a moment of pity on me. I would be back in Hell soon enough as it was.

11

R ed-XIII...
 It had surprised the hell out of me, the order to bring Dani
to my crib, but I took it for the damned blessing it was and got her the
hell out of there. It had caught me off-guard for sure, but I couldn't
and wouldn't be sorry. I was grateful now that the place had no electricity because it had given me the perfect excuse to give the place a
good once-over to hide anything Sacred Hearts-related before I let
her in. Everything was hidden safely in my secret stash, and she
would have to be pretty damned industrious to find the trap door, not
to mention off-the-charts intelligent, plus she'd have to be actively
looking for it, and she had no reason to.

Right now she was sleeping peacefully, her head on my shoulder,
her arm across my chest. I loved how snug and tight she'd fitted her
body against mine, her leg over both of mine. I had an arm curved
protectively around her body, my free hand high up on her thigh
beneath the covers. She felt so amazing and just so right, up against
me like this. Tomorrow I would have to let her go, and that was the
thing keeping me awake, long into the night. Nothing but the
shadows flickering across the cabin's ceiling kept me company while
Dani slept, oblivious.

I'd deliberately taken things slow with her, and she'd been so incredibly giving of herself, and brave. I admired her spirit more with every encounter that we managed to have together. I know it was ridiculously dangerous to let her get under my skin like this but I was a dangerous guy.

Still, cockiness had gotten more than one guy like me dead and the more I looked at her big picture the more acutely aware I was that I really couldn't afford to be cocky. If I were gone, she'd have no one to look after her. I mean, yeah, she'd done a halfway decent job on her own up until now and I was pretty sure, with as smart as she was, she had some kind of stash or exit strategy in place if the opportunity presented itself, but I had no idea what my brothers had done. My *real* brothers that is.

Whatever it was, it involved Ace and Deuce; Gordy had said Sacred Hearts had 'em pinned down. I'd passed along that the twins were going on a run and whatever other info I'd had on it to D, but I wasn't sure if D had told Grinder's bros or not. I was square in the dark on what was going on, on that side of things. I sighed softly. With Dani here it wasn't like I could pick up the phone and touch base, so for now I just had to play it by ear and adapt as I went along.

"What are you thinking about so hard?" she asked, and I tried to look down at her. ... No dice at this angle, and I damn sure didn't want to move her. She was comfortable and so was I, so I just settled back, my head on my pillows and smiled to myself. Little shit hadn't been asleep at all.

"I don't want to take you back to him," I said.

She chuckled bitterly.

"I know, but it has to happen. Do you regret prospecting for them yet?" she asked.

I kissed the top of her head. "Hell, naw, not when it brought me to you."

She sighed out and was quiet for a very long time.

"You make me feel safe," she finally murmured, and the words sounded almost like a confession from her lips.

"I'm glad," I said, and smiled. I kissed the top of her head again.

Her hair was like silk against my lips and the feel of it was sort of addicting. Hell, she was addicting. My perfect drug.

"It's not safe, though, for either of us. I've put you in terrible trouble with them if they ever find out. I swear I won't tell. No matter how drunk or high he gets, no matter how much he hurts me. I promise not to tell any of them about this." She sniffed and one of her tears dripped wet down my ribs.

I held her tighter.

"Shhhhh," I soothed and she sobbed gently against my chest, clinging to me.

"You don't understand. They'll kill you if they find out. I know, they've done it before. Which is why this can never happen again." She drew in a breath to keep talking but I stopped her.

"Dani, stop. We haven't gone back yet, you're not with them, you're with me, and until I have to take you back that makes you mine. If I only get you for one night then, damn it, I want it to just be about you and me and fuck the rest of the guys. Okay?"

She laughed brokenly through her tears and nodded.

"Okay," she agreed.

I silently held her, stroking her soft skin until she fell back asleep. Only this time, when she went, I went with her.

The next morning, and by 'morning' I really mean 'sometime after the noontime hour', we were woken by the shrill ringing of one of my cells from my jacket. I got up and dug through the pockets and pulled out the burner I used for the Suicide Kings and answered it.

"Hello?"

"You plan on bringing my bitch back here any time today, Prospect? Or you two been fuckin' and I need to kill your ass?" Pig growled into the line.

"I ain't been fucking your woman, man! I got mad respect for you, Bro, and I wouldn't do you like that. We were both up late is all, ain't been talking or nothing, just couldn't sleep. She's not used to a place like mine and was jumping at every damned animal sound out there."

Pig-Pen's laughter boomed through the line.

"She enough to drive you nuts?" he asked.

I forced a laugh as I stared into Dani's sorrowful blue eyes.

"Yeah, man, yeah. I'll get her ass up, we'll be on the road inside ten minutes. Be about an hour or so after that. That cool?"

"Yeah, just both of you get your asses back here," he said.

"Copy that, man." He hung up on me, which was nothing unusual.

Dani was already getting dressed.

"All good things must come to an end," I heard her murmur and I couldn't agree with her more.

With a heavy sigh I pulled on my clothes from last night, too. We didn't speak, and she was stiff at my back the whole ride back to the club. I kept stealing glances at her in the side view mirror and the closer we got to the club, the more withdrawn and shut down she became. That was good, as much as I hated to admit it. The guys wouldn't suspect anything if we didn't give them anything to suspect.

We were ten minutes from the club when it started to rain. I had some Gor-tex rain gear but there was just no point. We were soaked inside a minute, and I would have just given it to her. It was better just to make the final push to the club and neither of us wear it. We pulled into the lot and around to the back and dashed through the downpour, through the fire-exit door, into the bar. Almost all the guys except for the council were sitting around, grim.

"What's the deal?" I asked, "What happened?" Skid turned and looked over above the air hockey table where Grinder's cut was supposed to be. Instead, Ace's and Deuce's cuts were hanging and the hash marks had multiplied to ten in all. A message was scrawled along the back wall.

Keeping score? We're ahead. We're going to finish this.

"Oh, my God." I heard Dani breathe.

"Prospect, yer goin' with Pipes and Flyer tonight to finish what Ace and Deuce started. Coon, bring us the Hennessy's." Griz ordered from the doorway before disappearing back into the front of the club and the Suicide King's little round table council meeting.

I stared at the cuts with cold fury.

I was absolutely sure D had nothing to do with them; he was too smart for that. Now I was going on a run with the club's enforcer and one of Griz's lackeys, who I knew he was absolutely sure of. Dani slipped off to serve the council their Hennessy.

"This is some fucking bullshit," I muttered and Flyer looked at me.

"Yeah," he stated, flatly. I was suddenly glad I'd donned my body armor under my clothes when I'd dressed that afternoon. I'd asked Dani if it would make her feel better if I had some when I'd seen her side-eyeing me, worried. She'd thought I would need it to protect me from the Sacred Hearts. I knew different, but I'd humored her. It looked like the man upstairs was finally paying her some positive attention and I'd won out because of it.

I settled in and waited for Pipes to come out back and tell us we were moving out. I had a feeling it'd be a couple of hours, that we wouldn't be doing anything until dark. In the meantime, I waited to see if anyone would divulge anything about where we were going or who we were seeing. The men's silence told me, more than anything, that I was in some serious shit. I just had to go along with it, though. Nothing else I could really do for now, not without leaving Dani behind, and I wasn't going to do that to her.

Nope.

Fuck me.

12

Dani...

I was a shadow again. Thank God for that, because if I hadn't been forgotten, I never would have heard what they were planning. I put the Hennessy on a round tray with enough shot glasses for the men at the meeting and carefully went to serve them. I set the tray on the edge of the table and slid it more fully onto the scarred metal surface. Then I retreated to the deepest shadows of the hall, and listened. They were deep in to it and didn't check to see that I'd fully gone.

Gordy, a big, bald man with a steel-gray goatee down his chest, was talking, "I say the overlook. Yeah, it's open, but no one travels that pass this time of year, too early yet. I'll be waiting for 'em, Pipes and Flyer can bring him. We can have 'em pull off into the picnic area there, tap our rat, and git. Then we can call those Bleeding Heart bastards to come pick up their trash."

My breath caught in my throat. I'd heard all I needed to, and somehow I needed to warn Thirteen, but I didn't know how. I drifted off and away before anyone came looking for the bathroom and caught me eavesdropping. I wanted to know more but I just couldn't risk it.

I spent the next half-hour trying to carefully catch Thirteen's eye, with no success.

Finally I managed to, and I gave him a pleading look; I begged him with my eyes in that silent way we had, not to go. He looked stricken for a moment, then his handsome face settled into lines of grim resignation. His eyes, which were back to the blue of the storm-swept Atlantic, tried to reassure me that everything would be fine, and then he looked away, breaking our link. I felt my heart drop, plummeting into the pit of my stomach.

"Do you think Pig would mind if I went home and got some dry clothes?" I asked Skid softly. He looked me over.

"I ain't about to go ask him for you," he said. Finally he let out a heavy sigh and lit the end of his cigarette. I didn't have to try too hard to look soggy, uncomfortable, and downright pitiful. He nodded, finally, "Go on, git gone but make it quick! Get your ass back here. With as much dope as he's done? I doubt he'll even notice, 'less he wants a drink or something." I nodded and grabbed up my purse and jacket, along with my keys.

"Thanks, Skid," I murmured. He looked me over in that way he sometimes got, his eyes glassy with drink, like he was seeing an overlay of someone else where I was standing.

"My daughter was still alive, maybe I'd be a better man. Maybe I'd be more like them Bleeding Hearts," I thought I heard him mumble, but I couldn't be sure. I skirted around the end of the bar and slipped out into the back lot. I found my car against the back fence where they'd parked it, and got in. It'd stopped raining, the afternoon showers having moved off to let the sun shine through. It was still cold out, though.

I didn't really have a plan, but I did. It was half-cracked at best, and at worst was downright suicidal, but Thirteen had hit the nail right on the head. Some things were just worth the risks. If I had taken a risk like this years ago, I might well have been free of the MC, or I might be dead. Either way, I was beginning to realize, had its ups and the same end result. Freedom.

I drove home, threw some clothes into a bag, and scraped every bit of precious I had back into a Crown Royal bag. If we managed to live through the night, we'd need everything I could get. I didn't bother changing my clothes for real. I only had a certain amount of time to do this – as much time as it would take to change clothes, get down to my car and get back to the club...

I stopped.

I wasn't thinking about this clearly.

If I was going to do this, make a break for it, really run, I didn't need to go back to the club. I mean, I needed to go back, but not inside. I only needed to be there long enough to watch where Thirteen went, to follow them. I didn't have a fucking clue what I was going to do after that, but I was a smart girl. I had to be, with as much as I had gotten over on Pig and the lot of them over the last three years. I had survived this far without help from anyone. It had taken last night for me to realize just how much more I could have been getting away with.

I think what it really boiled down to was my conversation with Thirteen, about when I'd been sick and what I'd said; that crystallized it for me. He was right. I'd given up. I may not have been brave enough to commit suicide outright, but the Suicide Kings had pushed me to the point that when I'd gotten sick, I really hadn't done anything to take care of myself. I just let myself get sicker and sicker and had prayed for my own inevitable death. Then Thirteen had saved me. Now it was my turn to do everything I could to save him.

I drove back to the club and parked in an alleyway up the block, out of view. My phone had started ringing and I'd dropped it, stomping on it in my black and white Chucks with all the might my small frame possessed, until it was so much shattered plastic and broken glass.

No tracking me now, fuckers! I thought triumphantly. But that didn't assuage the uncomfortable pounding my heart was doing in my chest.

I coughed some, the last vestiges of the illness still hanging on even though I'd obediently finished all of the antibiotics that the doctor had left me. It was dark. Time kept marching on and the sick feeling in my stomach grew with every passing hour.

Thoughts like, *What if I missed them?* or, *What if they killed him inside and I'm already too late?* plagued me as I waited but finally, close to midnight, I heard the roar of bikes split the night air.

I watched as three headlamps, one in front, two in back, pulled around the clubhouse. Pipes was in front, and yes, Thirteen and Flyer were behind him. I ducked back as they passed the mouth of the alley I'd hidden myself in. I got in my car, and I waited for three minutes before starting it and pulling out after them. I knew where the overlook picnic area was. My granddad and I went there in the summertime when I was a kid. He would pan for gold in the riverbed while I played in the water and caught frogs.

I caught up to the three of them and tried to be smart. The men of the Suicide Kings MC never thought I was listening, but since I had little else to do but shamelessly eavesdrop for my own mental entertainment, well, I'd learned a few things over the years. One of those things was what to look for when you were on a run and how to detect if you were being tailed. I knew all of the rules and I broke every single damned one of them as I followed my quarry, so they wouldn't know they were being followed.

So far, so good. It helped that I knew where they were going. It really did. The hard part would be when they got there. I chewed my bottom lip and did something rather impulsive. I held my breath and when we hit the highway, when we were about halfway to the overlook from where we'd got on it, I passed them, along with a couple of other cars. My heart was in my throat as I glanced at their faces through a curtain of my hair but none of them looked at me or seemed to recognize my car as being mine.

With my heart pounding in my chest and the three motorcycles in my rearview, I drove on. I sped. I had to if I was going to do what I needed to do, which was drive up past the overlook a short ways and pull off so I could get back to the overlook on foot.

I was taking way too many gambles here for my liking, but I figured it this way from what I knew so far.

One, Gordy was already at the overlook waiting. Two, the guys had no intention of actually going over the pass and completing this run. If Ace and Deuce had fallen and it was so important to keep me safe and on reserve, then the Suicide Kings were out of money and out of options. This so-called run was just a ruse to separate Thirteen and take him out. Three, Thirteen had to be what they thought he was... a rat for the Sacred Hearts. I knew he was different from the men of the Kings. I could feel it to my very bones and last night had proven to me beyond any doubt that he was.

I passed the overlook and saw Gordy's bike parked there. He was sitting on a picnic table, smoking a cigarette, and startled when my headlights swept past him. I didn't slow, I didn't accelerate... I kept it steady and kept on driving. I didn't know how much time I had until the boys got to the overlook, but I planned on being set up and ready when they arrived. I still hadn't a single clue on what I was going to do when they got there.

Once I was around the bend in the road where it curved into the mountain, I pulled over and threw it in park, bailing out and pulling the keys with a silent prayer that once they were done with whatever they were going to do, Gordy, Pipes, and Flyer wouldn't come this way. I was hidden from the overlook, but a ways from it by foot. I took off at a trot down the hillside and when I was sure I could, streaked across the pavement and into the deep ditch, almost deep enough to be considered a culvert, on the side of the road the overlook shared. I kept low and moved as quietly as I could, the tall grass and low shrubs swishing entirely too loudly against my legs.

I was getting close to the overlook. My heart was beating an erratic staccato in my breast and I honestly thought I was going to have a stroke! I was close enough to see Gordy, and he turned in my direction. I froze and it seemed that luck or *God or whatever* was on my side, because just as he took a step in my direction to see what was going on, the distant roar of approaching bikes made him turn away from me. I let out my breath slowly and silently, and crouched even lower as the three of them turned into the overlook's lot.

The ditch was wide here and they'd buried one of those big metal pipes in it and paved over the top. The bikes went over it and I stayed low in the bushes growing tall to either side, using the rumble of the machines as cover to move over to the pipe and take refuge inside; it was more than big enough. I settled and listened as the three of them parked and shut off their engines. The mountain night was suddenly filled with the steady tick of cooling engines and the low voices of men greeting each other.

I risked a look when their voices grew distant, standing on tiptoe to peek over the edge of the culvert, across the blacktop surface. They'd wandered away from the bikes, closer to the picnic tables. Gordy had his hand on the back of Thirteen's leather coat and I silently prayed he wouldn't feel the bulk of the body armor he was wearing under his black tee shirt.

Suddenly, Gordy said something sharply and he kicked the back of Thirteen's leg. Thirteen cursed sharply and went to his knees, Flyer and Pipes grabbed him by his arms and stretched them to his sides. He struggled, but stilled when Gordy pointed his shiny gun at him. Gordy kept talking, asking questions, but I couldn't make out what he was saying from where I was. I pressed both my hands over my mouth as Gordy paced further and further away from Thirteen.

I felt tears slick down my face, hot and wet, tightening my skin with their salt as they dried there. Maybe he wouldn't shoot him. Maybe they would believe whatever he told them. Thirteen was brilliant, had been with the club for months, maybe – my thoughts were interrupted by three bright flashes, the foothills echoing with three catastrophically loud reports. I jumped and watched in horror as Thirteen jerked back between Flyer and Pipes, his head hanging limp, and the two men let him go. He fell forward into the gravel and lay there, still, not moving.

I ducked back into the pipe and huddled there, shaking. I had to wait for them to leave! I prayed hard and harder, and heard the crunch of their boots as they came across the gravel of the lot.

"... get back down to the club, we'll wait an hour and call the Bleeding Hearts to come pick up their trash," I heard Gordy say.

"Too bad about his bike, I would have liked to have that," Pipes remarked.

"Keys are in his pocket," Flyer shot back.

I heard Pipes snort, "I ain't giving up my baby! The fuck you thin..." his voice trailed off as they moved out of earshot. A short time later the bikes started up. I jumped and then held very, very still as they rumbled overhead, praying, praying, praying, *Please go left, please go left, please go left!*

They turned left, and my shoulders slumped in partial relief. I waited several heartbeats after the silence returned, knowing that with every pulse they put more distance between us and them. Finally, I scrambled out of the huge steel pipe and clawed my way up the embankment.

"Thirteen!" I cried, and flat-out ran in the direction of his prone body. I skidded to a halt on my knees and struggled to turn him over, the tears running down my face even faster when my hand encountered a patch of wet high on one shoulder.

"Thirteen! Chris, Chris! Please, oh, my God, please!" I screamed, and I about threw up with relief when he groaned. Oh, my God, he was alive! He coughed weakly and I kissed him. I kissed him hard.

"Wait here, oh, my God, wait here, I'm coming back. I promise you, I'm coming back!" I eased him off my lap and onto the ground where he groaned, and leapt to my feet in a dead run up the side of the highway to my car. I had to bring it closer! I couldn't wait for the Sacred Hearts to arrive, it would take them too long. I had to get him in my car! I had to! Or he might die.

Red-XIII...

Dani drifted back from delivering the President and his cabinet their booze, and she was a whiter shade of pale. I felt my heart drop into my stomach, but made no outward signs of it. I figured my fate was sealed. I had no fucking idea how I was going to get out of this or what I was going to do. Bandit was talking my fucking ear off, as usual, and I had to engage. I couldn't let these fuckers know I was onto the fact that they were on to me. I swore to Christ, if I got out of this, I was beating every single one of Grinder's bros' asses.

She moved, quiet and reserved, from behind the bar, and I could see her trying to catch my eye. Finally there was enough of a lull in attention on both me and her that I could meet her gaze. Her eyes were full of pain and pleading and screamed at me *Please, just go, just get away from here!* But I couldn't. Not only did I have to see this through for myself and for my club, but I had to see this through for her. I'd made up my mind as she'd slept in my arms that I wasn't done saving Dani Broussard just yet.

I tracked her out of the corner of my eye as she moved to the end of the bar and spoke softly to Skid, who was well on his way to drunk-ville. They exchanged words and with a final look in my direction, she gathered her purse, keys, and jacket, and slipped out the door. It was written all over her, in her tense posture. The girl was going to run. I felt a surge of fierce pride and relaxed. There wasn't anything I could do but let the afternoon drag on into evening. I was getting antsy by the time evening was dragging on into night. The more the minute hand crawled along the clock face, the more hash marks the hour hand passed by, the more resigned I became about my fate and the more hopeful I became about Dani's.

No one was saying word fucking one about where we were making the run to, which direction we were going. Nothing. Not. A. Damn. Thing. Which could mean only one thing for me: I was a fucking dead man.

I had nothing to pass on to D about where I was headed. I had nothing at all to tell my club, not even a fucking goodbye, which would have been worthless anyway. I didn't give up, though; I wouldn't give up until the bitter fucking end. I was a Sacred Hearts man and I was going to bleed my club colors - red, white, and blue.

Pipes eventually made his appearance. "Flyer! Prospect! Let's roll," he called, and I got up and stretched, racking my neck.

"It's about fucking time, man. I was getting bored," I said, and followed the two men out into the crisp night air.

We started our bikes and all the while we geared up to ride, I had the feeling we were being watched.

I hoped it was my club; that they had eyes on me, but I was pretty sure that was just fucking wishful thinking on my part.

"Where we headed?" I asked nonchalantly.

"Same fuckin' direction I am, shut up and fall in," Pipes said. It wasn't out of character for the dude. It was how he always was, so I couldn't say he was being intentionally obtuse.

We mounted up and rode out, and as we rode, I enjoyed it. It could be my final ride, after all, the wind in my face, the thrum of my bike underneath me, the steady rumble of all those horses as we rolled along the big slab.

We were headed up into the hills when a few cars moved on past us. I glanced at just the right time and *Holy fucking shit!* I had to pretend like I didn't see, but yep, there was my clever girl. *What the fuck was she doing?* I wondered as we powered up into the hills. I followed Pipes, Flyer to my right as we kept in formation.

I knew the jig was up when Pipes hit his signal and we turned into the overlook. Fucking Gordy was sitting on a picnic table smoking a cig, waiting for us. We pulled off to the left into the overlook's lot and I wondered briefly where Dani was, shooting off a prayer to whatever power that was that she was safe and would stay that way. I had to smile on the inside when I realized that I hadn't been paranoid or wishful, back at the club. We *had* been being watched, by one very curious, intelligent, and industrious Raccoon.

I didn't look for her as we crunched across the gravel towards Gordy. Instead, I tried to play my part.

"Hey, man, you comin' with us?" I asked the Kings' SAA.

Gordy fell in next to me and put an arm across my shoulders.

"We thought we'd have a little chat before you went runnin' off," he said jovially.

"Runnin' off? What do you mean, man?"

His smile faded and he squeezed me around my shoulders and shook me back and forth, putting me off balance. He laughed, but it was forced, and I knew what was coming. I just prayed he hadn't made the body armor I had on, through the bulk of my jacket and cut.

"Did you really fucking think we wouldn't figure it out?" he asked.

I kept to my role. "Figure what out, man?" I frowned and he abruptly stomped on the back of my knee. It hurt, but not too bad, but it wasn't meant to hurt necessarily, it was meant to take me down, to bring me to my knees, and it did that. Pipes and Flyer got a hold of my arms and I shouted "Fuck!" and struggled, but there wasn't shit I could do about it.

"Now, let's you and me have a little chat, Thirteen," Gordy said, and came around from the back of me to where I could see him. A shiny nickel-plated gun glinted in the weak moonlight.

"What the fuck, man? What're you doing? Is this some kind of joke?" I cried.

"Awww! Cut the shit, boy!" Gordy pointed the gun in my face and I looked up at him. If I had any fucking chance of surviving this, I needed to take any shots he fired to the chest. And, by the looks of the gun in his hand, he needed to back up.

"What's wrong? Nearsighted?" I asked, with a smug look.

Gordy barked a laugh, but he did what I needed him to do and began to put some distance between us.

"So, how long you been one of them?" he asked.

I lifted one shoulder in a shrug, which was only moderately effective with my arms held out like they were by two dudes.

"Don't know what you're talking about," I lied.

"Whew! Pig wasn't lyin' when he said you had a brass pair! Look at you and the way yer lookin' at me. Bet if I blow that horse dick of yours off, you won't look so fuckin' smug. Would yah?" He aimed his gun at me again, and this time I *really* didn't like where he was pointing it.

I struggled and almost got loose; score one for me. It was Pipes who muttered a curse and said, "Gordy, stop fuckin' with him, man! He ain't gonna tell us shit, but these Bleeding Heart assholes are slicker 'n owlshit, and he might have 'em out there right now. You heard Griz! They got at least one sniper in their crew. Just fuckin' do him and let's get out of here!" There was some real fear in his voice and I was betting dollars to pesos that he'd gotten a first-hand look at whatever Archer, Rush and Nox had done to Ace and Deuce. The fact that no-one who had seen it was talking about it told me just how bad it really was.

"Yeah. I get you," Gordy said, which wasn't at all what I expected him to say. I'd fully expected him to tell Pipes to stop being such a fucking pussy. Gordy took a few more steps away from me and had a decent bit of distance. My heart was hammering hard, the adrenaline flowing.

"It's really too bad. I thought you were a badass dude and that you'd be a good fit for us. Huh. Oh well." He lowered the gun and fired three shots that I knew of. I

It was the first that punched me right in the center of my chest, dead center in the ballistics plate I wore. Fucking agony! I felt a second thud into my shoulder, and that one really fucking burned. I think the third shot went wide. I tried to hold on, tried to stay conscious, but honest to God, mercifully, I blacked the fuck out.

"Thirteen!"

I heard a female voice scream. I groaned and tried to push myself to my feet. My vision was black – oh. I opened my eyes. White-hot streamers of pain streaked the gravel in front of my face. I coughed and groaned, and then the stars were whirling crazy among the trees. I was on my back and a fresh round of agony ripped through my chest. My hearing kept going in and out of focus; I was in so much pain I couldn't concentrate on a damned thing. Whoever or whatever was touching me, shaking me, hurting me, blessedly left me alone.

I lay on my back, panting. Every breath ripped new agony through my chest and my fucking shoulder burned and felt like I had broken shards of glass being ground into it. I ached, my whole fucking chest ached, and I had a brief moment where I was totally cool with dying, as long as the fucking pain just stopped.

Light fell across my face and I put up my hand to ward it off. Strong fingers, feminine hands, closed around my forearm and I heard a woman's voice, commanding, but high with panic.

"Come on, Thirteen! You have to help me, you're too big! I can't lift you!" But she was trying and I would give anything, anything at all, for her to fucking stop. I heaved myself to my feet and she got under my uninjured arm. The light was coming from her car. She got me into the passenger seat, I don't even know how. All I knew was that there was this fucking angel from God and that she was helping me. The door slammed shut, the light went out, and I think I went out with it.

14

D ani...

I was terrified. He was bleeding and I couldn't see how badly, but I didn't dare stop to look. I knew where the Sacred Hearts clubhouse was and as I drove, I couldn't help but fear I would be too late, because it was at least an hour, an-hour-and-a-half back the way we'd come and over the county line. I wanted to speed but I didn't dare. If I were pulled over with a bleeding man who'd been shot in my passenger seat, they would search the car and find the stolen jewelry, and with Thirteen obviously a biker, they would blame him, and then it would be all my fault, and this was such a mess! I drove five miles an hour above the speed limit, crying and jumping at shadows all the while.

I felt a triumphant surge when I saw two riders coming in our direction, a tow truck behind them. I laid on the horn and they startled, gunning their engines past my car and continuing on their way. I let out an inarticulate, frustrated scream, pounding my steering wheel.

"Just hold on, okay Thirteen? We're almost there." He didn't answer me; he was unconscious, and that just made the tears flow faster. I counted the mile-markers and watched for number fifty-eight. From everything I'd heard, the clubhouse was about a quarter of the way between mile-markers fifty-eight and fifty-nine, on the left. There! I pulled into the turn lane and onto the inclined drive, braking hard in front of the heavy iron gates barring my path.

No! I'd come all this way!

Not to be deterred, I opened my door, jumped out, and laid on the horn. I screamed, I yelled, I cried, and I looked wildly for a solution. I finally spotted it, perched high on a pole to one side of the gate. A camera. I jumped up and down, waving my arms wildly while the tears poured down my face. I must have looked like a wild crazy woman and right then, I was! I would do anything to get Thirteen the help he needed and if they didn't open the damned gate then I would call the police. Except – I didn't have a phone!

"Pleeeease!" I screamed, and bent at the waist, sobbing.

The gate kicked to life and began rolling aside and I straightened. I didn't waste any time, but jumped back in the car and pulled through in a spray of gravel, up into the Sacred Hearts' clubhouse driveway. For me, into the belly of the beast.

I skidded to a stop in front of the club's front door and jumped out, to men pouring from the front door, guns drawn and pointing at me and my car. I didn't care, I threw myself around the back of my car and wrenched open the passenger door, all the while screaming at them.

"Help me! Help! It's Thirteen! They shot him! I hid and I saw and they shot him!"

"Slow the fuck down, bitch! What the fuck are you saying?"

I looked up, and behind the man giving me a dark look and hard words was the doctor from my apartment. I nearly caved with relief.

"Doctor, help! Doctor, help me, please! Please!" I cried; he came striding around the front of my car to where I was trying to get Thirteen to help me again.

"Doc, wait, man, we don't know who this – "

"Aww, hell! Fucking shut up and help me! It's R.T.!" the doctor yelled, and I was suddenly swamped by a whole lot of men in a whole lot of black leather. A big, huge man with blonde hair in a braid moved me aside and the man who'd snarled at me first grabbed me by the arm. I went with him, moving aside, getting out of the way of the men who were trying to help Thirteen.

We went into the club, Thirteen carried limp between the big blonde man and a Mexican man. The doctor yelled to a tall, young and skinny brother with lots of tattoos, "Disney! Get my bag and come help me." He then turned his attention to the other two. "Take him to his room," he told them and they obeyed immediately. I went to go with them, to go with Thirteen, but I was savagely pulled back against the snapping man's chest.

"Whoa! Where do you think you're going, sweetheart?" he demanded, and swung me around hard, slamming me face down onto a table. I was bent at the waist, one of the chairs digging painfully into my stomach when another man wrenched my hands behind my back and began to tie them. I collapsed into sobs and tried to wrestle my way free, but there were three of them now. One held me down, the other tying my wrists, and the last patting me down.

"Nox, let her up," one of them said. One of my arms was pulled free and they jerked my purse away from me. I was shoved down again and my wrists were retied. I struggled and screamed and fought, but there wasn't any way I was getting free. I knew that, deep in my heart, but I was so damned tired of being manhandled and mistreated and I so desperately wanted to get to Thirteen, to know he was being cared for, to know if he was alive.

"Knock it off, sweetheart! You ain't going anywhere," one of the men grated, and I kicked out with my foot and met shin and he cursed.

With my hands firmly tied behind my back I was wrenched up by my arms, my shoulders painfully jerking in their sockets and protesting the unfamiliar strain. I was carried, hissing, spitting, screaming and crying, between two of them while the third followed us through the club. I didn't make it easy for them but I was outmatched, by, like, a lot.

They carried me outside and across grass to another building. I almost got away once, getting one arm free from one of my assailants. The one on my left crushed down harder with his grip on my other arm and cursed at the one on my right, "Fucking hold her, Rush!"

The third man opened the door at one end of the building and held it for the other two to carry me through. We passed down a narrow hallway with doors to either side, before the third man: Nox, the nameless man had called him, opened one of them. The two thrust me into the empty room and I stumbled, falling to my knees. With dark looks from all three, like they were the Devil's own, they swung the door shut. I screamed in rage and anger and sorrow, and threw myself against it. I kept screaming, long and loud, and kept throwing myself at the door until I just didn't have any fight left in me.

An hour passed, one of the longest of my life. I had finally settled in the middle of the room on my knees, bowed forward over them, my forehead to the floor. It was the only way I could get comfortable. My hair hid my face, not that it made much difference. The room had no lights, not a stick of furniture, no nothing. The carpet was that mat kind, super-low to the ground and might as well not be called carpet at all, the kind you found in office buildings, easy to vacuum or whatever.

My face was hot and tight from crying so damned much and I didn't care. I was miserable. I was scared for Thirteen and I hadn't seen a soul since they'd thrown me in here. Every once in a while I heard low voices on the other side of the door, but they were indistinct, low and muffled by the walls and the door. I couldn't understand what they were saying. My hands were cold, my shoulders stiff from the unnatural angle my bonds pulled them into, and I was just incredibly drained from everything. Physically, emotionally, mentally drained.

The door opened and I looked up through a curtain of my hair. The man was slender, with short, light-brown hair and grey eyes. He frowned down at me. I glanced at the name flash on his cut. 'Blue'. He had a small bottle of water in his hand and he stepped into the room.

The door was pulled shut behind him by the third man, who had long brown hair in a ponytail and a five o'clock shadow along his jaw. He gave me the dirtiest look before closing the door behind Blue, who knelt down in front of me. I looked away from him.

His hand cupped my chin and I stiffened. He tugged on my face, gently but insistently, and just waited me out until I complied and looked up at him. He set the water down and with one hand under my chin, he smoothed my hair out of my face with the other. It took a few seconds, with as wild and as much hair as I had, and I took the time to study his face.

He had a slight furrow between his brows and his eyes held a tension around them. The cool gray depths spoke -as loudly as his voice was silent- that he didn't like what was happening to me, that he didn't like what he was seeing. I stilled and let him move my hair, I didn't try to bite him or beg him for anything; instead, I waited to see what he was here for, to see what he was going to do.

He lifted the bottle of water and cracked the seal in front of me. I was suddenly dying of thirst, my mouth dry and full of cotton from screaming, my lips cracked from the salt of my tears. He put his hand gently back under my chin and placed the mouth of the bottle to my lips and helped me take a sip. It was cool and refreshing, and slid down my throat soothing the rawness. I couldn't remember the last time a drink of water had tasted so pure and so sweet.

He stopped for me to take a breath, and I asked him, "Is Thirteen okay? Is he all right?" I begged and pleaded with my eyes for him to tell me something, anything about Thirteen's well-being. He frowned and looked torn, and finally put his finger to his lips in the classic sign for 'hush', then, with a glance over his shoulder at the closed door, he turned to me and nodded. Relief exploded through my chest and tears of relief flooded my eyes and slipped down my face.

Thank you, I mouthed, and he nodded and helped me finish the little midget bottle of water. He stood in one fluid motion and knocked on the door. The same man opened it and glared at me, giving me a tempestuous look that screamed *I want to hurt you.*

"I've already been through hell! So give it your best shot. Not only will I survive, I'll win!" I snarled at him. I don't think he was expecting that, because his expression went from mean-mugging me to surprised, his eyebrows meeting his hairline. He looked at me and his face smoothed out into lines of careful consideration, to an expression of thoughtfulness. I spit at him and he closed the door with a soft thunk. I bowed my forehead back to the floor.

Thirteen was okay. I sighed in relief. If Thirteen was okay, then my work here was done. They could do whatever they wanted to do to me. I'd gone above and beyond the call of duty and I was tired. Thirteen had saved me and I had saved him back. Everything else was just window-dressing.

As I knelt on the hard floor, my feet and legs gone numb, my hands gone numb, too, I wondered what would happen to me.

Would they rape me, or just kill me? When they killed me, would they draw it out? I supposed I should be grateful the demon from the lake run was dead. By the looks of him, he would have drawn it out, made it painful. I knew that he'd liked knives and, from all the blood on him that night, I bet he had made Sparks' death long and slow. There wasn't any doubt in my mind that they'd killed him, and I was grateful to them for that. He'd deserved to die.

I wondered if I was going to meet the same fate. I mean, I had turned on my club and there were some things in the MC world, I'd learned, that were unforgivable sins across the board. Turning on your club was one of those things. I mean, if I were capable of turning on their enemy, then I was capable of turning on them later down the line, and so it really only made sense to kill me, to make sure that wouldn't ever happen.

The door opened and I looked up through my hair again, which had fallen back in my face. The blonde giant who had carried Thirteen into the clubhouse had opened the door, and another man stood in the doorway in front of him. He wore a zip-up hooded sweatshirt, his hands buried deep in the pockets. I couldn't see anything but his mouth and chin; the hood obscured the top half of his face. That, and it was still dark outside, and so it was dark inside too. I swallowed hard and tasted the bitter tang of fear. I guessed it was time, then.

"Oh, now that's nice," the man in the hoodie said, and he sounded genuine, not a trace of sarcasm in his voice.

"Reave, don't fuck with her," the big blonde warned.

The man pulled back his hood and his face stole my breath. I hissed and stiffened up and his lips curved up into a feral grin. He pulled his other hand from his pocket and stepped toward me, flicking the switch on his knife. He knelt down next to me and I closed my eyes.

The demon wasn't dead; somehow, he was alive, and I was going to die. I felt my shoulders sag as I accepted that this was the end of the line. I didn't have any more fight left in me at that point. I just didn't. He touched my shoulder and ran his hand lightly down my arm to my cold and numb fingers. He massaged my hands with one of his warmer ones and I figured he was trying to figure out where to make his first cut.

I was waiting for the kiss of his blade, for the sting, for the blood to start flowing, when whatever bound my wrists gave way.

The big man was suddenly there, his arm curving beneath me across my chest, helping me to sit up. My shoulders cried out in agony, stiff and angry at suddenly having to move as I brought my hands from around my back. I met the wintry, sky-blue eyes of the demon, who was smoothing the forelock of his hair down against his forehead. He crooked a smile at me.

"You remind me of my wife," he said, and I blinked. *This thing had a wife?*

"Who would marry a monster like you?" I blurted, and he gave me a sad little smile.

"You don't know me, so I'm going to let that slide. Mad respect, though, most people aren't brave enough to call me a monster to my face." His eyes were cold and distant, and I fought not to show any trace of fear.

"It's not bravery," I told him and the big blonde sighed.

"You okay?" he asked me. I looked at him next. He was their Sergeant-at-Arms, his name flash read 'Trigger'.

"It doesn't matter," I told him truthfully, which made him frown. "Is Thirteen okay?" His eyebrows went up in surprise.

"Yeah," the demon said, also surprised. "Yeah, he is, thanks to you."

"Come on. Our Pres, he wants to talk to you, and then you can go see Thirteen." Trigger helped me to my feet, which felt weird because they were both still numb. I shook out first one leg, then the other, and looked at the tattered remnants of the black bandanna that'd been used to tie my wrists. The demon had his hands back in his pockets.

"Were you at the lake run?" he asked me quietly, as first the giant SAA went out the door, then me. He followed behind me closely, the demon did, and I nodded.

"Yeah."

"Ah, okay." He nodded, and I think he was blushing. They led me out of the building and back across the grass, into a back door and down a dark hall, past bathrooms and, I thought, more sleeping quarters, though I couldn't be sure. The common room of the club looked like a bar, except there was a glassed-in room to one side. That room contained banks of video monitors and computer equipment. One of the monitors was the camera focused on the front gate.

There was a group of men all around a big table in the center of the room, and I faltered. The demon, his hands still deep in his hoodie pockets, lightly ran into my back as I stopped, and I jumped.

"Easy, Dani," and I startled that he knew my name. "No one's gonna hurt you here."

"Don't lie to me," I said tartly.

"He ain't lyin', darlin'. C'mere and have a seat."

The man who had spoken was seated at the head of the table, and he patted an open seat to his left. He was probably in his late forties, early fifties, and had long black hair in a loose ponytail down his back, and a neatly trimmed, but full, black beard. He was just barely starting to go gray at his temples and at the corners of his mouth, which tipped his age slightly younger, not older, for me. He was Hispanic, and his deep, dark eyes burned like coal in his face.

The man seated to his right might as well have been the older man's younger carbon copy, except for the beard. He was clean-shaven, but his eyes sparkled with intelligence and burned just as fiercely as what had to be his father's.

The demon put his hands lightly on my shoulders and steered me past the big Sergeant-at-Arms, and into the vacant seat. I tried not to look at the three men at the end of the table: Nox, Rush, and the unnamed man who had frisked me, tied me up, and thrown me into that room alone. Once I was seated, the big man at the head of the table introduced himself.

"I'm Dragon, President of the Sacred Hearts," he said.

"I wish I could say it was nice to meet you but considering you're probably going to have me killed and I don't care anymore, I'm just going to stick to the truth from now on and say it's really not," I said, with false bravado. I was scared as hell on the inside, but if there was one thing I had learned while with the Suicide Kings, it was that 'scared' didn't matter. None of it fucking mattered. They were going to do what they were going to do, and there wasn't anything I could do about it. I was small and I didn't have a weapon, and even if I had, I didn't know how to use one and ...yeah... there were just plain more of them than there was of me. I just had my smarts to rely on and I had to be more clever than them. So, what would be, would be.

I was sunk. I had nothing left to lose except for Thirteen, and I didn't really have him to begin with. He'd been lying about who he was the whole time, but he'd saved my life and I had returned the favor. I owed no-one anything, except myself, and so I would try to figure out a way to weasel out of this, and if I couldn't, then I would at least try to see Thirteen one more time to say goodbye. For some reason that was important to me.

Dragon and the rest of the table gave a laugh at my words and when the chuckles had settled down he got down to business.

"Archer, Rush, and Nox," he said, and he sounded pretty stern. The three from when I arrived shifted in their seats. So the third one was 'Archer'. Interesting. "I believe you owe the little lady an apology, Brothers," and the look he gave them was hot enough to burn right through them.

Archer growled, "She's got their VP's name inked into her back, what the fuck were we supposed to think?" I flinched at his words and Dragon the younger, the name flash on his cut reading 'Dray', looked at me curiously from where he sat across the table. I shifted uncomfortably and a large hand fell on my shoulder. I jumped and looked up into the SAA's face, his silver-blue eyes kind despite his hulking frame.

"Steady," he told me, and everything about him radiated reassurance.

"It's Pig-Pen's 'tramp stamp of approval'" I said bitterly. They must have seen it when they'd had me bent over the table. I suddenly felt weary, just bone-tired. "I got lucky. He tried to brand me with an iron. Skid stopped him, and he had me tattooed instead. Not like I want it there." I shrugged, but new tears started. The humiliation, it just never stopped.

"What's your story, princess?" Dray asked, low and careful, inviting me to talk, to make them understand. I studied him for a moment or two and, deciding he was sincere, I told them. I told them about Jared, about Pig-Pen claiming me, about how things were with the Suicide Kings, and about Thirteen.

Then I looked at them all in turn.

"You almost got him killed, whichever of you nailed Ace and Deuce's cuts to the wall. Your little message? Taunting them? Gordy, he isn't into the drugs like Pig. He isn't stupid; he figured it out. That the only way you would know about your brother's cut and the score-card was if you had someone on the inside. Newsflash for you, you'd already taken out the low-ranking members of the club, so that just left Thirteen." I felt a rush of emotions, fear and frustration, and sheer anger at the situation.

"You keep saying he's okay!" I reined in my outburst before asking, "Can I see him now? Can I say goodbye or whatever, before whatever comes next?" More tears welled up, hot and fresh; I had a headache from crying so much but truthfully, I hadn't really cried much in the last three years, and I think that the dam had burst and that was all coming out now, too.

All of them looked solemn and the three, Archer, Rush and Nox, looked guilty as hell. They were receiving some unfriendly and downright hostile looks from the brothers around the table and I swallowed. I hadn't meant to start anything and if I managed to survive this, I was pretty sure I'd made an enemy for life of at least Archer. Nox and Rush, I wasn't so sure, they wouldn't look at me, but Archer... if looks could kill, I'd be incinerated where I sat. Whatever had given him pause when Blue was giving me the water was gone now.

"Enough of this. That's just enough for one night. She's told you the truth about everything. If it weren't for her getting him here so quick, we'd have lost another brother tonight! I'm taking her back to see him." We all turned; the doctor was standing in the archway by the end of the bar where I'd been brought in from.

"Doc's right, and you are, too. Go on," Dragon uttered and nodded at me. I looked around and stood up slowly. No one stopped me and so I carefully rounded the chair and slipped past Trigger, who made no move to grab me. I drew closer to the doctor, who held out his hand to me. I bit my lips together to stop their trembling and stopped close to him, but didn't take his hand.

I didn't trust any of them, and with a sharp ache in the center of my heart I realized that I couldn't really trust Thirteen, either. I mean, could I? I followed the doctor through the labyrinth of doors to an open one that led into a bedroom with cool gray walls and a low bed, neatly made. Thirteen lay on one side, shirtless, the covers pulled up to his ribs. A big, deep, ugly bruise, so deep a purple it was almost black, stained the center of his chest. High up on his right shoulder, a snowy square of gauze, a splotch of red at its center, was taped in a patch that just looked wrong.

The doctor waited by the door as I crept into the room. I knelt down by the bed at his side and slipped my hand into his where it rested at his side. It was warm, and his chest rose and fell in shallow, even breaths. I sobbed in pure relief that he really was alive, realizing I hadn't quite believed them when they'd said he was okay. I'd needed this, needed to see it with my own eyes. I pressed my lips to the back of his hand as I knelt on the floor by his recovery bed, and then rested my cheek there. I just wanted to feel him.

He took a breath out of time from his original cadence and I looked up. His green-blue eyes were open and a slight smile curved his lips, "There's my clever girl," he said, then, "How you doin', Rocket?"

I laughed brokenly.

"I'm okay," I promised, and with him looking at me like that, I really was, because the way Thirteen was looking at me screamed two things at me: that he'd believed in me, and that he loved me, which I completely understood and finally had to admit to myself. I loved him, too. There was just something about this man. We connected on some deep sub-level of our beings. I hadn't felt anything like it before, and I was absolutely certain I never would again.

Some things were just worth the risk and whatever kind of rare connection Thirteen and I had wasn't just worth a risk here and there, it was worth risking it all. He took his hand from mine and, wincing, smoothed it over my hair. I smiled at him, and he whispered, "Come up here and lie next to me." I nodded and struggled to my feet. My body was as tired as everything else. A voice stopped me from the doorway as I went to round the bed.

"Brother, if you're gonna have her do that, she might as well have a shower and get changed now, so she can stay with you." The Vice President had spoken and I was startled to realize that Thirteen and I had an audience.

"I don't want to leave him," I said.

"We can see that, baby, and we're, uh… We're trying, here. So how about it? You grab a shower, get cleaned up, and we'll bring the rest of your stuff in from your car."

I blinked. They'd gone through my car?

I shook my head. Of course they had.

I worried my bottom lip between my teeth and Thirteen grasped my hand in his. His eyes weren't on my face, though. They were on my wrist and the dents made from the bindings that still hadn't smoothed out all the way.

"What the fuck?" he demanded and cast his eyes at Trigger.

"We'll talk, Brother," he said.

Thirteen looked at me.

"Grab a shower, take one of my tee shirts from the drawer. No one's going to hurt you–" I snorted and he scowled. "Any more," he amended. "Hurry up, I want you back here with me where I know you're safe."

"C'mon. I'll stand watch while you're in the bathroom if it makes you feel better." The demon gave me a wink and a mock-lecherous grin. I scowled and quailed on the inside but it must have showed some; his expression went cold.

"Wow, never quite had one of those reactions to one of my jokes before. For serious. I'll make sure you're okay." He beckoned me forward towards him and Thirteen gently shook my hand and let go, urging me to go. I took a reluctant step away from him.

"Dani, baby, I know I haven't been exactly honest about who I am and shit, but have I ever lied to you?" he asked me. I looked down into his very serious face and shook my head.

"I promise, you're going to be okay. Go with Reaver, he'll make sure you're left alone and then he'll bring you right back here. I promise," he said.

I nodded and went towards Reaver, the demon sent straight from hell. He smiled at me and held out his hand, a switchblade resting on its palm.

"This is my new very-favorite-knife. I gave my old very-favorite-knife to my best friend's girl a long time ago. I just got used to making this one my new very-favorite-knife but it looks like you could use a bit of trust and an insurance policy, so I'm going to give my new very-favorite-knife to you. Okay?" he said and I met his eyes with mine, blue on blue.

I plucked the knife from his palm and gripped it tightly in my fist. He smiled, and it was a slightly haunted and sad thing, and I got my first inclination that maybe *just maybe* he wasn't as monstrous as first impressions led me to believe.

I gave him a tentative smile back, and he turned sideways so I could go past him, out into the hallway. As we moved across it to what was presumably a bathroom, I heard the Vice President say, "He makes friends in the weirdest fucking ways sometimes," which made me smile for real.

15

Red-XIII...

I watched Reaver lead Dani across the hall and, with just about every reserve of strength depleted, I gave up the brave show which I'd been putting on for her benefit and laid my head back down. Trigger and Dray brought in a couple of chairs and sat down by the bed. We only had a little time before Dani got back and there were things I wanted to know.

"What. The. Fuck?" I growled out.

Dray sighed. "Doc saw her, and it was a good thing he did, too. She was jumping up and down, screaming and crying and laying on her horn outside the gate, but nobody heard shit. We were all inside. Doc happened to see her on the camera and said he knew who she was and to let her in. He gave us the 4-1-1 that she was the Suicide Kings' girl you'd called him in to help, and Archer, Rush, and Nox went Own Fucking Program while we were tied up helping you."

Trig picked up when Dray left off. "Dragon had got a call that you'd been taken out and where to find you; he took Duracell and Ghost and they were out, going for the overlook, when she showed up. And then it took me and Dray to get you in where Doc could look at you. Reave was passed out, Dis was following Doc's orders, and

Archer, Rush, and Nox were left to deal with Dani. We had our hands full with you and they weren't hurting her–" I stopped him.

"She doesn't look unhurt to me. You see her wrists?" I demanded.

"Yeah, okay, fair enough," he conceded.

"Finish the fucking story, man," I demanded, and Dray picked it up.

"They locked her in one of the unfurnished rooms out back and posted up outside the door. They wouldn't let anyone near it until Dragon got back; wanted to put it to a vote on what to do with her. We didn't know what happened, you were out, and we had nothing to go on until we could talk to you. She was alone in the room and we figured her being locked up wasn't the worst thing that could happen until this entire shit-show could be sorted out."

He had me there, but just because he was right didn't mean I had to fucking like it. Trig pressed on. "We fucking argued like a mother-fucker, but these guys are still new to our ways, so we tried to give them a little leeway. They finally agreed to let Blue in with some water, because the dude doesn't say shit anyways." That was the truth.

"By the time Blue came out, my dad was back with Duracell and Ghost –with your bike, by the way." That made my lips twitch. She would have been a bitch to replace, but honestly, she was just an object, a thing; if anything had happened to Dani... Dray must have read the look on my face because he didn't dwell on that point any longer.

"We decided to bring her out and have a fucking chat, Dragon's orders," he said.

"You got a fucking hellcat there," Trig observed. "Dragon pretty much matched up everything that came out of her mouth with what you told us about her, and she gave every one of us fucking what-for over you getting shot. Put it together rather neatly for us. Dragon's out there with Archer, Rush, and Nox, living up to his name. He's fucking livid, man. They went OFP in a big fucking way, and that's what compromised you. We're sorry, dude. We thought we could trust them to believe in the brotherhood, to follow the plan, but they just had revenge on the brain and fuck everybody else." Trig looked heartily sorry.

"They'll be lucky if their patches aren't pulled," Dray added.

"Don't do that." Her voice was gentle from the doorway. She looked like a tiny, fragile china doll, her hair dripping, making darker patches on the gray tee shirt of mine she had on. I knew these guys all had women that they were mad for but that didn't make me feel any better. The tee she had on didn't cover near enough for my tastes, barely skimming the tops of her thighs beyond where it would be considered indecent. Reaver stood behind her, a hand gently on her shoulder, and I didn't like that either. She gripped the knife he'd given her in one of her hands, took a deep breath, and let it out slowly.

"Why not?" Trigger asked, eyeing her speculatively.

"I just don't think it needs to go that far," she said evasively. But I could see her fear.

"Come here." I patted the side of the bed that was vacant and she hesitated. Reaver took his hand off her shoulder, belatedly realizing it was what was stopping her, which made him really frown. He came around and, with his right arm drawn against his ribs, he used his left to pull back the blankets for her. She got into bed and swallowed hard.

"Relax, Dani, these guys aren't here for a show," I said softly. I pulled her into my side where she belonged and pressed her head into my uninjured shoulder. She was careful where she put her arms so she wouldn't hurt me, but I didn't care. I just wanted her close to me. My smart and clever and ridiculously brave girl.

"You're cool, Sweetheart. You can take what Trig – hell, what any of us - asks you at face value," Reaver said, and helped himself to a seat on the foot of the bed.

"They hate me," she said, bravely. "At least Archer does. Nox and Rush, I think they follow him. If you take their patches, they'll blame me, come after me. I don't know what they did to Ace and Deuce, but it was bad, for Skid to get that drunk that early in the day. Please, don't make me a target. I don't know who the one Ace and Deuce ran off the road was to them, but he had to have been important to them."

Trig sat back in his chair and Dray looked thoughtful. "You got all that from where?" he asked.

I kissed the top of her head and couldn't suppress the proud smile on my face.

"Smart girl," I said.

She shook her head. "If I were half so smart, I would have left a long time ago," she said.

"Nah, you just needed the stars to align and give you the right motivation, and a place to run to," I said. She closed her eyes and sighed.

"Come on, let's leave these two alone," Doc called from the door. Trig, Reave, and Dray left, my VP and SAA taking their chairs and shutting the door behind them.

Dani and I were alone.

"You okay?" I asked her, and she trembled against me.

"You know, I don't know. I want to say I'm not, but with you holding me like this... I am. It's so confusing. I just... Who are you?" she asked.

"You comfortable?" I asked softly, and she nodded against my chest. "Okay, then. Close your eyes, I'll tell you a bedtime story."

She huffed a broken laugh that held bitterness at its edges.

"Fairy tales aren't real, Thirteen. If you lose a shoe at midnight you aren't a princess, you're drunk."

I laughed and pain seized up my chest and ribs, like the entire cavity had filled with shards of broken glass. Doc had told me that between the shot to my center chest plate and how close Gordy was, I'd been damned lucky the blow hadn't stopped my heart. I closed my eyes and breathed Dani in. She smelled fresh and clean, with that subtle hint of fruit and musk that was whatever soap she used.

"You smell like you," I murmured.

"They went through my car. My stuff was waiting in the bathroom for me."

I could hear the frown in her voice and I fought not to laugh again, instead concentrating on telling her what she wanted to know.

"My name really is Chris, my last name is Welker, and I was born here in the state," I started. "Family life was good, but not great; went to high school, didn't graduate; went to trade school, got my GED and picked up welding. Moved to Tennessee for work, started working as a deckhand on a river boat. One month on, one month off." I sighed. "One of the crew was a Sacred Heart man and introduced me to the life when I was twenty. I took to it like a fish to water.

"Joined up with the chapter out of Memphis; my bike was my dad's, and when I was seventeen and found it rusting in our barn, I restored it. Got tired of the boat, had made plenty of money, got tired of the bullshit and petty backstabbing going on in my club, and so I went nomad. When D. put out the call that the mother chapter needed some help, I figured it was time to come home. Was here all of a couple of weeks before your boys blew up Trig and Rev's business. D. took me aside, since I hadn't been around much, asked me if I'd be willing to infiltrate the Suicide Kings. I'd done it before for the Tennessee chapter and said sure, that I'd give it my best shot. Never thought it would be so easy and never in my wildest dreams thought that it would find me you."

I lay staring at the ceiling as the room started to grow light with the coming dawn through the high window. I thought she'd fallen asleep, but then she spoke.

"So other than the whole 'belonging to a rival club thing', you never lied?" she asked softly.

"Not to you, not ever," I promised. She nodded against my shoulder.

"Chris?" she asked gently when enough time had gone by. The sound of my name, tremulous and softly spoken from her lips, both aroused me and put me into a perfect state of peace.

"Yeah?"

"Can I ask you something?"

I smiled.

"You can ask me anything, Dani."

"How do you feel about me?" she asked, and I could hear her swallow. This was important, and not the time for me to question anything, or buck up and try to seem cool, or to overthink shit, either. She needed the truth and so I gave it to her.

"I think you're amazing. I think you're smart and kind and incredibly brave. I think you're beautiful, I'm finding that you're funny, and I think it's a combination of all of those things that first attracted me to you, but it's the fact that you are so damned willing to try and to trust, no matter how many times those assholes gave you a reason to never do any of those things again... I think it's that, that makes me love you." I said, and kissed her hair.

She sniffed and trembled slightly at my side.

"You really think those things?" she asked, and I could hear the waver in her voice.

"Yeah, Dani, I do."

She was just so damaged and yet, even when I found her at her worst, so sick and knocking at Death's front door, she fought not to be, to choose her own way. Dani had a will under there as strong as iron and, yeah, I think I could safely say I was in love with her.

She could have just gone. She could have made her escape and put the Suicide Kings and the Sacred Hearts and their stupid war firmly in her rearview, but she didn't. She'd stayed and followed me into the lion's den, stood by, waited for an opportunity, and seized it, saving my life, saving her own life, and standing up to every damned one of them in the process. That was sexy as hell.

"Why didn't you just leave, baby? Why did you put yourself in danger for me? Why did you follow us? You could have been caught! If Flyer and Pipes had seen you when you passed us-" She gasped, a sharp exclamation of sound.

"You saw me?" she asked.

"Yeah," I said grimly, leaving off that it had scared the shit out of me. "Just... why?" I asked.

"Because you saved me, and you were gentle and kind even when it could have gotten you in trouble. Because you treated me like I was worth something. And because of all those things, I just... I needed to save you back. I owed you at least that much, and because I'm in love with you too," she explained.

I sighed out, content.

"Promise you'll stay with me, that we'll figure this out. It's gonna take time, so to start with that, just promise you'll be here when I wake up," I murmured.

"I can do that, I promise," she said softly, in return.

"Okay, good."

We both drifted to sleep in each other's arms; I needed to heal and so did she, me physically, her emotionally. I thought we both had a better shot of doing it together and as much as I didn't want to be anything like that asshole, Pig-Pen, I couldn't deny to myself or my brothers that Dani Broussard was mine. My woman, with all the weight and responsibility that carried.

Right now, I had her; right now, I could hold her; and as soon as I was able, I was going to make sure that she was mine by blowing a hole in every single one of those fuckers. Whether it was by my own hand, or one of my brothers', it didn't matter. Every last one of them was going to die, starting with any one of them that I had ever seen touch her. Together, Dani and I made a whole, and where she hadn't been strong enough to punch or kick or knock a motherfucker out for laying a hand on her, I had no such problem doing so. And I was going to make damned sure that when I did it to them, that I was operating as her hands and from her heart to theirs. You reap what you sow, and they were about to reap three years and more of pain, all at once.

16

D ani...

"Kiss me before you go?" Thirteen asked.

I smiled and went to his bedside. Leaning down, I placed my lips gently against his. His hand cupped the side of my face, his thumb gently edging my cheekbone, and peace settled into my heart. I straightened reluctantly and smiled a bit wanly.

The Sacred Hearts wanted to speak to me again, and had sent Reaver and Blue to fetch me. I was dressed in my own clothes, which had been brought in from my car along with just about everything else in it, which made me feel marginally better. I was comfortable, in jeans and a long-sleeved black top that fit me like a second skin. It was simple in the front, a scooped neckline and plain, but the back plunged low and I loved the feel of the sweep of my waist-long hair against my skin.

I couldn't wear a bra with this particular top but that was all right. While I wasn't ungifted in the bust, I wasn't small-breasted, either. I'm just one of those women genetically lucky enough that wearing a bra wasn't mandatory all of the time. I walked with Reaver and Blue out to the common room. Blue kept giving me these sidelong looks to check and see if I was okay, and I suppressed a smile.

"I'm fine, thank you," I murmured, and Reaver raised an eyebrow.

"You talking to yourself?" he asked.

"No, Blue asked," I said quietly. Reaver looked at me as if I was crazy.

"They sent you–" I stopped at his look and amended what I was saying. "No, you volunteered to come get me because you want me to like you. You work very hard at being liked, and it bothers you when you aren't trying to be scary and someone is still scared of you. It makes you feel bad. Blue came because he didn't like what was happening to me; he genuinely feels bad about it and wants me to feel safe. Am I right?" I asked quietly. I'd stopped in the archway and Reaver was looking at me in a new light. Blue was smiling.

"Smart, and perceptive," Blue said and I looked at him. He smiled a secret little smile, and went to the table and pulled out a chair for me.

"Living with them, you have to be perceptive." I took the seat, acutely aware that I was further down the table and on its opposite side this time, and closer to Archer, Rush, and Nox. I bit my lips together and tried very hard not to look at them, focusing instead on their Sergeant-at-Arms. He was huge – tall, blonde, and broad of shoulder, with silvery-blue eyes, and as Nordic as they came.

"How's that?" he asked.

I told them about Pig's moods and about how it was common-place to be roughed up or slapped around for simple mistakes, "They started calling me Coon a few months into my being..." I struggled for the right words and came up empty, settling for, "...being with them. They thought it was cute, on account of me just about always having two black eyes." Stormy looks were exchanged.

"We found *this* in the door of your car, and *this* in your purse. We can't figure it." Dragon said, after a long pause in the conversation. Reaver set down my bottle of perfume and the Crown Royal bag.

"It's, um... it's how I kept myself valuable to Pig when he started to get bored with me. My grandfather was a Frenchman and a custom jewelry-maker. When the people who bought their drugs from the Suicide Kings on the street started bringing them jewelry, most of it stolen, Sparks got pissed. I told Pig I could melt it down, refashion it into things more valuable that they could pawn without a trace or sell online to turn their profit."

The table was quiet and I felt the need to fill the silence.

"I know it was wrong, but it was mine, you know? I didn't want to die. They left me alone for the most part, to create new things, and they couldn't hurt me too badly anymore. At least, when Sparks was alive... If they broke my arm or my fingers, I couldn't work, and Sparks would be pissed. I was stupid for thinking they might stop beating on me altogether that if I was more valuable to their bottom line, that maybe..." I turned my face so I wouldn't have to see some of the more pitying looks.

"This something you like to do, darlin'?" Dragon asked from the head of the table.

I sniffed and nodded weakly.

"I miss my grand-père. I had to leave all my tools in my apartment and my workshop downstairs there. I thought if I could take this stuff when I ran, that I could pay Thirteen back somehow and if he didn't... if we... I thought I could use it to start over somewhere."

The men exchanged some looks and a silent decision was made.

"How heavy and how much of this shit is there?" Dray asked. I told him about everything that I had for my grandfather's trade and what it required.

"Do you want me to do for you what I did for them?" I asked, finally.

Dragon started laughing and so did some of the other guys.

"Darlin', all our business is legit; we don't have any need for you to flip stolen jewelry. None at all. I think we're all thinkin' the same thing, though. If we go out with you and get these tools and supplies, and bring it back here to store it where those fuckers can't sell it or do whatever, would that earn us some trust and maybe a smile or two out of you?"

I stared at him open-mouthed.

"You'd do that for me?"

Archer cleared his throat. "No. We would... Consider it our apology," he said, and I dared to look at him. Rush and Nox were nodding their agreement and I found myself nodding as well.

"Okay, um... Yes." I nodded.

"Rev and Data should be back any time now. We'll wait for them and go to it. Might as well spend some time with R.T. and get something to eat while we wait," Dragon said. I nodded. I couldn't really remember the last time I ate, but with everything happening the way it had been and my stomach all in knots, I wasn't exactly hungry.

"I'll throw a couple or ten frozen lasagnas in the oven." The tall, slender tattooed man who had followed Doc's barking orders the night before got up and went through a doorway behind the bar.

I got up and stood patiently as the guys started milling and talking, until Trigger noticed me just standing there.

"You okay?" he called down the table.

"Um, don't I need an escort or something?" I asked.

"Honey, you're not a prisoner here," Dragon said.

"Do you know your way back?" Trigger asked. I nodded. "Well, go on, then."

Dragon smiled, and as I turned, I heard Trigger sigh and mutter, "This would be so much easier if Sunshine were here." There were murmurs and grunts of agreement and I frowned and decided to test the waters a bit.

"Who is that?" I asked, turning back around. Trigger straightened and I held my ground, my heart hammering as he came towards me. He pulled his phone out of his pocket and turned on the home screen, and there was a picture of a beautiful, petite woman with auburn hair as long as my own, her eyes a peculiar golden color, smiling at the camera. I blushed furiously and handed the phone back, and Trigger grinned. She'd been nude, and from the perspective, I gathered she'd been on top of him.

"Sorry, we like to be watched," he said.

I felt myself turn a shade or two green and nodded, leaving the men and hurrying back to Thirteen.

"You okay?" he asked as I shut the door behind myself.

I turned and nodded.

"I think so," I said uncertainly.

He frowned and held out his hand. I sat on the floor beside his bed and held his hand.

"Talk to me," he urged gently, and I did, easily. I told him about the exchange from the beginning and he smiled that his brothers were going to help me get my stuff. And then I told him about Trigger and Sunshine. His smile collapsed.

"Oh, hey, Sunshine and him are into that sort of thing, but you and me? No way. Never. It's just you and me behind closed doors. I don't share and I wouldn't do that to you." I nodded and kissed the back of his hand, laying my head on the mattress beside where our fingers were entwined.

"You going with them when they go to get your jeweler's things?" he asked softly.

"I think I have to; they might miss something important if I don't." I swallowed hard.

"You'll be okay. They'll protect you, baby. They know what you mean to me."

He took his hand from between mine and smoothed it over my hair. I closed my eyes and relished the touch. Being touched in this way was so different from what I'd been living with for the last three years. It was taking some getting used to, but for the most part I was starved for it. So thirsty.

I looked up. "What are we going to do, Thirteen? After all of this?" I asked.

"I don't know, Rocket, but we got time, lots of time, to figure it out," he answered, his green-blue eyes searching mine, and he struggled to sit up.

"Help me up," he said.

"What are you doing?" I asked.

"Coming with you. Come on, help me up." He reached and I stood up.

"You were just shot last night!" I cried.

He laid back down and tried to catch his breath.

"I know, babe, but you've been tested past your limits. I'm not letting you go by yourself."

I dropped onto the edge of the bed and gathered his hand between mine, into my lap.

"We don't have to go anywhere right now. They said they wanted to wait for someone named Rev to get back."

He nodded. "Not a bad idea, he can handle himself and some heavy lifting. I'm still coming with you, though."

I pursed my lips and sighed. I figured it was best to say nothing and to maybe let the doctor or his other brothers argue with him. Instead I toed out of my Converse and came around the bed, getting in with him.

"Please don't hurt yourself for me," I whispered.

He smiled and let me cuddle into his side.

"Can't think of anything I would rather hurt myself for. We'll talk about it later when Rev and whoever he went off with gets back. Deal?"

"Deal," I murmured.

We lay close in his bed and talked softly until he fell asleep. I lay beside him, listening to his even breathing, and wondered how this would all come together in the end. Would the Suicide Kings let me go? Would they have a choice? Their numbers were greatly diminished compared to the Sacred Hearts, so it would seem. I mean, they thought Thirteen was dead, and they thought the demon... *no, Reaver*, I reminded myself, was dead. I wondered if the Old Lady had really died or if they were hiding her somewhere, too.

I knew that Archer, Nox, and Rush's brother had died. Their rage was too pure, too raw for it to be otherwise.

A soft tap came at the door, and the doctor poked his head in.

"He sleepin'?" he asked. I nodded. "Good, but I need to check his shoulder." He came in and set his bag on the floor next to the bed. He snapped on a pair of white latex gloves.

"How you holdin' up?" he asked me quietly, as he laid out what he would need on the bedside table.

"Okay," I said, just as quietly.

He sighed. "You look like you got a lot you're thinking about." His comment was an invitation for me to speak.

"I was thinking about how this would all play out. I mean, the Kings think that Thirteen is dead, and Reaver, too..." I swallowed hard.

The doctor paused and closed his eyes, a pained look flickering across his face.

"They got Grinder and they got my woman, Chandra, when they broke in here."

I blinked back tears in the face of his pain. *His woman.* I looked up at him. His woman had been killed and yet when Thirteen had called, he'd come. He'd come and healed me, when I was technically one of their women.

"I'm sorry," I said, and he gave me a crooked but sad smile.

"Not yer fault. Wasn't like you was in their cheer squad or anything." He looked me up and down.

I shook my head. "I hope you kill them all," I said truthfully.

"Ain't a single damned one of 'em you would spare?" he asked.

I thought about it; really thought about it. The only name to come to mind was Skid's... I chewed my bottom lip thoughtfully. Skid had, on one or two occasions, stood up for me. But there were a lot more of them where he'd stood by and let Pig...

"Maybe Skid. He stopped Pig from branding me, and would sneak me pain medicine from time to time, but he's just as guilty as the rest of them in his own way," I murmured.

"'The only thing necessary for the triumph of evil is for good men to do nothing.' A man by the name of Edmund Burke said that. Sound about right?"

I looked at him and nodded finally.

"I think that would fit Skid, but he isn't exactly a good man anymore. I think he used to be once and that it's down in there somewhere, but it got scoured away somehow," I scraped my bottom lip between my teeth.

"That was us once, the Sacred Hearts." He sniffed and shook Thirteen gently by his good shoulder.

He jolted.

"What? What're we talking about?" Thirteen muttered sleepily. I smiled and laughed a bit.

"Asking your woman who she would spare out of the Suicide Cunts, if she had her way," the doctor said. I choked at his name for the Kings and smiled broadly. I liked it. "I've gotta change that shoulder, you ready?" he asked.

Thirteen struggled into a sitting position and nodded. The doctor carefully peeled the square of bandage off of Thirteen's shoulder and Thirteen hissed.

"Pussy," Doc chuckled, and looked through his half-moon spectacles at the carefully-stitched wound.

"It's awfully red," I murmured. It was, around the edges, the black stitching neat and spiky. It was slightly swollen, but not too badly. The doctor took his time cleaning it off with some more gauze.

"Eh, it looks pretty normal actually. Still gonna get a shot in the ass, there, got some antibiotics and a tetanus booster," he said and slathered more antibiotic ointment over the wound.

"Tetanus? What the fuck I need that for?"

"Dunno the last time you had one, and the last time I checked, the slug I dug outta there was made out of metal. You're a lucky son of a bitch. The Kevlar mostly stopped it. You had one grade less ballistics plate over your heart, you wouldn't be here. I'm still not sure how that blow didn't stop your fucking heart. Chalk it up to you being one tough son of a bitch." The doctor spoke low and intensely as he redressed the injury.

Thirteen locked eyes with me and, dead serious, he said, "Naw, she was there and had my heart in her hands. It was safe enough."

I nodded and laid my head on his good shoulder, the doctor's words haunting me. So close, I had been so close to losing the only person who had ever stepped up and looked out for me, before I could fully explore what we had developing between us.

"It's okay, Rocket," he murmured into my hair, "It didn't happen and I'm here and we'll figure all this out, one day at a time." He kissed the top of my hair and I nodded. I liked the sound of that. I really did.

Eventually, Thirteen had a visitor of a different kind. Two brothers I hadn't seen yet came to the door and knocked at its edge as Thirteen and I played a game I'd never heard of called 'Never have I ever', which was supposed to be some kind of drinking game, but we were playing with M&M candies instead.

"Hey, Rev, Data." Thirteen smiled.

"Hey, man. Heard you got into a hell of a scrape," 'Rev', a stocky man I could swear was some kind of familiar, said.

"Oh! The fighter!" I said, when where I'd seen him before clicked into place.

He smiled.

"Saw me whoop your boy's ass, did you?" he asked, and his grin was one that was open and carefree and that, were I an ordinary girl, would have made me instantly smile back. But I knew how deceptive some smiles could be.

"Not mine," I said, and dropped my eyes to Thirteen's lap.

"Sorry, darlin'. Didn't mean it that way, just heard where Thirteen found you," he said.

"Yeah? They telling stories out there?" Thirteen asked sharply.

I glanced at his face and caught motion out of the corner of my eye as Rev put his hands up. 'Data' leaned against the door. A lanky fellow with greasy brown hair and a goatee, he had his arms crossed and coolly appraised what was going on inside the room; his warm brown eyes skated over me where I knelt on the bed beside Thirteen, assessing, but making no judgments, not yet. I instantly liked him for that.

"Not listening to any of the bullshit gossip out there until I hear it from the horse's mouth," Rev said, and dropped to the carpet, sitting Indian-style. He wore shorts, which I found strange, given how cold the weather had been and still was. We were into spring but the polar vortex wasn't keen on letting up and was holding on by its fingertips. It was unseasonably cool outside.

He gripped the toes of his red Converse high-tops and leaned all the way forward, stretching his back. He leaned back up and caught my eyes with his warm brown-gold ones.

"So, what's your story?" he asked me directly. It was so forthright and honest, so open and so refreshingly nonthreatening or menacing in any way that I had to smile.

"I'm Dani, Dani Broussard," I said.

"Revelator." He nodded in the direction of the man at the door, "That's Data." Data tried a smile on me and inclined his head.

I shifted and made to settle in, leaning back against the simple flat headboard and shoving pillows behind my back. Thirteen shifted and used me as his cushion. I smiled down at him and held him lightly to me, mindful of his shoulder.

"I'm not sure where to start," I murmured.

"Got all night, Dani. Why don't you start from the beginning?" Data suggested, and slid down the wall to sit down.

I looked at Thirteen and he gripped my wrist lightly, planting a kiss in the palm of my hand.

"Just talk, babe. You're here, the guys want to know about you... Just stick to what you're comfortable sharing."

I nodded and realized that was why Rev's approach was working for me. He wasn't demanding, he wasn't asking about anything specific, he just was...

"Okay..." And so, I started over, from the beginning, for their benefit. It was so strange. I wasn't used to being able to speak my heart and mind truthfully. Not without some kind of physical pain resulting. I was finding it to my liking, though.

As we talked, Rev would make us laugh with sarcastic comments and some of the funniest facial expressions. Some of the other club members filtered past the door, stopping and listening for a time before moving on, a couple even coming inside and joining the conversation.

"So I hear you want to get some of your stuff out of your place. Don't blame you. You wanna do it now, or is tomorrow morning good?" Rev asked.

I thought about it for a heartbeat or two and decided that the morning would be best. I said so, and that's when Rev got up and stretched.

"Okay, good deal. I'm gonna go rack out then; it's been nice talking to you, Dani. See you in the morning." I smiled and looked down at Thirteen who was dozing lightly where he lay against me.

"'Night, Rev. 'Night, Data." I smiled at Blue, who pushed off the door frame. He gave a short little inclination of his head and wandered off with the rest of them. I sighed and Thirteen chuckled a bit.

"Do me a favor?" he asked and I smiled. He hadn't been dozing after all, just relaxing.

"Anything," I said, suddenly very attentive.

"Get ready for bed, shut that door, and get in here."

I smiled and nodded, and he carefully moved off of me so I could get up.

His cool green gaze followed me as it usually did, only this time his expression wasn't unreadable. His lips curved in a smile of pleasure as he watched me move around his room. I took the time to go brush my teeth and comb my hair in the bathroom before returning and shutting the door.

"If you're comfortable with it..." he said, and I turned, cocking my head to the side to indicate that I was listening, "...skip the tee shirt," he said softly, and there was a longing and a subtle heat to his gaze. I slipped out of my clothes, a little self-conscious about my body. I mean, I know he'd seen it all before and I wanted to be with him, but that didn't stop my heart and my head from being screwed up from everything that came before.

"Hey." His voice was velvet and slightly chiding. I looked over.

"Put on a tee if it makes you feel secure. I want you to feel safe with me. You don't gotta do anything I ask." His green-blue gaze was completely sincere. He meant every word. I turned out the overhead light and came to bed, the cotton sheets cool against my skin when I slid between them, Thirteen's body warm and inviting, still strong despite his wounded status.

"My brave girl." He kissed me, a soft thing, almost reverent, definitely full of respect. I kissed him back and his hands smoothed gently over my skin beneath the covers. He shifted to hold me closer and grunted with pain, freezing in place. He broke the kiss we shared and cursed Gordy six ways to Sunday.

"I want to love you, to make you feel good," he admitted, his green gaze sparking with something undefinable. "Will you let me touch you?" he asked. I swallowed and nodded carefully. I wanted him to touch me, even with how hurt he was, with how crazy everything had been. "Lay back," he whispered, and I did what he told me.

17

R ed-XIII...

The fact she trusted me so implicitly was such an amazing turn-on. I was hurt, and if there were an Olympics for bad ideas, this would probably take the silver. If I actually tried to love her properly, now, *that* would take the gold. But I just wanted to touch her, make her feel good, use my hands to make her come undone and have her forget for a minute everything that was crazy. She needed to relax and I knew I felt relaxed as hell after an orgasm. The way Dani was wound up, she'd probably need forty. But I was pretty sure I had at least one or two in me, for now.

It wasn't perfect, that was for sure. I lay on my good side and found that if I moved slow and careful, my bad shoulder was going to permit me the position that would put my hand between her thighs. I didn't go there right off the bat, though. I had more class than that. I leaned over carefully and caressed her cheek, kissing her softly to start.

Her mouth moved against mine, tentative and careful, as if she were afraid her kiss would hurt me further. She slid closer to me until we were pressed lightly against one another, her body's heat soaking into mine. She was so warm, and so soft. I closed my eyes and lost myself in the feel of her for a second, trailing my fingertips in a ghostly touch across her skin, down the side of her throat, over her throbbing pulse-point, along her collarbone, between her breasts, diverting and following one's curve. I circled her tit in a light spiral pattern of touch leading inward to her nipple, before grasping and rolling it between my forefinger and thumb, palming the rest of her breast. God, she was a nice handful. Not too small, just barely over-flowing my grasp.

"You have gorgeous breasts, you know that?" I whispered against her mouth. "So perfect." She was getting into it now, relaxing, her beautiful blue eyes closed, and she savored my words. I was pretty sure that Dani wasn't used to getting compliments, and I vowed to shower her with them more often.

I spent some time teasing her, caressing her body, playing with her, exploring every inch of her supple curves and taut planes with light little touches, ghostly caresses that raised her skin in a sweep of goose-flesh. I carefully hooked one of my legs over one of hers and swept it in tight between mine, opening her up so my hand could roam lower.

My patience in this endeavor had paid off. When I'd captured her leg, she cried out into my mouth and arched a little off the bed, but the sound I swallowed from her didn't taste the slightest bit fearful. Oh, no, it was absolutely laced with desire, fraught with trust and with need. I drank her desire like one of Mandy's fine chocolate drinks, rich and decadently sweet, and I dipped a finger into her folds, teasing her outer pussy lips with a light caress.

Dani moaned and writhed, grinding her hips into my hand, demanding a deeper, more concentrated touch. I obliged her; she was so wet and ready, I slid my middle finger into her sleek heat and stroked as deep in her as I could. She broke her mouth from mine and gave a half-gasp, half-moan that lit me on fire from the inside. I was painfully hard where I was pressed against her thigh and hip, but I probably wouldn't be getting any relief of my own tonight. There would be plenty of time for that later, when I was healed up and she was more settled into the new and beautiful life I had every intention of giving her.

"That good?" I murmured, and it took a little adjusting, but I managed to massage her clit with the heel of my hand. It was a trick and a half, being gentle while still staying up inside her, but I had this. She arched and I felt her spasm around my finger, which made my dick twitch in an answering spasm of its own. God, I wanted inside her so bad, I wanted to love her right, but I couldn't, so for now this was the next best thing.

"Oh God, Thirteen!" she gasped, her voice deep and breathy with passion. I smiled, and since her little pants spoke of a need for more oxygen, I stopped depriving her of any by kissing her and put my mouth to good use elsewhere. I took the nipple closest to me into my mouth and rolled it with lips and tongue, giving it a good hard suck. She cried out, an inarticulate sound that was still music to my ears, and I decided it was time to really bring her.

I added my index finger to my middle and Dani rocked her hips into my hand. God, she was so perfectly tight! Her silken body wrapped around my fingers, her walls pressing in so damned hot and perfect. I let her swollen nipple go from between my lips and just looked at her, her head thrown back, raven hair a silken wash across the stark white pillowcase, long dark lashes fanning perfect against her smooth and creamy skin. She was just so damned beautiful, it was almost painful to look at.

"God, Dani, you kill me," I growled. Her eyes opened, and the piercing blue met my gaze though her eyes remained hooded, leaden with love and lust in equal measures. Shit, that look alone had me almost coming, myself.

Her fingers wrapped around my shaft up near the head and she slid her hand up and down firmly but gently, running the head against her palm. It felt good, it felt real damned good and it took every bit of my self-control not to thrust. I held very still, which was its own kind of painful when I wanted to move so badly, but I didn't dare.

I groaned and closed my eyes, my hand faltering in my attentions to my girl's body for just a second while I let her have her way. It felt good but at the same time, oh, God, she was short-circuiting my brain. I bowed my head and I kept still, concentrating very hard on keeping my breathing shallow and even, and on wrestling control back from Dani. I changed the angle of my hand, going deeper with my fingers, grinding more insistently against her clit.

She cried out, and her hand stilled. I brought her up to a fever pitch and with a final pure, clean shout she bowed back, arching as though I had pulled her up by a string at her center. Her walls tightened around my invading fingers. Her jumping with her climax jolted me hard, and I gritted my teeth from the pain that radiated from my shoulder and through my chest.

"Oh!" she cried and tensed beside me, going very still. Her blue eyes locked with mine, radiating concern.

"'S okay," I hissed between my gritted teeth. The pain passed and I unlocked my muscle groups one by one.

"I'm okay. Promise." I kissed her and she kissed me back, my chest and shoulder throbbing miserably in time with my heartbeat.

Yep, definitely, solidly a silver medal in the Bad-Idea Olympics but at the same time, so worth it. I slipped my hand from between Dani's thighs, her breath coming in deep, even pants as she tried to catch it.

"You're really good at that," she gasped.

"Thanks," I replied simply. I'd had a lot of practice but I wasn't going to tell her that. It wasn't something she needed to hear. When you had a dick the size of mine, you had to be careful. Too many times, I'd accidentally hurt a girl without meaning to. Also, too many times, my cock had come out, the girl had gotten a good look, and left me cold. I'd gotten good with my hands to compensate. The more aroused the woman was, the easier it was for her to take me, so I made sure to go above and beyond before getting my willy into the mix.

I removed Dani's gently stroking hand from my cock and kissed her until she was a languid puddle of relaxed goo in my bed. Slowly I untangled my legs from hers. She held very still, so careful not to jerk or jolt me. I smiled.

"Be right back," I whispered, and climbed out of bed.

I stuck my head out the bedroom door. When I was sure the coast was clear, I padded into the bathroom and washed my hands with soap and hot water. We needed to get her tested so we could be sure where we stood with each other, but now was so not the time to broach that topic.

I returned and slid into bed carefully. She immediately cuddled carefully into my side.

"Did you wash your hands?" she asked, without a trace of reproach or judgment in her voice.

"Yeah." I know I didn't sound any happier about it than I felt.

"It's okay. If you hadn't, I would have made you."

I didn't say anything. I mean what the fuck could I say? I'd already gone down on her back at my cabin, so it was a little late now. I should have just held her close, should have just not thought about it. But I had, and I did, and now she was so very still and so very quiet in my arms, withdrawn back inside her own head, retreated inside her damage. I twisted my head and kissed her hair and she sighed and relaxed a bit.

I wish I could say that I came up with something to say, something good that put her at ease and made her feel better, but I didn't. Honestly, I was so... just... tired, on both a physical and mental level. At least I managed to keep my arms around her, if nothing else. I needed to do better. To be better than this, for her. But in order to do that, I needed to be back on my feet, and the only way to that end was time. I was impatient, not going to lie. I wanted to fix it, but I was new to trying.

I had a taxing day ahead of me tomorrow. I'd decided that even if I couldn't be much use, that I needed to be there with her, go with her to get her stuff. I'd stay in the truck but I had a feeling that I was going to face an argument about it not only from her, but from Doc. That was okay, though. I needed to man up, to show with my actions the things my words failed me on, that she'd caught me, hook, line, and sinker, and that I wasn't going anywhere any time soon. I dropped into a deep and dreamless sleep far quicker than I would have liked, while turning all of this over in my head. Dani was safe and so very still beside me.

18

Dani...

I didn't sleep well; I kept waking at every new sound and I wasn't used to sleeping with anyone in the bed with me. Not that it wasn't nice, just the opposite: I felt warm and safe curled against Thirteen's body. It was very nice; I just simply wasn't used to it. I slipped from the bed and left him, to get a shower and get dressed before anyone else was up. I was surprised to find the doctor with a cup of coffee and, of all things, a thick romance novel in his hands, sitting at the bar in the common room, his half-moon glasses perched on the end of his nose.

He looked over at me. "Chandra loved these damned things. Read 'em all the time. Suppose I just miss her." His blue eyes grew vacant and bleak, and I nodded. I slipped up onto the bar stool beside him. "Got something you wanna ask me?"

I nodded. "I need an STD test." I swallowed hard and he sighed, nodding.

"Lemme ask you something, and I'm sorry for being indelicate here but, you been with anyone since I was at yer place?"

I pursed my lips and blew out a breath.

"Thirteen, once, and we used a condom," I confessed.

"Anyone else get to you?" he asked. I shook my head. "Good deal, I can take care of this once and for all with a blood test, then. All the antibiotics I pumped into that IV would kill anything short of the Herpes virus, any of the hepatitises, and HIV or AIDS, and all of those I can test for with a couple of vials of blood. Want I should do it now?"

I nodded and kept mute, because if I opened my mouth I was pretty sure that I was going to start screaming and crying. I was a lot of things - scared, angry, and frustrated were at the top of the list - but there was a whole lot more going on in my heart and my head. I settled on cold fury for now, an anger so deep and so cold, it numbed all the rest of it out for now. I was angry at Pig, for sure, and the rest of the MC, but I was angry at me, too.

Doc left for a few minutes, and came back with what he needed in prepared sterile packs, setting up right there on the bar as he peeled this and that open. I shoved back the sleeve of the black hooded sweatshirt I wore, exposing my inner arm, and closed my eyes as he went to work with the needle. I hated needles, was terrified of them, which is why Pig-Pen tattooing me had almost, *almost*, been worse than taking the brand, but truthfully, the only thing higher on my list of fears than needles was burning. Reasonable, given how much I worked with fire to melt, warp, and shape the metal I worked with to make my jewelry. I knew very well what fire could do.

"All done." Doc pressed a cotton ball to the crook of my arm and bent it at the elbow to keep it in place.

"Me next." We looked over, startled.

"You shouldn't be out of bed yet." Doc scowled at his wayward patient.

"Had to get up to piss, saw what you were doing. Now do me. Let's get my girl some closure and some peace of mind." Thirteen looked good in just a pair of jeans and the gray hooded sweatshirt he was wearing. It was the zip-up kind and he'd left it open over his bare chest.

"Sit yer ass down, then," Doc ordered with a sigh. "Sooner I do this, the sooner you'll go back in and lay down, right?"

Thirteen chuckled but it was half-assed at best. He winced hard. I bit my lip, feeling guilty that what we'd done last night may have something to do with his discomfort today.

"Yeah, whatever you say."

I helped him with the sleeve of his sweatshirt and Doc drew his blood, too.

"Hey! Look whose up!" Reaver crowed from the archway leading back towards the rooms.

"Yeah, he shouldn't be," Doc grumbled.

More people started coming out and going for the coffee.

I shot a questioning look to Thirteen and he nodded.

"Cream and sugar?" I asked quietly.

"Yeah," he nodded, and I went and fixed two cups, bringing him one.

Before I knew it, bowls, cereal, and milk were being passed around.

"I miss Sunshine," Trigger griped, and the look on his face, in his eyes, sheer misery.

Dray laughed, and then winced as he took a sip of the coffee. "I miss Em; breakfast will never be the same without her coffee. She's ruined me for this swill."

Trigger laughed at that and the colorfully-tattooed Disney sat down, shirtless, his brown hair in a messy ponytail. He looked good, but the way he carried himself told me that he was completely unaware of any effect he had on anybody. I studied his tattoos and wondered why anyone would permanently ink a zombified version of the Disney princess Ariel from *The Little Mermaid* into the skin of their ribs. I couldn't imagine for the life of me, with how bad Pig's tramp stamp of approval had been, that the ribs were a comfortable place to tattoo, especially with how lean Disney was.

"What's the plan for today?" he asked, his brown eyes firmly on his bowl of cereal. He'd been completely oblivious to my study, which I was grateful for. I'd been rude for staring.

"Got the crash truck emptied out?" Dragon asked, lighting a cigarette.

"Last night, like you asked," Duracell, a man with bright red, close-clipped hair, affirmed.

"Then we're going and getting Miss Dani's stuff moved, before those cunts get any ideas about what's hers and what's theirs," Dragon drawled, sucking on the end of his cigarette.

"Thank you," I said, quietly.

"No trouble at all, we take care of our own. It's what we do," Disney said and smiled, his light brown eyes warm.

"I wouldn't be calling her one of ours just yet," Archer muttered in a sullen tone of voice.

"Man, shut the fuck up. You don't know shit," Thirteen blazed at him, covering my hand with one of his. I drew strength from the touch but kept my eyes fixed on my coffee mug. I wanted to shrink into my chair and just disappear if they were going to fight about me. I wanted no part in any of it.

"Jesus Christ, man. You need to learn to keep your fucking mouth shut. Look at her!" Dray demanded, glaring across the table at Archer, who turned his cold green-gold eyes on me.

I raised my eyes to meet his and swallowed hard, gathering my courage.

"Right now, it seems you have more in common with the Suicide Kings than I do," I said softly and he recoiled. I stood up, my cold fury finally cracking, its molten core finding an outlet. "They hate me just as much as you do! I'm just a means, a way to line their pockets and a receptacle for their VP's penis!"

I raised my eyebrows at him. Archer stood up, his chest heaving.

"Oh! Big man!" I taunted. "I told you to give it your best shot, that not only would I survive, that I'll win! You want to hit me? Fine! Hit me!" I stayed seated, Thirteen's hand around mine keeping me grounded as I railed, "You want to bend me over this table? Fine! You can do that, too. It's nothing that hasn't been done before! You want to know everything about them from someone that's been living under their thumb for the last three years?"

Archer stilled at that. I looked at him hard; now he was interested. God! He was just like them! I made a disgusted noise. "Oh! Now I have your attention! Good. While I have it, a few things! One, fuck you! Two, I'm not their fucking whore anymore. And last but not least, stop being such a fucking asshole! I've had enough!"

We glared across the table at one another and finally it was Rush who spoke. He was shorter than Archer, not quite as broad through the shoulder, with short tawny hair and light brown eyes.

"Nobody knows better 'n me and Nox how pissed you are about Grinder, but look at her, bro. *She* didn't fucking do it. I mean, are you listening to what she's saying? Shit," he shook his head and looked me in the eye, "breaks my fuckin' heart what happened to a pretty girl like you. As soon as you're done eating, I'd like to help you move."

I nodded and sniffed, angry tears stinging the back of my eyes. The silence stretched out along both sides of the table and Archer slowly sank into his seat.

"I'm sorry I yelled at you, Archer," I murmured and looked down to find my hand that was tangled with Thirteen's mottled and white. Somehow, his strong, sure fingers had found the spaces between mine. He smiled an endearing, crooked smile at me. He winked and leaned over carefully, kissing my temple, breathing "Brave girl," against my ear, his warm breath a caress that made me close my eyes and wish I were as he said. If I were brave then I would never have been Pig-Pen's toy, not for so long as I'd been. Finally, someone spoke.

"Archer's a dick," Nox said bluntly. "But he's our brother and its better'n being a pussy. I'd like to help you move, too."

Archer got up abruptly, his chair crashing backwards to the floor. He stormed around the table and out through the archway leading back to the rooms. A moment later we heard a back door crash open and shut.

"He and Grind were close. That doesn't really excuse his being a dick," Rush murmured, Nox nodding in agreement.

"No, it don't, and he might wanna calm his tits. I'm running low on good graces," Dragon stated, and gave the two a meaningful look. There were grunts of agreement almost all the way around the table and everyone quietly went back to eating. I closed my eyes and felt my shoulders droop.

Thirteen shook my hand, where it was entangled with his, gently, to get my attention; I met his sea-green eyes and he tried that smile that always had my heart doing flips on me.

"Not your fault, Rocket. Don't worry about it." He pressed a kiss to the back of my hand and I nodded, but inside I felt like I was falling down a well of despair and I was beginning to wonder if this roller-coaster of emotions I was on was ever going to slow down or stop. I just wanted to crawl back into bed and sleep for a week. Instead, I found myself washing everyone's dishes just so I would be left alone long enough to try and sort through everything I was feeling.

"Here." Doc leaned a hip against the counter and set down an orange pill bottle with just a few small white pills in the bottom, maybe five or six.

"What's that?" I asked.

"Xanax. I want you to take one. It'll even you out. You start to panic or lose control, you got a few to get you through. You're trying to take on too much all at once, Dani. You need to slow down and breathe."

"You sound like you're speaking from experience," I said softly.

"Maybe I am... Maybe I am," and with that, he pushed off the counter and went back out into the common room where the guys were all getting ready to head out with me to get the rest of my things.

"I'm going to the hospital, see if I can pull a shift. I need a break from all this shit," Doc declared and, shrugging into his jacket and cut, swept up his medical bag, where he'd stowed my and Thirteen's blood samples, and went out the front door.

I took one of the pills, but I didn't feel any different at first. Then things did start to even out. I felt the tension ease from my shoulders and my heart didn't feel like it was being crushed in my chest, like a fist was squeezing it. I felt a little calmer, a little less overwhelmed. I found Thirteen back in his room, sitting on the edge of his bed, trying to pull on his boots. He was dressed. I set the bottle of pills on the nightstand on my side of the bed. He looked at me with worry in his eyes.

"Better?" he asked, gently.

"Better," I affirmed, and he let out his breath.

"Kills me that I can't do anything for you right now."

"What are you doing?"

"Going with you and the guys." He held up his hand when I opened my mouth to speak. "I'll stay in the truck, but, babe, I'm not leaving you at a time like this."

I sank down onto the bed beside him and nodded. Truthfully, I'd been scared to go without him. Thirteen was the only thing familiar in an otherwise-unfamiliar world right now. It was sad and twisted and fucked-up to have him go with me in his state; I felt incredibly selfish, but I really didn't want to go without him, and so I didn't argue. Thirteen grabbed his leather jacket off a hook set into the wall behind the door. The Suicide Kings prospect's cut was conspicuously absent from it, which made me smile. Thirteen smiled at me and let me go ahead of him, a question in his eyes.

"They really weren't your colors anyway; I think you're more of a summer," I quipped, and he laughed, which made him grimace.

"Don't make me laugh, Rocket."

"I'm sorry."

"None of that, either. You're fine." He got the jacket onto himself, with a lot of ginger movements and my eyes immediately went to the shoulder.

"Nothing to see, the way they had a hold of me pulled it to the side. Good as it ever was except for a few blood stains in the lining." He pulled the jacket to the side, revealing a thick black satin lining; of course there was no blood, that I could see. Still, I felt my face fall into solemn lines again.

Thirteen's smile faded around the edges. "I'm fine, Dani; you're safe, I'm here; you're free and here with me. It's all that matters."

I considered him a moment and found myself nodding slowly. He was right. Could it really be that simple?

"Where the fuck you think you're going?" Dragon demanded.

"With you."

"I can see that, but ain't you forgetting something?"

Thirteen arched one brow in confusion, and Dragon brought out his cut from off the back of his chair. The guys in the common room cheered and Thirteen went to get it. Dragon helped him shrug it on and patted him on the back. Thirteen winced and gave him a dirty look. Dragon grinned and pulled his own jacket and cut off the back of the chair.

I looked at Thirteen in his Sacred Hearts colors and waited for my feelings to give an uncertain roll, or really, for any single one to present itself. I was surprised when the paramount emotion that rose to the surface in the center of my chest was pride. I was proud of Thirteen, standing there, regal in his colors, 'Red-XIII' emblazoned on the name flash over his left breast.

It looked right on him and I was struck by just how different these men shrugging into their own coats and their own set of colors were from what I was used to.

For one thing, despite some of their cuts' ages and rougher appearances, they were all clean. Some were freshly-showered, some freshly-shaven, and while a few wore stained jeans or work pants, they had clearly been freshly-laundered – or, at least, recently laundered.

For another thing, very few of them smoked; Dragon really being the only one who stuck primarily to paper-and-tobacco cigarettes. Trigger had an almost ever-present electronic cigarette, and Data could usually be seen sucking on one of those vaping mechanisms that always reminded me of the piece the caterpillar from Alice in Wonderland was constantly sucking on. The club, though, Dragon smoked inside, was relatively easy and clean-breathing, well-ventilated, and that's when it struck me – the place was immaculately-kept.

There were no fetid beer and alcohol spills on the floor, the furniture was all in good shape, even if a few of the pieces were aged or outdated. The building didn't have sloppily done paint in here, or graffiti like the Suicide Kings'. This place, these people in this place, treated everything and everyone with respect, and the surroundings and their appearances reflected that.

"You look like you just had an epiphany." Thirteen commented dryly.

"I think I did."

"Care to share?" He took my leather jacket and hoodie from my hands and held it so I could slip in to the pairing, and I stared for a long, hard moment at his work-rough hands holding the black cotton and leather.

"Dani, you okay?" he asked, concern wrinkling his brow.

"No one's ever held my coat for me," I said, and turned and let him help me in to it.

"No one? Ever?" he asked, surprised.

I shook my head. "Not that I can remember."

"That part of whatever you were thinking?" he asked. I nodded and he smiled, "Get used to it, Rocket. Life is gonna get a whole lot better for you from here."

"We ready to go, or what?" Rush demanded. Nox smiled ruefully to himself and held open the front door. Men started piling out into the bright morning sunlight to a panel van, a box truck, and their bikes, and I slipped the big bug-eyed sunglasses out of the inside of my jacket pocket and put them on. As I stepped out into the bright sun there was some laughter.

"Those look ridiculous," someone commented.

"I agree. I hate them but I needed something to hide the shiners, and they're the only pair I have." The chuckles stopped abruptly and I sighed. "I'm sorry, I don't mean to be a killjoy..."

"Hey, stop," Thirteen had me face him, a grave expression on his face. "One of the things I love about you is that you're always two or three steps ahead, that you think about everything, and everything you do has a purpose, if not two. I've seen it, I know it, and you're doing just fine." He shook me gently.

"Can we get a move on, please?" Rush called through the passenger-side window of the van, with Nox at the wheel.

"I think I'm beginning to understand how he got his road name," I heard Dray gripe behind me. I smiled and bit my lower lip.

"Yes, please, let's go," I chuckled. I rode in the box truck. Disney drove, Thirteen sitting still beside me. He'd taken the middle so I could look out the window, he said, but I think it was more so I didn't have to sit beside someone unfamiliar.

We were in the lead, the panel van behind us, other Sacred Hearts following on their bikes. The truck and van were more than enough to fit everything. I wasn't taking anything but my grandfather's equipment; I didn't care about anything else. I'd brought away the clothes I'd wanted to keep and the photos and mementos I'd managed to keep out of Pig's hands the last time I'd been there. Pig had sold off most of my jewelry for drugs or what have you, except for the few heirloom pieces I'd managed to hide away under a piece of loose baseboard.

Thirteen held my hand as we rode and I gave Disney directions, our fingers intertwined and resting atop my denim-clad thigh. It was nice; I wasn't used to having my hand held or public displays of affection. I wasn't used to affection at all, really. I thought that my chance at that, at any kind of happiness, had died with Jared, until I found an outlet through my jewelry making. That was honestly the only thing about leaving my old life behind that I had thought I was going to miss and now, here we were, going to get it. I smiled and hope bloomed in my chest. Thirteen looked over and down at me, and his face lightened and a smile broke out over his lips at the sight of mine. He raised my hand to his mouth and kissed the back and I caught Disney smiling faintly in the driver's seat.

"You have someone?" I asked him.

His smile got wider. "Yeah, name is Aaron," he said.

"She must be really special," I commented, and Disney's face flamed.

"Uh, he is," he said and Thirteen laughed.

"Aaron, baby. As in A-A-R-O-N."

"Oh! I'm so sorry! I just assumed you meant E-R-I-N, as in the female spelling." I was blushing hard now and Disney broke out into a wide grin. He proceeded to tell me all about Aaron and how he had been on the west coast in California to play in an orchestra that was doing the score for a movie. About how he was excited that he would be seeing him soon because after California, he'd joined the rest of the Ol' Ladies in Florida.

I grinned. "Oooooh, Griz was *pissed* about that. He didn't know where you'd sent them. I figured that you'd sent them to wherever the other MC at your lake run came from. Their leader seemed really close to the demon." Both men's heads swiveled in my direction, matching looks of surprise on their faces.

"What?" I asked.

Disney looked decisive. "Look, I saw him that night too, but Reaver, he ain't like that all the time. He was my mentor when I was a prospect, and he's a really good guy and good friend. The girl that Sparks hurt that night was Reaver's baby cousin, so yeah, he kind of went off the rails. Believe me, it scared even me. Just... do me a solid? Don't let him hear you call him that, please? It'd really hurt his feelings."

I was embarrassed. When all the pieces were together, it was a different situation.

"I'm not saying Reaver isn't fucked-up, or scary... he's both of those things, in spades. I'm just saying that, underneath it all, he's more good than bad. He loves Hayden, Sunshine - hell, all of the girls - and he loves this club. He'd do anything for any of us and he's loyal to a fault. Just wait until you get to see those things before passing any judgment."

By now I'd fixed my gaze out the window, turning all of these things over in my head, worrying my bottom lip between my teeth as I thought about it. Reaver was trying awfully hard to get on my good side, spending time around me, volunteering to do things to make my stay more comfortable, giving me what was supposedly his favorite knife, which I gripped with the hand that Thirteen wasn't holding. Still, all of those things served to make me more suspicious of his motives, not less. I felt a nagging worry in the back of my mind that my suspicion said much more about me than his kindness thus far said about him.

"Pull up here. The one with the green awning." Thirteen said, and I realized with a jolt that we'd completed the ride in silence, that we were here and I'd spent the entire rest of the trip puzzling out the conundrum of 'what was the real Reaver? Man or monster?' I was still thinking about it when I slipped out of the truck, my Converse thudding against the cracked sidewalk.

Thirteen scooted over and I glanced up at him.

"What happened to 'staying in the truck'?" I asked.

He gave me an impish grin and stilled.

"Yes, ma'am." He gave me a little half-assed salute and I smiled.

Rush was opening up the back of the van and I opened and propped the gate into the courtyard.

"So, what're we taking and what're we leaving?" Trigger asked me, following me through the gate. I fished my keys out of my pocket and went to the workshop shed in the corner of the courtyard, sliding the correct key into the MasterLock holding the hasp on the door closed. I flung open the door and let loose the breath I hadn't realized I'd been holding. Everything was exactly how I'd left it.

"Everything in here. The kiln, the centrifugal casting machine, just – all of it. The wax, the plaster; everything, wall to wall." I said. "The rest of it is upstairs in my apartment." I stepped aside to let Trigger and Revelator past me. There was a lot of equipment in here. In addition to what I used to melt and smelt, there were various cutting and polishing machines, and surfacers for stones.

Revelator gave a low whistle, "You're serious about this shit. You ain't playin'!" he said. I smiled and put my sunglasses up onto my forehead.

"My grand-père taught me everything he knew, and I made up a few things of my own. I wish I could show you how it's done, or something that I've made, but I took all of that with me, seeing as it was both valuable and portable. I didn't think I would see any of this stuff again." I felt an overwhelming rush of gratitude for their help in this.

"We'll get you taken care of down here. Why don't you show Blue and Reave what's what upstairs while we get this started? Reave ain't supposed to be lifting anything too heavy yet, but maybe you can put him to work boxing shit up or something." I raised my eyebrows and Trigger laughed. "He's my best friend, just lookin' out for him," he explained. I filed this away with everything else I'd learned about Reaver in the last hour and still had a hard time equating that highly-lauded individual with the crazy, blood-covered man I'd seen just last summer.

I went out, and up the stairs to my apartment, again pondering just how differently this MC operated from the Suicide Kings. I didn't notice when Blue paused in the courtyard to retie the lace on his work boot. I just went up the metal and concrete stairs and fit my key first in the deadbolt's lock and then in the lock in the knob, throwing back the tumblers. I opened my front door and stepped through into the dim interior of my apartment.

I didn't know, I didn't think, and it cost me when thick fingers snagged me by the back of the hair. He'd been in the kitchen, he must have heard the key in the lock, and Pig-Pen had me fast and was growling out, "Bitch! Where the fuck have you been?" I cried out as he steered me toward the dining room table, one fist knotted in my hair and the other gripping my arm with bruising force. I ground my teeth together, my eyes watering from the pain as he slammed me face-down across the dining table's gleaming, dark wood surface.

"Answer me!" he demanded, shaking me. His hand left my arm and I knew where it was going. He pinned me fast between his body and the table, keeping control of my head as he fumbled at his belt. He was shirtless and there was no telling how long he'd been here, and I knew I was in trouble. I put both palms flat against the table, but he was too much. I tried to push myself up, but he was too strong, and my hands just slid against the high-polished wood.

Suddenly the pressure on me lifted and my scalp smarted terribly as he pulled me up by my hair. I screamed and he turned me around, gripping me by the throat. I knew what he had planned. I was wearing jeans, and face-down there was no access. I glared at him and both my hands went to the one still wrapped in my hair.

"What, you going to fight me?" he asked close to my face, then he licked me, from my chin, up my cheek, to my temple. "Go on an' fight, fucking turns me on when you struggle," he said and he let go of my throat, his hand going to the front of my jeans.

He froze at the same time I heard the hammer cock on a gun.

"You know, my buddy Blue here has a twitchy trigger finger. I'd let her go if I were you." Thirteen's voice was as flat and dispassionate as I had ever heard it.

Pig-Pen's head was shoved forward.

"Okay, let me rephrase, because it wasn't really a suggestion. Let. Her. Go."

Pig let me go and I stumbled a pace or two away from him. Blue had a gun to the back of Pig's head and Thirteen stood in the doorway to my apartment, his chest heaving, his arm tight to his ribs, Trigger at his back.

"Shoot him!" I blurted. "Please, for the love of God, shoot him!" Blue blurred, and I stumbled over to Thirteen, who had his hand out for me. He pulled me into his side and leaned on me.

Pig-Pen looked poleaxed.

"Not sure how you're alive."

"You think *that's* a neat trick?" we heard, and Thirteen moved me and himself aside. Trigger turned sideways in the doorway, and Reaver stepped into the apartment past him. Pig scowled, but not before I saw the glint of fear in his eyes. Reaver grinned from ear to ear.

"Hey, Dani, nice area rug! It really pulls the room together. Mind if we take it with us?" Reaver asked me, entirely too cheerful.

"If you promise to kill him," I said, looking Pig-Pen square in the eye.

Reaver's expression turned icy-cold in a blink, just, nobody home. "Oh, I don't think any of us is going to have a problem with that, baby," he said and gave a nod to Blue.

Pig-Pen sneered, but never got the chance to say anything, because Blue hit him with the butt of his gun so hard I could swear he broke Pig's skull. Pig dropped like a stone, sprawling half in my kitchen and half in my entryway. I closed my eyes and huddled into Thirteen's side miserably. He grunted and I went to pull back, but his arm tightened around me.

"You're okay, Rocket. I got you," he said, and I nodded.

"You gotta move," Trigger said, and I opened my eyes and let Thirteen take me outside.

It took Blue, Trigger, and Revelator to carry my area rug down to the van. Thirteen kissed the top of my head and palmed my cheek. "I need to go with Reaver, you gonna be okay here, with Trig and Rev and the rest of the guys?" he asked me. I pulled on my big-girl panties and nodded.

"Kiss me," he ordered, and I looked up into his green-blue eyes and complied. He broke the kiss gently and kissed my forehead.

"You solid?" Dragon asked me, leaning against the stair rail. I nodded numbly and he looked at Thirteen.

"You and Reave head to Point Nowhere in the van. Duracell, Blue, you follow 'em. We'll finish up here and come meet you." Dragon gave a meaningful look to Reaver. "Don't mind if you get carried away," he said and Reaver nodded and I saw the most peculiar thing. A look that was half gleeful anticipation and half crushing remorse or defeat flickered through his bright blue eyes.

"I really want to go wash my face," I mumbled and all eyes turned to me. "He licked it. Right before he told me to fight him harder." I felt queasy, and Reaver's, and everyone else's, expressions crushed into dark frowns.

"Can I borrow my old, new very-favorite-knife?"

I reached into my pocket and held it out to him.

"Thanks." He held it up in front of my face. "I give this back to you, you know you never have to worry about him again." I blinked, but before I could say anything, Reaver was headed down the stairs. Thirteen let me go and, with a final squeeze of my hand, went down the stairs slowly after him.

I went into my bathroom and washed my face something like six times, but it wasn't good enough. Finally I gave up, stripped down, and got into my shower, staying in it until I ran out of both soap and hot water. When I got out, I was a prune, but I didn't care. I dried off and got back into my clothes, and when I went out into the living room, it was to find that my workbench was gone. The living room looked very empty without it or the area rug in it.

"Feel better?" Trigger asked.

"Yes and no."

"We're ready to go when you are, Rocket," Revelator said, shrugging his massive shoulders, his fists buried deep in his jacket pockets.

"Did you get it all?" I asked.

"Every damned bit of it's boxed and in the truck. Just waiting on you to give the word on if there's anything else."

I looked around me. "I grew up here. Just me and my grand-père," I murmured.

"You want we should take it all?" Dragon asked from the front door. "It'd take a couple of trips, but we can do it."

I looked around me. "Is it crazy that I want you to burn it? I don't want any possibility of coming back to this life... None."

The president of the Sacred Hearts exchanged looks with Trigger and Revelator before settling his dark gaze back on me.

"You sure about that?" he asked.

"Never been more sure of anything in my life."

"Go wait down at the truck with Disney, Nox, and Rush. Rev, go with her, make sure she's straight." Revelator walked up to me and nudged me with his shoulder; he didn't grab me or turn me or do anything, just walked up and bumped his shoulder lightly into mine. I turned around and went down the stairs, peeking into the shed to make sure nothing important was being left behind. Assured that there wasn't, I slipped out the gate and onto the cracked sidewalk.

"That it, then?" Disney asked, his brown eyes travelling over me, concerned, noting my wet hair.

"That's everything," I promised.

"You good with riding with me or Trig or someone on back of one of the bikes?" Rev asked. I smiled faintly.

"I will gladly save one of your male egos from having to sit bitch for one of your brothers."

Rev's eyes sparkled with mirth. "Nah, I would've just had Dis be my bitch, he's used to it. Ain't you, Puddin'?" Disney glared, but couldn't maintain it and broke into a grin.

"Man, fuck you! I keep telling you, you aren't my type."

Rev laughed, and Nox and Rush shifted a bit, obviously uncomfortable.

Revelator 'tsk'ed. "Man, what'd Dragon tell you two when you came on board? Shit, Grinder didn't have a problem with it." He crossed his arms which, with as big and built-out as he was, was a touch awkward on his frame.

"Rev, dude, its fine," Disney said, and looked uncomfortable himself.

"No, it ain't, Dis…"

"Stop." I felt my shoulders drop and I pinched the bridge of my nose. "Just, stop right there." The four of them considered me.

"Grinder is the one Ace and Deuce ran off the road?" I knew it but I wanted Rev to see my point. Rush and Nox both nodded and the pain that weighted them was apparent. "I'm sorry you lost your friend," I said softly.

"He wasn't just our friend." Rush said plaintively. "He was more 'n just our Brother, too. He was our *brother*. We grew up in the same foster home as him and Archer. Rush and me are brothers by blood, but Archer 'n Grind, they protected us." He bowed his head and I considered Nox and Rush. They looked the same age. I startled, breaking into a wide grin.

"You're twins."

The two men exchanged a look.

"How the hell do you get that?" Rev asked.

"She's right," Nox shrugged.

"You two don't look a damned thing alike," Rev frowned.

"It's called fraternal twins. Identical twins come from the same egg that splits in two. But sometimes a woman's body lets go of two eggs at the same time; if they both get fertilized, then you end up with two babies, sometimes two boys, sometimes two girls, other times a boy and a girl at the same time. They don't look alike, but they shared the same womb, so they're twins." Revelator looked like he was turning a little green the longer my explanation went on. Disney started cracking up.

"Rev's girl, Red, is pregnant," Disney said, and, Boom.

No, really. *Boom!* Something in my apartment upstairs exploded. We all jumped, and Dragon and Trigger calmly walked out the court-yard gate.

"Let's roll," Dragon ordered and, before any more conversation could be had, we moved. Revelator climbed astride his custom rig while Nox and Rush piled into the truck along with Disney. I ghosted up the sidewalk behind Dragon and got on his bike behind him without a word. He handed me his helmet and I put it on as he pulled away from the curb, but, honestly, my gaze was affixed to the orange flames licking inside my bedroom window.

I turned forward and caught Dragon considering me in his side-view mirror. I inclined my head, my expression grim but determined, and he laughed to himself, shaking his head.

"You and Thirteen are going to make a hell of a pair!" he shouted over the wind.

"How's that?" I shouted back.

"You got a matched brass pair!"

I considered everything that had just happened and I could see his point. For three years I'd been a girl who'd done as she was told, who lived in fear and under the thumbs of mad men. Then I had met Thirteen, who'd shown me that risks were worth taking and I'd suspected that he wasn't all that he seemed. I'd certainly known he was different.

I closed my eyes. I didn't know the Dani I was now. She just didn't jive with the Dani of a year or even three years ago. Never had I been an incarnation of myself that had been okay with murder, let alone condoning the murder of a man right in front of me, staring me in the face, in the eyes, as I begged someone to put a bullet in his brain. I'd straight-up seen the bloody aftermath of what Reaver could do, with my own eyes; yet I'd handed him a knife willingly, knowingly, gladly and let him go off with Pig-Pen. I thought about Pig-Pen, thought about the flames consuming my childhood home, and couldn't scare up an ounce of remorse or sorrow.

I felt stone-cold and empty. I felt powerful. I felt in control of my own destiny for the first time since, well, ever. And it was all because I finally felt supported. Thirteen had given me more than just the gift of finding my own bravery. He'd given me the gift of my freedom, of the ability to dream and plan and scheme for something better for myself. His brothers, the Sacred Hearts, were backing not only Thirteen, but also myself in laying the foundation for a future free of terror and pain at the hands of not only Pig, but the Suicide Kings.

I thought about all of this on the ride back to the SHMC's club house. When Dragon pulled up into the drive, he turned right, into the expanse of parking lot and around the club's building, waving Disney to follow him. He pulled around the building and down a blacktop lane wide enough for just one car. We followed that around the expanse of grass and stopped in front of a tall, corrugated metal building with three big roll-up garage bay doors. He cut the engine on the bike and put down the kickstand.

I got off and unbuckled his helmet from my head and handed it back.

"It's illegal in this state to ride without one, you know," I said, with a faint smile.

"Do I look like I give a fuck, pretty girl?" he asked, grinning.

I laughed and turned to look up at the building.

"What is this?"

"Well, that far one there is a garage bay, the middle one is mostly storage, though we ain't got nothing in it, and this one," he said, waving a gloved hand at the bay door in front of us, "is yers now."

I turned back to him.

"Mine?" I asked.

"We'll get you set up in here, so you can do whatever it is you do. No charge, nothing like that. You get yourself back on your feet with what you got. Get some money in your pocket. Figure things out with our boy on if you're going to stay or if you're going to go... Just do us all a favor?"

"What?" I croaked, my voice very nearly betraying me.

"Thirteen is a good man. He's a boon to this club, a better brother none of us could ask for and he risked his ass for you in a big way. Now if you can't handle it, I get it... but really try before you do anything like try to make him choose, because I know enough about Thirteen to tell you, if you asked he'd probably hand in his cut, and it would be a damned shame if he did." Dragon's dark gaze held mine and at the same time held such sorrow.

"I wouldn't do that…" I said, deathly quiet. The bay door was raising and the men who had stayed behind at the club were coming out to help unload. I was surprised to see Archer among them. Nox and Rush stood aside with him, talking to him. They looked in my direction.

"Wouldn't do what, honey?"

I turned back to the Sacred Hearts President.

"I wouldn't make him choose. I would just… I don't know… I would just go away, disappear. I know this life, the bonds that you're supposed to have with your club. The Suicide Kings don't have it, they just have this violent, perverted, half-assed facsimile of it. I see it here, though. You all had no reason to help me, to come to my house, to put yourselves in danger, burning it down simply because I asked. No reason at all except…" Dragon's mouth quirked up in a one-sided grin, "Except for Thirteen. You didn't do it for me. You did it for…" I stopped because it was scary to say it out loud.

"Let me ask you something, Dani?" I nodded. "You ever give yourself willingly to that son of a bitch?"

"Who? Pig-Pen?" I very nearly physically gagged. "No!" I said, horrified.

"Listen here, you're a lot like my late wife, like a lot of the fine women we have attached to this club. You belong to Thirteen, you're Thirteen's woman because you choose to be." He poked me in the chest with a gloved finger. "You ever choose *not* to be anymore, that's up to you. But as long as you belong to Thirteen, as long as he stands strong and takes on all comers in your defense, well then, you belong here with us, too. Anything happens to Thirteen, you still belong with us. Bein' a part of an MC is more 'n just a buncha guys wearing black leather, lookin' and actin' badass on the back of a Harley, drinkin' and fuckin' and generally tearing it up. You get what I'm sayin' here?"

"You just described the Suicide Kings to perfection there; you realize that, don't you?" I mused.

He snorted, "Just one in a long list of mistakes those assclowns have made, and look where it got them." His dark eyes blazed with an absolutely unholy light, and it was a scary look.

"I thought for sure you were going to kill me, when I brought Thirteen here."

"I know."

"Why didn't you?"

"Honestly? The old version of us, the misguided, cocky, and just generally arrogant version of us would have."

"What happened to that version? If you don't mind my asking..."

"It wised up in a big goddamned hurry about six, seven years back when it got my wife, Dray's momma, killed." His expression clouded with a long-held deep sorrow and grief.

"I... I'm sorry that happened to you." I swallowed past a hard lump that developed in my throat.

"Just listen to what I'm tellin' you. You're a smart girl, Dani, for all you got mixed up with the wrong people."

I nodded. I think I understood perfectly well what Dragon was telling me. Everything about his actions, everything that he was doing pointed to one thing, *Here is your second chance. You're safe, you're sound, now build a life for yourself.*

"You might wanna go on and tell them how you need that stuff set up, otherwise they're just gonna drop it wherever," he said, and put his helmet on his head. This entire time he'd been straddling his bike, comfortable.

I nodded.

"'Thank you' just doesn't cut it," I said, dubiously.

"Just give us a chance," he said, and started his bike back up. "That's all the thanks we need."

I stepped back and nodded again, and he followed the blacktop loop around the grassed-in area and back out to the lot. I heard a couple of other bikes join the chug of his over the main building and then listened as they faded into the distance, mulling over everything he'd said.

"Dani, how do you need this stuff to go?" Disney called, distracting me.

I went over.

"Um, I think the kiln needs to be more like... Um, yeah! That'd be great..." and I immersed myself into accepting Dragon and the SHMC's kindness, all the while beating down the voice inside my head that was telling me *It was too good to be true...*, resolutely telling it to shut up because after everything they had done so far, and after so long under the tyrant's spell, I was ready to believe again.

19

R ed-XIII...

    Point Nowhere was as deserted as a church in the heart of a red-light district. Reave and I let Blue and Duracell do the heavy lifting after pulling the van into the building. Really, we just opened the back doors, handcuffed Pig's hands in front of him, and let the ceiling-mounted engine hoist do the rest. Now he was hanging from the ceiling, feet around a foot off the floor, still unconscious. With as hard as Blue had cracked him, I was starting to wonder if he'd ever wake up. Blood ran in a slick wash down his back from the cut on his scalp, rivulets spilling over his shoulder and midway down his chest.

"Think we should get some salts under his nose?" Duracell mused. Blue frowned and shook his head.

"Naw," Reaver answered. "Best wait for the others. Let sleeping..." he wrinkled his nose, "yeah, not even going to finish that thought." He glowered.

"I want to hurt him," I stated simply. "First time I ever laid eyes on Dani, he had her backed into a corner, threatening her. She looked so damned small and so afraid, but she stood her ground, smarted off to him, and he backhanded her." I sniffed. "Last time he really laid his hands on her was around a month ago. Backhanded her again.

Months back, I had to watch this animal fuck her on the clubroom's pool table so's everyone could watch. I don't even know what she did to piss him off, but the look on her face, just blank and staring... It was like she was dying inside, a little at a time."

Blue was scowling and Duracell was giving Pig a decidedly unfriendly look, but Reaver was looking at me. "That what made you wanna save her?" he asked.

"I think it was the start. Honestly, what sealed it for me was after Rev gave me that cover-story ass-whoopin'. She got saddled with patching me up, and she wraps these two Oxy in a piece of paper and stuffs 'em in my pocket." I pulled out the receipt with her note, which I had carefully folded in my wallet. I handed it to Blue, who read it, raised his eyebrows and passed it on to Duracell.

"She stuffs that in my pocket, then writes on my arm to check my pockets. Man, if this scumbag or any of the others had caught her dipping into their stash on account of helping me, they would have beat her ass into next week and maybe even into the week after that. Not going to lie, when I felt her hand go in my pocket, I thought sure she was going to roll me, but no. She was trying to save me some pain."

We talked, mostly about Dani, what I'd seen and what I'd heard from the Suicide Kings about her. I didn't share anything that she'd told me out of turn, but I could tell, the more I talked, the hotter and deeper the water Pig was sittin' in was getting. Finally, we were interrupted by his groaning and coming to, just in time for the roar of pipes to drift into the building from outside.

Dragon, Trig, and Ghost came through the door and I nodded in their direction. I was stiff and fucking uncomfortable as shit where I stood, leaning heavily against an old metal work table.

"Just in time, he's just waking up," I called out. Trig and Ghost stood off to one side; Dragon took the lead on this one. He marched up to Pig and grabbed him by a fistful of hair, hauling his head up to look at him.

"Only got a couple of questions for you, boy," Dragon rumbled in his deep baritone voice. "Where can we find the rest of your crew?"

Pig spit in our President's face. Dragon socked him in the ribs. Pig grunted. I leaned back. "You know what? I'm gettin' too old for this shit..." Dragon uttered, walking away from Pig and wiping his face with a spare bandanna. "Reave, you go ahead now."

Reaver stepped up and I swear the dude was made of fuckin' ice. He just exuded 'creepy motherfucker' as he stepped across the concrete floor in his soft-soled sneakers.

He brought out the switchblade he'd given to Dani, "This here is my very favorite knife. I gave it to Dani..." Pig frowned and there was no recognition. I snorted.

"Coon, you jackass!" I called over.

Reaver frowned at me and turned back to Pig. "You've been tormenting that girl for years and you can't even recognize her name when you hear it?" He looked disgusted and started carving.

Pig started screaming and I don't think a single damned one of us really felt all that damned bad about it.

I scrubbed my face with my hands after about an hour of it. We weren't getting anywhere.

"Stop! Stop! Stop! Stop! Stop!" I called, "I got a better idea." I went over to the supply bench and plucked off a handheld propane torch. I opened the valve and got it hissing and used a spark lighter to get it to catch. Once it was ignited, I walked towards Pig, adjusting the flame until I got a nice, steady blue burn on her.

"Tell us where the rest of 'em live."

"Fuck you!"

"Get his pants off him."

"Wait, wait, wait, wait!" Pig started screaming and thrashing, as Ghost and Trig did what I told them with grim faces.

When he was hanging there nude, I asked him, "Have I got your attention?"

"Yes!"

"You going to tell me what I wanna know?"

He was crying now, and it was pretty fucking pathetic watching a grown-ass man cry, but I was thinking about Dani's tears. He would need to cry a hundred to match a single one shed from her corn-flower-blue eyes and I still didn't think that would be enough.

"Yes! I'll tell you what you wanna know!" and he did. He spilled everything.

I took the torch to his balls anyways. The smell of his flesh cooking drove Blue and Ghost out into the night retching, but I stood there and burned the motherfucker. It was Dragon who stopped the high and piteous screaming; he blew a hole right through Pig-Pen's head. I shut off the torch and stood there grimly. It was Reaver who took it from my hand.

"You're going to need a while before you go back to Dani. Trust me," he said quietly. I nodded and went with him out to the edge of the property. We sat quietly.

"That's the most fucked-up thing I think I've ever done." I sniffed. "I've done some pretty fucked-up things, too."

Reaver gave me a reassuring look. "It isn't so fucked-up by half, Brother. You're good. Still human. I promise," he said.

I stared up into the star-shot sky. We'd been at it a good long while.

"How do you do it, man?" I asked.

"I just don't care..." he said honestly, and shrugged. "That's what it is, really. I care that I don't care. I know it's wrong and I know it's fucked-up and I just don't feel anything. Get to that place with this before we go back. You have to, but get to that place only for this, you understand me? Don't make a repeat visit. I've made too damned many." He got up and went back to the ugly metal building as I nodded.

I didn't have a fucking clue how I was going to do that. Not clue one.

20

D ani...

I woke, so late at night it was the wee hours of the morning, to Thirteen sliding into the bed behind me. He drew me back into the curve of his body and kissed the back of my shoulder, sighing as if the weight of the world was upon his shoulders.

"Are you okay?" I murmured, concerned.

"No, babe. I'm really not, but I will be." He kissed the back of my shoulder again.

"Is he...?"

"Yeah." He sounded terse, incredibly so, and so I dropped it immediately. We were silent for a very long time and I thought maybe he'd fallen asleep.

"Thank you," I whispered and my tension eased. I melted into the hard warmth of him.

He murmured back to me,

"Don't thank me, babe. Not for that. Please?" he said.

I nodded and bit the inside of my cheek.

"Okay."

I was a complete coward. I didn't want to know. I'd asked Thirteen to do something so terrible that he came back to me in such a state, and I didn't want to know. I closed my eyes and slept, but it was far from soundly, and fraught with twisting nightmares and dreams.

We spent the next two days, essentially in bed, rising only for meals, forget showering; most of the time we spent together was spent facing one another, hands clasped, sometimes speaking softly, sometimes just searching the other's face, communicating comfort through gentle touches and meaningful looks. We kissed, but that was all; the day's events from my move were taking a real and exhausting toll on Thirteen physically, and both of us emotionally.

On the third day, Doc came to Thirteen's room and said, "Get your asses out of bed, the both of you, and come out here," before he turned on his heel and strode out into the common room. Thirteen and I exchanged a look and got out of bed. He pulled on a pair of flannel pajama pants and I put on his robe, and we went out into the common area. Doc held out two tri-folded pieces of paper, one to me and one to Thirteen.

"Yer results," he said.

I swallowed hard and unfolded the page with shaking fingers. Negative. Negative all the way down the line. I sank to the floor, my legs folding under me with relief.

"Well, I'm clear," Thirteen said and looked over to me and down. "Shit, Dani, what's wrong?" He snatched the page from my hand and read it over, and frowned.

"You're fine," he said, confused.

"You might wanna hold her or something, she's having the same deal Em had." Dray commented dryly.

Thirteen crouched and folded me into his arms, and I burst into relieved sobs.

I was clean. Last hurdle vaulted. I was clean and I was clear of the Suicide Kings. I was free. Thirteen held me and looked at Dray, helpless and horrified.

"It's cool, man. Just let her vent," Dray said and he motioned to the others sitting around to get up and get out, leaving just me and Thirteen alone.

He smoothed a hand over my hair and made me look at him.

"You're okay, baby, you're fine! Shhhhhh." He soothed and held me until the last of my tears dried up.

I was elated. As soon as I had my shit together from my latest meltdown I felt lighter. The cry had been cathartic and I felt cleansed in a way that no shower or bath could accomplish.

"You okay?" he asked me.

I nodded against him. "Yeah," I said and my voice sounded piteous, even to me.

"Okay, come on, let's get you up off the floor, then." I rose with him and he took me into one of the bathrooms and sat me on the closed lid of the toilet.

"Be right back."

He returned with towels and we showered together. He held me and I held him, and we traced each other's forms with delicate touches of fingertips and lips, and in some cases tongues. There was no sex, not yet. The time wasn't right for either of us. We still needed to heal. Once showered, we dressed comfortably.

"Guess we should rejoin the land of the living, eh?" he asked.

I smiled and nodded. We joined a bunch of the other guys in what was dubbed the media room, where a couch and recliners and a few oversized beanbag chairs resided.

"What're we watching?" Thirteen asked, pulling me down between his legs and against his chest.

"Trying to figure that out," Archer grunted. He looked me over and there was no trace of hostility this time, just a thinly-veiled curiosity.

"We got *Guardians of the Galaxy*?" Thirteen asked him.

"Yeah, why?"

"Put it in; Dani doesn't get why I call her 'Rocket'."

Archer shrugged and obliged him, sliding the disc into the tray. The movie was funny and the raccoon named Rocket a brazen little guy for his size. I laughed and enjoyed myself thoroughly.

When the movie ended, Reaver looked at us. "Okay, now we don't get why you call her Rocket. Fill some of us in who missed it."

"The Suicide Kings called me Raccoon, on account of my always having two black eyes," I murmured.

There were several dark looks traded.

"Gotcha," Reaver said and no more was said about it.

We went to bed after the movie. I waited for Thirteen to initiate anything sexual but he simply held me, kissing my forehead. I slept better that night than I had ever slept before.

The next day, he found me in the first bay of the large garage outbuilding, straightening my workbench and firing up my equipment to ensure the circuit would take it.

"What're you doing?" he asked, and dropped into a seat nearby.

"Making sure the system you have in place can handle the load; so far, so good." I shrugged and continued sorting my tools carefully.

"Getting back into it?" he asked, sounding wary.

"Going to try. I'm not going anywhere, if you're worried," I said.

"You and me have been under one hell of a strain," he admitted.

"Together," I pointed out. "I don't want to see this fail before I've given it a chance to start, Thirteen."

He pulled me between his legs and held me lightly by my hips.

"Me, either." He looked up into my eyes, "Wanna show me how some of this works?" I gave him a tiny smile and nodded, surprised that he grasped things rather quickly.

"I never asked you what you did for a living," I said finally.

"I'm a welder. Worked on a riverboat for a while. One month on, one month off. Brutal schedule but for a single guy not so bad, just wanted to move on to something new, put down roots. This place seemed like a good place to start. Dragon is a solid Pres, it's the mother chapter, and they'd gone legit. Was supposed to be no more violence, until the Suicide Kings brought the fight to our door."

"When it's done?" I asked.

"Figured I'd do what I could to help you. Maybe pick up a new trade, or go back to welding, someplace land-based." He shrugged.

"Okay." I humored him, "Where are we going to live? Here?"

"For the time being, until we've finished what was started, then I figured we'd talk, figure out what we wanted and go from there. The possibilities are endless, baby. We can do whatever we want."

I narrowed my eyes, and cupped his face with my hands. "Apartment or house?" I asked.

"I'd like to buy a house, what do you think about that?" His voice had grown husky and I drew closer to him.

"Never lived in a house; I think it sounds nice."

"All right," he said against my lips, and then we were kissing. His mouth moved, sure against mine, and I sighed, and eased into his embrace.

"I want you," he growled.

"I'm right here," I told him. He swept some things off my worktable and boosted me up onto it. It was the perfect height and soon our mouths were crashing together. His hands went to the button and fly of my jeans just as mine scrabbled against his. There were several frantic jerking movements as we unbuttoned and unzipped. I raised myself off the worktable, putting my hands flat against the metal.

"Shit! I don't have a condom," he griped.

"I had an IUD put in," I gasped.

He growled, a deep and appreciative sound, and nipped at the side of my neck as I kicked off my shoes and he got rid of my jeans. The metal of the worktable was cold against my ass, but I didn't care.

I was careful of his one shoulder, pulling him against me by his ribs, the cotton of his tee so soft beneath my palms. He smelled ridiculously good, of clean male and fresh laundry. His hands found my hips and pulled me to the edge of the table, and I moaned as I wrapped my legs around his hips. Just as he was about to enter me, the side door opened.

I shrieked and tucked myself against Thirteen, hiding. I had no clue who had come in but hiding seemed like a really good idea.

"Oh, shit! Sorry!" a male voice cried and I heard the door slam. Thirteen held me close and started laughing. I gave him a baleful look.

"Oh, come on! We finally go there, and this? How is that not funny?" he asked.

I gave him a light shove and he handed me my pants and panties, hauling his own jeans up. It took a ridiculous amount of him rearranging himself to get his jeans on comfortably. I raised an eyebrow, noting that underwear wasn't really his thing. He shrugged, "Too constrictive. Never liked it." I laughed and hopped to the floor, buttoning and zipping myself up.

The side door opened and a voice called in, "Is the coast clear?"

"Yeah," I called back.

Revelator came through the door, his eyes squeezed tightly shut, bitching, "Oh God! It burns!"

"What does?" Thirteen asked, grinning.

"The sight of your naked ass! Straight into my brain!"

Thirteen laughed. "That's what you get for not knocking first."

"Duly noted. No worries, Rocket, I didn't see anything." I nodded, and the uneasy tension in my shoulders loosened.

"Did you need something?" I asked.

"Uh, yeah. I wanted to talk to you, actually." He slid up onto one of the tall stools near my work table and I pushed myself back up onto it, swinging my legs.

"What about?"

"I asked my girl to marry me before I found out I knocked her up, but it was sort of half-assed and impromptu. Anyways, I told her I would ask her again, properly, but I sort of need a ring, so I was wondering if you maybe wanted to trade?" He buried his hands in the pockets of his long, denim shorts and leaned back on the stool precariously.

"Trade, how? I mean you want a ring, obviously, but what do you want to trade me for it?" He'd piqued my interest with his approach, and the grin that spread across his face told me he knew it.

"Swap you skills. You make my girl an engagement ring, I'll fix your tattoo."

I stilled. "What do you mean you'll fix it?" I asked quietly. *Could something like that be fixed?*

"It's what I do. Me, Trig, and Dis, we're all tattoo artists. I mean,

I'm the resident piercer, too, but yeah. Trig and me are the best cover-up artists in the state."

"Cover-up?" I echoed. "How do you cover up something like that?"

"Well, I'd have to see it but generally, using pattern and color and by doing something bigger... you okay?"

I'm pretty sure I looked ill, because Thirteen took me by the hand.

"I'm afraid of needles," I confessed. "It was hell being held down and having this one put on. Only thing I'm afraid of more is burning, which is why Pig tried to brand me in the first place."

Revelator considered me. "Was it bad?" he asked, "The sensation, I mean. I mean, of course it was bad, being afraid and all."

I thought about it. "Yes and no."

"Guess the big question is, do you want to live with that thing the rest of your life?" He met my gaze and I stilled.

"I'll start your ring now, today. Do you have a picture of your girlfriend?"

He gave me a winning, victorious smile and pulled out his phone.

"Don't tell her I showed you these, they uh, they're supposed to be just for me, but they're the only pictures I have right now." He handed me his phone and, oh my! The pictures were very erotic in nature, but also very tastefully done.

"Wow, that's quite the tattoo," I commented.

"It's not, actually. It's Sharpie. Come to think of it, I can do the same thing on you to show you how we can disguise that thing on you before you commit to any needles. I mean, the tattoo will look way better and be a lot cleaner, but it'll give you an idea... Is she listening to a word I'm saying?"

"I'm listening," I said, but my voice sounded faraway, even to me. I knew exactly what I wanted to do for this ring and was already taking tools to wax to carve out a three-dimensional image for a mold.

"Okay. I'll uh, I'll come back," he said.

"Okay. Leave the phone," I said, when he went to pick it up.

He gave an amused laugh, said something to Thirteen, and left. Thirteen kissed my temple and went and sat down.

I kept Revelator's phone awake but finally the screen went dark and I frowned. "Damn!" Thirteen chuckled, unlocked it for me, and went back to his little video game on his own phone.

The images inspired me. So full of love and light and trust, the ivy vines drawn onto his woman and her coloring spoke to me. I had visions of white gold and a diamond solitaire. The wedding band, when the engagement ring was slipped into it, would bracket the solitaire, with three marquis-cut emeralds to either side forming twin ivy leaves. If I did this right, then the bands would be the vine, and I planned on making it thin, but strong to support the daily wear an engagement-and-wedding set got.

I worked diligently and I worked late, getting the wax into the clay and into the kiln to bake overnight and form the mold required to cast the pieces. This was not going to be an easy set, but I could do it.

Thirteen and I finally wandered back into the clubhouse, where we found several of the guys indulging in fried chicken at one of the tables. Rev was one of them, and I gave him back his phone. Disney was sitting with an open sketchbook at the next table, drawing.

"Here," Rev turned a chair around so the back faced the table. "Straddle this and have something to eat."

I sat, and squeaked as he lifted my shirt and tucked it under the band of my bra, up out of his way. My jeans rode low enough that he had a clear view of my lower back.

"I'm gonna move these down." He plucked at my underwear, and I nodded and he tucked them down into the waistband of my jeans. I heard him suck his teeth.

"Hey, Dis! C'mere, Puddin'." Disney got up, came over, and stood behind me. I was ravenous, so I had a piece of chicken and tried to settle my creeping nerves over feeling so exposed.

"Shouldn't be too hard. What do you want to cover it?" Disney asked me.

I swallowed chicken. "I don't know. Never thought about it. Didn't even know it could be changed."

"You really should be asking Trig, not me," Disney commented.

"Flowers would be nice, though. Like, a drift of them down this way. Something feminine, something pretty."

"Yeah, go get Trig, let's brainstorm." Disney wandered off to find him as I worked at finishing my meal.

I ate silently as the three of them stood or sat around behind me talking. Thirteen sat beside me, smiling at me, this secret little encouraging smile that put me at ease.

"That'd be cool. Hey, Dani?"

"Mmm?" I asked, my mouth full.

"You be cool if we took this back to Thirteen's room and busted out the Sharpies?" Rev asked.

"Uhhhh..."

"Please," Disney made a slightly rude noise. "I'm gay and Trig and Rev would lop their own dicks off before they'd cheat or hurt their Ol' Ladies. We promise to be nothing but professional."

Thirteen captured my eyes and the perfect trust I saw in his green-blue eyes had me softly agreeing,

"All right."

We went back to his room.

"Ever get a massage?" Trigger asked. I shook my head. "Well, crap. Okay, I know this sounds bad, but get naked, get under the sheet and lay on your stomach, and when you're set have Thirteen let us in."

I blinked at them, bewildered, but they were out the door, shutting it behind them.

"It's cool, they trade in slinging ink under skin; they need to see the skin to see what they're doing. This is the best way to preserve your modesty and they know it," Thirteen explained.

"How come you don't have any tattoos?" I asked, kicking off my shoes.

"Just never could settle on anything I wanted permanently inked under my skin. Too indecisive, I guess." He lifted the blankets for me to get under. I lay on my stomach and he motioned for me to get in the center of the bed. Once I was settled, he draped the sheet up to my shoulders and folded the rest of the blankets down at my feet.

"Gonna let 'em in. I'll be here the whole time."

He let the guys in. They were talking about flowers and trees, necklaces and little girls and all manner of different things, shading and color and light source and shadow, all of it in rapid succession, to where I just let my fatigued mind wander rather than try to follow it.

"Gonna fold down the sheet, you cool?" Trig asked.

"Yes."

They all sat around me chatting and finally Revelator said, "Might tickle," before he started to draw over the spot on my back marred with Pig-Pen's name.

I closed my eyes. It did tickle faintly but wasn't too bad. The four men sat on the bed, the three artists arguing jovially about colors and design elements, and I had to smile. They weren't seeing me as a person at all, but it wasn't upsetting or malicious. I really was nothing but a raw canvas to them and there was something soothing about it. They didn't see pussy, tits, and ass. They were just working, playing around with their craft, being artistic, and I let them. It put me at ease and before I knew it, I was fast asleep, Thirteen's hand grasped loosely in mine.

I don't know how long I slept but Thirteen was whispering in my ear, "Dani. Dani, baby, wake up." I opened my eyes and stretched, slightly stiff from being in the same position too long.

"Mmm, what time is it?" I asked, yawning.

"Time for you to look." Revelator was grinning, a long mirror in his hands. Trigger handed me a hand mirror and I positioned it over my shoulder. The guys held the long mirror over the bed and I gasped.

The entire left side of my back from my shoulder to my ass was a tree, the branches sweeping up and onto the rest of my back, jagged and black; stark, with no leaves covering them and no flowers either; but in a drift at the tree's bottom were gorgeous lilies and a myriad of other flowers. What really caught my attention was the locket hanging from one of the tree branches, swaying in a mythical wind, the face of the locket open and inside, a facsimile of my grandfather's smiling face.

"Oh, my God... It's beautiful! But how did you..?" Thirteen held up one of my photo albums.

"Sorry," he stated simply, but I could tell by his smile that he so wasn't, and I wasn't either. It was gorgeous. It was also huge. My whole back had pretty much become the canvas for it.

"You wouldn't sit for it all at once. We'd do all the outlines in one sitting, then give it time to heal, then do the shading, let it heal, then do the color, a section at a time. Depending on how well you sat, you'd be looking at five, maybe six sessions, less if you can hold still and don't need breaks. I don't think it will be as bad as you think. Getting a tat is a lot different when it's something you want and nobody's holding you down," Rev said.

"You're a smart girl. If we show you the equipment and explain how it works, logically, I think that would help and go a long ways, too." Trigger said.

I stared at the image they'd painted on my skin with permanent marker.

"When can we start?" I was convinced. I loved it. I really, really loved it, and I could and would do it. I would erase every last trace of Pig from my body with an overlay of something beautiful that commemorated my grandfather, who meant so very much to me.

"Tomorrow night, if you want. Not going to lie, it's a big decision. Are you sure?"

"I'm sure," I said, marveling at the image.

The four of them exchanged looks.

"Okay. We're going to bed. You two have fun." The other three left me with Thirteen, who closed the door behind them.

"I like it," he said truthfully.

I smiled. "Can we please finish what we started in the workshop?" I asked.

He grinned.

"Absolutely."

21

Red-XIII...

Her request made me instantly hard the rest of the way. I'd be lying if I said the sight of all that smooth skin, of her sitting up in my bed with the sheet grasped coyly to her chest, hadn't gotten me at least halfway there already. Goddamn, she was gorgeous and goddamn, did I ever want to be inside her.

I stripped my shirt over my head, grasping it at the back and pulling it off in one smooth movement. Her eyes shone, traveling over my shoulders and chest with a liquid heat, dimming for a second when she reached the stain of the bruise in the center of my chest.

"Dani," I said softly, and her eyes snapped to mine. The smile I gave her reignited the warm fire, the need in her expression. I stripped the rest of the way in record time and when I came to the bed, she reached for me, the sheet dropping to pool in her lap. She knelt up and met me in my descent, our mouths meeting in the middle, the kiss everything it had been in the workshop and more. She molded her soft, almost-too-thin body to the front of mine, her arms twining around my neck and shoulders, and I put a knee on the edge of the bed. She scooted back and I went with her until we were both kneeling on the mattress, kissing, taking our time. The heat between us increased to a steady boil.

I broke my mouth from hers and lay on my back, and without missing a beat she straddled my hips, her upper body dipping low so our mouths could meet once more. I smoothed my hands over all that damned satiny-smooth skin of hers and as we kissed, unconsciously rocked my hips, sliding my shaft against her hot, slick lips.

Dani broke our kiss with a frustrated cry and pushed herself up.

"Condom?" she asked, breathless.

"Fuck no," I growled, and she didn't argue. She rose up on her knees and reached for me, guiding me into her body. She lowered herself agonizingly slowly, until I caught her wincing. I put my hands on her hips and gripped her firmly.

"Stop," I told her gently. "You feel fucking amazing, babe. You ain't got to take it all. I told you that."

We locked gazes, her cornflower-blue eyes something to really behold, wide and so big and beautiful. She wiggled her hips and I sucked in a deep breath, and with the sweetest, purest smile, she rolled them just right. Fuck, man, I knew I was damned. Damned to want her, and only her, for the rest of my fucking life, and I would gladly go straight to hell for her. I let my head fall back to the pillow and I moaned. Good Christ, she felt incredible! Hot, wet, velvet heat, so pure, so sweet, clenching tight, her beautiful pussy gripping my dick as she drew off me, milking me for everything I was worth.

Dani collapsed forward, her hands on my chest, down low where there was no bruising. She looked down at me, her black hair loose and tousled around her face, in a wash down her back, cloaking her shoulders. She looked like some sort of goddess, like the goddess of crows, made flesh, something mythical and fantastic, and she had me so damned firmly under her spell.

She loved me hard, she was all-in, and it was amazing. Still, it was hard not to notice the fine trembling in her lithe frame. She was getting tired, so I swept my hands up her body, cradling her before I put some of my strength to use. With a wild and surprised cry from my girl, I spun her, putting her beneath me. While her riding me was fucking beautiful to watch and felt incredibly good, it just wasn't going to put me over the edge.

The sudden movement on my part had hurt more than I'd like to admit. I guess I wasn't fully healed yet, but I couldn't and wouldn't care. I pulled out of her and she gave me a dirty look. I laughed.

"Turn on your stomach for me?" I asked.

With a look like she was about to mutiny if she didn't get me back inside, she complied, getting up on her knees. I shook my head and guided her with gentle hands into the position I wanted, her on her stomach, flat on her stomach, legs together. I nudged them apart, my hands on her ass, just enough to get myself situated and, with a triumphant smile, slipped back into her warm and welcoming body.

Dani cried out and I bowed my head. I loved this position. I was so long I could do it easily but it kept me from going too deep. Still, it felt like she took all of me this way. Her soft thighs stroked my shaft near the base when I thrust, the head of my cock and a decent amount of my length buried and getting the attention that would get me off inside her. Bonus? I seemed to be stroking right over her g-spot, because the feral sounds of passion pouring from her throat damn sure told me I was hitting all the right buttons.

I kneaded her delectable ass with my hands, my eyes roving over the artwork inked onto her back and I had the stray thought that I was glad she'd chosen this design. I really didn't think I would ever get tired of looking at it. It was really beautiful.

"Oh, God! Thirteen, I'm gonna come!" she cried, her voice high and breathy, and I smiled. Oh God, indeed. She jerked, her beautiful cunt putting a stranglehold on the head of my dick before her pounding orgasm swept me into a damned frenzy of one of my own. I shouted and buried myself deep before coming myself, glad that her orgasm riding her would ease things.

"Mmm!" She jerked beneath me and I pulled back a bit.

"You all right?" I asked breathlessly.

She hummed in satisfied pleasure and nodded. Her face was turned to the side so she could breath, her eyes were closed, and her expression was pure, relaxed bliss. I smiled and braced myself on the bed, leaning over her. I drew back my hips and withdrew from her body and she shuddered, moaning in pleasure.

It made me laugh, a slightly prideful sound, and I leaned down and kissed the back of her shoulder that bore no ink.

"Like that?" I asked her softly, a whisper against her warmth. She nodded, completely wordless and boneless beneath me. I pressed soft kisses to every bit of her soft skin while the dew of sweat cooled on our bodies. She giggled and jerked a bit when I made it to the back of her knee. I spent some time there and her giggles quickly turned to moans and groans of approval.

Shit, my turnaround this go-around was fucking amazing. I was getting hard again already.

"You good to go some more so long as you don't got to move?" I asked her.

She nodded, her arms tucked beneath her, hands holding her hair back from her face. So fucking trusting, so fucking beautiful. I smiled and kissed my way to her foot. I planted a kiss to one sole and then the other, and kissed and licked and nipped my way back up the other leg. Dani's eyes were closed, her face serene as she relished the little touches and the attention I lavished on her, and I loved that.

My girl wasn't much of a talker during sex, which was fine by me. Her reactions were more than enough, fucking priceless, such a turn-on. I straddled the back of her thighs and pressed into her slowly. She pressed back onto my cock, her hips rising subtly off the bed, and she moaned. The sound went straight to my blood, and I closed my eyes. I took her much slower this time, took my time, loved her more gently until both of us came with much less intensity, sure, but for what felt like much longer.

I was spent. My girl was spent. There just wasn't any more room for a round three in there. We'd loved one another just that thoroughly.

22

Dani...

They'd pulled Thirteen into a room in the back near the media room the next morning after breakfast. They called it the council chamber. I pretty much assumed that was the equivalent to the Suicide Kings' war room. I drifted out to the shop and picked up where I'd left off on Revelator's wedding set for his woman, when a slight flicker of movement out of the corner of my eye made me turn. I damn near came out of my skin.

"Sorry." Reaver looked apologetic and, as silently as he'd entered, glided over to the chair that Thirteen had occupied while I worked. I watched him, the ring I was crafting forgotten in my fingers.

"Got bored." He lifted a shoulder in an inelegant shrug.

"How are you still alive?" I blurted.

He crooked a grin and bowed his head, smoothing his hair down in front. He looked at me.

"What do you think?"

I frowned.

"If I had any idea, I wouldn't be asking."

"Touché, fair enough." He nodded and then looked at me, "It was pretty stupid, actually. I got married and changed my name, but no one that was there bothered to tell the EMT's that. They looked at my driver's license and checked me in to the hospital under the name on it." He made a distasteful face.

"Dragon and Doc talked about it; Doc issued a phony death cert in my old name and they kept it quiet. Used my 'death'," he put the word 'death' in air quotes with his fingers, "as leverage, both to get the girls to agree to go to ground and in hopes that if the Suicide Kings believed I was dead that they might back off." He twisted his lip wryly.

"Yeah, not going to happen, you're going to have to kill them all," I said succinctly.

He got a wicked gleam in his bright blue eyes and a slow grin curled his lips. "With pleasure," he stated dryly, and I felt the first fingers of icy dread tick down my spine. He must have read it in my posture, seen it on my face, because his smile got a little broader.

"I thought you were one of their cabinet, why aren't you in there?" I asked, in a bid to change the subject.

He shrugged.

"Had to make everyone believe. I didn't mind giving it up, it never really suited me anyhow. Especially, now that there's Hayden." He slipped his phone out of a pocket, and showed me a picture. She was small against his front, her head tipped back as he kissed her. The photo was tastefully black and white. They were surrounded by glass and metal but I couldn't tell where they were. It didn't take a PhD to see that they were completely and madly in love with each other.

"She still doesn't know," he said softly and withdrew the phone. "I want this over more than I can say. She's down south, being looked after, safe, but every day away from her..." he shook his head.

"When you meet the right woman, it stops the rage and the pain, and she's the right woman for me. I don't know that she'll take me back after this one." He slipped off the chair and stretched, his white tee riding up, the edge of a long pink scar riding over his ribs and down towards his stomach on his left side. He lifted his shirt so I could see.

It was bad, the scar tissue puckered where the bullet had gone in, two long scars radiating out from the site and a couple of more puncture-looking scars higher up between his ribs. Likely from chest tubes or something.

"How is your recovery?"

"Doc says I'm real fucking lucky. Should do just fine. Almost out the other side of this thing. Ready to get back in it."

"Why'd you come out here?" I asked.

"You hit the nail on the head. I want you to like me. That, and I promised to give you this back." He held up the switchblade he'd taken back from me after giving it to me the night I'd come here. His eyes were clear and cold as a winter's sky, and nothing but a wasteland of frozen tundra peered out of them. No emotion, just nothing there. Like a wolf would look at you. I bravely reached out and plucked it from his long fingers.

"I keep my word, Rocket. You can count on us here," he said softly. I nodded mutely and took a shuddering breath, a little overcome with emotion. I hit the switch and the blade snapped free, flakes of dried blood sifting to my workbench. Pig's blood. Tears of relief flooded my eyes and I sniffed. I looked up to Reaver's emotionless eyes and said the only thing I could, even though it didn't even begin to cover it.

"Thank you."

"My pleasure." His eyes thawed, warming back up into human temperature, and he put a hand on my shoulder.

"Almost over," he said, and I nodded, the 'I promise' hanging in the air between us.

"Can't wait for you to meet the rest of the girls," he said with a smile, and the thought earned a smile from me in return.

"I wonder what they're like..."

He laughed and started telling stories, the heaviness dissipating with every word spoken, the fear diminishing with every laugh shared. It's where Thirteen found me, laughing at something Reaver had said, and I was struck by something I'd heard the VP say.

"Do you always make friends this way?" I asked.

Reaver gave me a cheeky smile and bounced his eyebrows a few times, which made me laugh again. I was finding that he was quite the character.

Hours later I held Thirteen's hand while Revelator and Trigger sat across from me, showing me how their tattoo guns went together and how far the needles penetrated the skin. Doc, who was wearing his cut for the first time that I could remember, looked on. He had an 'In Memory Of' patch with his woman's initials sewn where an old patch used to reside, the edges of the leather slightly raw to either side of the newer patch, which was narrower but taller than the old one had been.

Doc sighed and pushed off the wall. "I got a better idea. Ain't no way she's going to make it through this without panicking... I can see it in her eyes."

I looked up at Doc and swallowed hard.

"I'll make it. I have to. I want it off, gone, hidden or whatever... I really want to do this," I said.

Doc gave me a sad little smile.

"I know you do. Let me hook you up to an IV to keep you hydrated." He sighed again, before adding, "Now, I can't put you under, but I can give you a pretty good case of the feel-goods and push some Fuckitol. By the time the boys get going, you won't give two shits what's going on."

I considered. I had thought about taking one of the Xanax he'd given me before anything started but this was another possibility. I finally nodded. I mean, he was a doctor, a real one. What could be safer?

"GOOD DEAL, THANKS, DOC." Thirteen smiled at the older brother and Doc nodded.

"Sweet, let's do this." Rev grinned at me, the chip in his front tooth making it positively endearing.

"Where you doing this?" Doc asked.

"Thirteen's room, that way we can leave her to sleep. We'll get as far as we can, don't want to traumatize the skin too much in one go, but we should at least get the outline in, maybe some shading," Rev replied, and Trigger nodded, his ever-present e-cigarette dangling from the corner of his mouth.

We went back to Thirteen's room. Thirteen put fresh, clean sheets on the bed and Rev turned his head this way and that, finally shaking it.

"Great for after, but we're going to need the massage table."

They set about making preparations and I sat, Thirteen holding my head and shoulders while I shook, my face buried in his chest as Doc started an IV in my arm. I really, really hated needles. I'd bounced so nervously when he'd drawn my blood it was ridiculous, and this was no different. He introduced things to the line and pretty soon the world had gone hazy and I don't remember too much after that except rhythmic buzzing, cool air against my skin, and an ever-growing sting to my back, like somebody had gone and slapped the worst sunburn I had ever had in my life.

True to Doc's word, I was so high I simply didn't care about any of it.

23

R ed-XII...

Reaver caught my eye from the doorway and lifted his chin. He was dressed and ready to head out. I nodded and held up a finger, and he nodded, his eyes coolly sweeping the back of my girl. She had a sheet hiding her from the hips down and Rev was bent over the low-riding massage table from his perch on a chair beside it, his brow furrowed, deep in concentration. He had a small tray-table set up next to him with all his inks and guns and shit as he worked the image stenciled on Dani.

She was going to be miserable in the morning and uncomfortable as hell while she healed.

I knelt by her head and smoothed her hair back from her face. I whispered that I loved her in her ear and kissed her cheek. Trigger nodded at me and Disney echoed the gesture. They would take care of her while I was out. I shrugged into my jacket and cut, still a little stiff, my shoulder was not quite there yet, but Doc and I were already rehabbing it. The slug had had a shit-ton of its momentum stopped and hadn't gone deep at all. Really, it was just a damned flesh wound; the stitches were out already.

Reave and I passed Doc sitting at the club's bar reading one of his woman's books. We each clapped him on the back as we passed and he said, "Be careful."

"As careful as a virgin on her wedding night!" Reave called over his shoulder, and Doc snorted.

We mounted our bikes outside and strapped on our helmets. The deep night air was comfortable, warmer than it had been in a while, just this side of chilly. Still, there wasn't a cloud in the sky, the stars were out, the roads dry and clear, and it was just about as perfect as it could get when it came to riding.

"Ready?" I grunted.

"I been ready, let's bury this."

I kick-started my bike and he hit the switch to start his and we rode out, along the highway, deep into East County and into the heart of Suicide Kings territory. Neither one of us had the intention of dying for real tonight. Nope. We were the reapers this time.

We pulled up and backed into an alley a good distance from the Suicide Kings' club. We only had to wait an hour or two before Flyer came stumbling out the back.

"Winner, winner, chicken dinner," Reaver breathed. I looked over at him like he was fucking nuts, but he just plain wasn't home. He leaned over his handle bars, watching the man the way most people watch a fascinating insect. I shrugged, more to myself than anything. To each their own.

We didn't hear it, but rather saw it. One second Flyer was standing there trying to keep his feet under him, and the next second there was this puff, almost like he let out a breath of that vapor shit that was popular nowadays. Then he just keeled over.

"That's our cue," I sang out under my breath and Reave and I dismounted our bikes. I checked my guns and, satisfied they were ready to go, glanced at Reave. He shrugged his shoulders and I rolled my eyes. "Seriously? The last time you brought a knife to a gun fight you got yourself shot."

The crazy fucker just grinned at me and we set out along the street, skirting cameras, and went up to the side door of the building. Reave nodded and we slipped in, unnoticed.

We were here to finish this as much as we could and with Flyer down, that left Gordy, Pipes, Skid, Bandit, and Griz.

Reaver and I walked into the big expanse of open space where Griz had his table set up, his 'war room' as he called it, and I gave a sharp whistle, gesturing with my gun. Gordy straightened up and stood, calm, his hands in the air.

"Mmm, eleven -- you can write off your VP. Your guy outside was twelve, and you'll make thirteen." Reaver ticked each downed man in turn on his fingers and cocked his head to the side.

"Well, I'll be dipped in shit," Gordy said.

I snorted, "Please, you had to know this was coming."

Ghost, true to his name, drifted into the room from the back. He shook his head. Skid, Pipes, Bandit and Griz were still MIA. Ghost took a position where he could cover things, taking steps two at a time to the catwalk that ringed the room.

"So, what now, boys?" Gordy asked.

A flash of movement at my side and Gordy's eyes went wide open, his hands going to his throat, and he found one of Reaver's throwing blades in his neck, dead center. A cruel fucking blow if you ask me. I hadn't even seen Reave go for it.

"Go ahead, pull it out," Reaver said.

Gordy choked, blood coating his chin, and went to his knees. I slowly lowered my gun.

Reaver went walking to Gordy, who was struggling to pull air through a windpipe that no longer worked the way it was supposed to. He was going to die slow this way, and I can't really say I felt one way or the other about it.

Reaver crouched by him and looked him over, smiling his secret little smile, like he was listening to a music only he could hear and the sound of it pleased him, soothed him somehow.

I glanced up at Ghost, who had a better view of Reaver's face than I did, and the man looked like he was shut the fuck down, like the soldier he was. Still, a hint of unease flickered in the depths of his gaze as he looked down at the scene below him.

I followed through with the plan, and ducked into the bar and added three more hashtags to the count on the wall, which hadn't been touched since Archer, Rush, and Nox had put it there.

I went back, and Reaver was murmuring something to Gordy as the light died in the other man's eyes.

We loaded the bodies into the van but left the cuts near the bloodstains on the floor. We rode out ahead of Ghost, to Point Nowhere, and buried the fuckers in Cicada Woods before heading back to the club.

Ghost got out of the van, his sniper's rifle slung over his shoulder. Reaver, as quick as he'd gone fucking scary, was back to his normal, lighthearted self by the time the gate rolled shut behind us. He got off his bike and we went inside and had a stiff drink before parting ways.

I went to my room. Doc sat in a chair beside the bed, his glasses perched on the end of his nose, reading a thick paperback. Dani lay on her stomach, her face turned to the side, one arm gracefully following the cascade of her dark hair over the edge of the mattress. Her other arm, the one without the IV hooked to it, was curled to her chest as she slept on, oblivious. Her back was raw and puffy where the ink had been forced under it. The whole thing was pretty much done except for color.

She could get up tomorrow and decide she couldn't go through another session, and it would be okay, would look like a completed piece. I stood, looking down at my girl for a long time.

"It was a good idea," I said to Doc, keeping my voice low so as not to disturb Dani. "Thank you, man."

Doc looked over his half-moon spectacles at me, over the top of his novel, before lowering it.

"Some awful shit?" he asked.

I sniffed and nodded. He grunted and nodded too. Nothing really needed to be said about it.

I stared down at the beautiful piece of art inked under my woman's skin and sighed.

"This is going to seriously suck for her, come morning."

"Shouldn't be too bad, I'm keeping her hydrated, she'll need to be cleaned up some and Dis, Rev, and Trig already have it worked out, timed so someone can go to her, wherever she's at, to keep the tat lubed enough to keep her out of too much discomfort while it heals. She couldn't take any more of it. We decided it was best this way. . She won't have to, but the guys didn't want her going around with no half-assed tattoo the rest of her life." Doc voiced just about every thought I'd just had, and it made me smile.

"Dani's tough. She'll finish it," I said, with confidence.

"Well, gonna say g'night then, now that you're here." Doc heaved himself to his feet and I nodded, my eyes still only for Dani, sweeping the curve of her back where it dipped just before the swell of her ass. You couldn't even see the original ink. It was like it had never been. I heard the door shut softly and I sighed. If only erasing some memories were as easy. The pain from the tat would dissipate, but the pain in her heart, well, that shit would take a lot longer to heal.

I finally tore my eyes off of her long enough to strip down and get into the bed on the other side. I wanted to hold her, to touch her, but I didn't want to wake her or hurt her so instead, I lay on my side and stared at her beautiful face.

I stared for a really long time.

24

Dani...

The morning after the first part of my tattoo had been done was sheer misery. Not only did my head feel like it was full of cotton from the drugs, my back felt this odd combination of burning and like the skin was too tight. I'd whimpered when I'd woken, and Thirteen had startled awake beside me. He'd helped me into the closest bathroom so I could take care of business, which pretty much involved bathing, except I couldn't shower. Something about not getting the tattoo directly in the spray.

Instead I had knelt in the tub while Thirteen gently poured water on the back of my neck, letting it wash down over my back. That was not fun. But what really wasn't fun was when he'd used his fingertips, laden with an antibacterial hand soap to wash me. No matter how gentle, how ghostly the touch, it was sheer misery. The only thing worse was patting the affected areas dry.

Still, even after the entire ordeal, it had been completely worth it once I had gotten to look at the sweeping image in the bathroom mirror. They'd completed it, every line, every bit of shading; it was a whole, complete image and what's more, you couldn't identify a single trace of Pig's mark. No matter how hard I looked for it, even knowing it had been there, I couldn't see it in the drift of lilies at the bottom; the flowers and foliage perfectly disguised it.

I'd spent the entire first two days of the healing process on my stomach in bed. The guys would come at regular intervals to slather this thick, petroleum-like moisturizer over the inked-in areas of my back, and I looked forward to those moments. It was the only time the infernal itching eased for me.

I couldn't have put on a shirt if I wanted to in those first few days, and then, while it took the rest of the week to get to a point it no longer itched, I could only wear one of Thirteen's oversized tees. The lotion that had to be continually applied made an absolute mess of things and so I was doing laundry almost as much as I was spending any time in my shop.

When Thirteen couldn't come to apply the lotion to my skin, it was usually one of the three artists, though it had been a few days since I needed any. The skin had healed and finished peeling. Finally, I'd been able to spend serious time at my workbench.

I had just finished polishing Revelator's wedding set for his woman and was about to get started on shining up the white gold band I'd fashioned for him when Blue had entered.

He smiled and waved a hand up and down and I nodded. He didn't speak and I didn't feel the need to fill the silence with useless prattle.

I lifted the back of my shirt and he traced a fingertip over my back along the tree.

"Thirteen in church?" I asked.

Blue made a face and nodded.

"Thanks."

I put the shirt back down, and he raised an eyebrow in question.

I nodded. "I think I'm going to go for it."

Blue smiled broadly and I smiled in return. He nodded happily and left me in the shop to myself. He was the only one to check on me regularly just for the hell of it, other than Thirteen, and was becoming a true friend. I think it was because I understood him clearly without his ever having to speak. Only Duracell shared that particular talent.

I smiled and finished polishing the three individual rings, proud of my work. I slipped them into two small velvet bags left from my grandfather's defunct jewelers business, and shut off the lights and equipment. That was enough for one day.

The afternoon sunshine was warm and the unseasonably cool spring and early summer had turned over into a string of beautiful midsummer days. I stretched and tipped my face into the sun, drawing in a deep breath that smelled of sunshine and freshly mowed grass. The men of the Sacred Hearts kept the grounds of their club meticulous. It was a welcome change from the dilapidated, rusting industrial building surrounded by a rutted gravel lot.

I looked across the grass, past the long, low, cinderblock building that housed more rooms for brothers, either in the club who lived here, or visiting from out of town. The back of the main building had an asphalt track, a giant access loop from the front lot that could be followed past the garage outbuilding my shop was housed in and past the low outbuilding full of rooms. It could also be used as a running track, which I often saw Reaver and Trigger do; sometimes Revelator and some of the others used it for that purpose as well.

On the opposite end of the oval from where I stood was a low bench, and in front of that stood Archer, Rush, and Nox. It was a homemade outdoor shooting range. A berm of dirt piled high providing the backdrop for their targets, quite a ways out from where the men stood checking and readying weapons.

Nox, Rush, and I had grown to get along but Archer remained hostile; an enemy for life, that one. I shook my head as he glared in my direction. I was disappointed. I wanted Thirteen's brothers to like me. Hell, we all want to be liked, but Archer just plain wasn't having any of it. I shrugged to myself and struck out across the grass to the back of the club's main building. Coming in from the bright sunlight into the club's dim interior always took a period of adjustment for my eyes and this time, I crashed headlong into someone coming out the door. I put up my hands, against slick leather and rough felt patches. Gentle, supportive arms curved around me, pulling me in.

"Easy, Rocket, I got you," Thirteen's voice was smiling. "I always got you."

I lost my stiff posture in his arms and sank against him, a smile touching my lips. I tipped my head back and he met my mouth with his in a gentle yet persistent kiss.

"Hmmm, do we have time to..?" I let the question hang, hopeful.

"Wish we did, babe, but I was coming to get you. The guys were getting things set up to finish your tat, you up for it?" He stared into my eyes and I smiled; his were a warm spring green, and held such a confidence in me. I nodded happily.

I liked the colorized version of the tattoo too much not to do it. I wasn't sure that I would have been able to go through with a piece so big, let alone twice over, if Doc hadn't come up with the idea of making me so high I didn't care. Thankfully, he had, and I was willing to do it.

I loved the black and white image; don't get me wrong, it was beautiful. But for the last two weeks, as I had contemplated it in the mirror, I had realized that this tattoo was much more than just a cover-up.

For me, it went beyond just making something pretty out of something ugly. It had become a physical representation of leaving my old life behind, of laying old ghosts to rest, and of a new beginning for me. I needed, very much, to breathe color and life into the image inked under my skin. I needed vibrancy and happiness to follow in my wake, not the bitter ash of memory. ...And so, I would do this.

Thirteen pulled me tight against the front of his body and kissed me thoroughly, his tongue stroking alluringly against my own, teasing my body awake, making me shiver with a wanton neediness. I pulled back and slapped him playfully on the chest of his cut.

"Ow, hey! What was that for?"

"No getting me all excited if you can't or won't follow through." I wrinkled my nose at him and he laughed. We walked for his room, his arm slung around my shoulders.

"Gonna be a minute before we can again, you do this," he reminded me. "Wanted to make sure you'd know what you'd be missin'."

I snorted, "Somehow I think it'll be more of a hardship for you than for me." Last time I had been so miserably uncomfortable in my own skin I had barely wanted to be touched. The thought of sex in that condition had made me cringe, no matter how much I was in love with Thirteen.

"Damn straight!" Thirteen was saying, but he faltered when I stopped.

"Baby, what's wrong?" he asked.

I looked at him plaintively. "You know I love you, right?" I asked quietly.

"No, but it does me a lot of good to hear it," he said just as quietly. He took me back into his arms. "I love you too, Rocket." His fingertips were gentle where he cradled my cheek, his thumb grazing along the skin in a simple caress.

We kissed again, only this time it was a thing weighted with promise and emotion. Heavy with words unspoken, with admiration and care and a strong mutual respect for one another.

It was the single most spectacular kiss of my entire life and it left me breathless, my heart swollen within my breast to a point where I no longer needed air to breathe... I just needed him.

Someone cleared their throat nearby and Thirteen and I jumped. Revelator looked at us, apologetic.

"We're all set, ready when you are," he said.

I smiled, Thirteen scowled. I gave Thirteen a playful poke in the shoulder and he grinned, laughing at me.

"You shouldn't scowl at him when he's about to turn me into a human voodoo doll," I complained.

Revelator laughed, "Not like you're going to know the difference," he remarked.

We followed him in to the bedroom and it was set up like before.

Doc stood by the massage table, laying the plastic tubing he would be hooking to an IV.

"Ready when you are, sweetheart," he said kindly.

Trigger, Rev, and Disney left the room with Doc and I stripped down, pinning my hair up in a messy bun like I was wont to do when I worked or what-have-you.

"Here, give these to Rev after he's done," I whispered, and handed the little velvet bags to Thirteen. He smiled and looked inside. I was so pleased by the look of impressed, soft wonder on his face over what the bags held.

"You're incredible, Baby," he murmured and kissed the top of my head, pocketing the offerings.

I smiled and sat on the edge of the massage table wrapped in a towel that covered me from armpits to knees while Thirteen let Doc back in.

He started the IV, my eyes squeezed shut, face pressed into Thirteen's stomach, his arms wrapped protectively around my head and shoulders. He made soothing sounds while the deed was done and then let me go when it was over, thumbing some stray tears from under my eyes.

"Hang in there, Dani, y' won't care soon enough," Doc murmured encouragingly.

I lay down on my stomach and Thirteen brought the sheet to my hips before taking the towel away. My modesty was perfectly preserved.

"You good, baby doll?" Doc asked.

"Yes." My voice was a little high and tight with panic, but then he pushed the drugs and that euphoric foggy feeling started in my brain. A couple more minutes and you could have told me the sky was green and I would have believed you. Sometimes drugs were a wonderful thing. Especially when administered by a doctor, oh, and with no availability and thus no danger of repeating them or becoming addicted. Yes, indeed. I could do this.

I let my brain ramble on with these thoughts, startling slightly when the tattoo gun gave an angry buzz as Revelator situated himself.

A latex-covered hand pressed to my back after I jumped and stayed there for a time. A comforting weight, warm, secure... I think I may have drifted off to sleep at that point. I don't remember. I certainly don't remember the gun starting back up or the point he began to dig at my flesh with the needles.

Oh, yes. Drugs were so not bad... Mmm-hmm.

25

R ed-XIII...

   "What the hell you got in there?" I asked Doc as Dani's true-blue eyes glazed over and she stared off into space. She'd turned her head to the side, her arms on the table, and looked like she was lost in the Land of Oz somewhere, a tiny, drugged-out, creepy-as-fuck smile on her sensual lips.

   "Horse tranquilizer; I left the elephant tranqs in my room. She just ain't that big," he commented with dry sarcasm. Revelator paused the buzzing of his gun and chuckled, refreshing the needle with bright pink ink. He'd started right in on the lilies on her lower back. Trig and Dis looked on in fascination. This was the first project they'd done together, the three of them.

   They'd taken pictures the whole process, shown Dani when she'd rejoined the land of the living, and asked if they could keep them to do a big framed job in their shop to promote their business. She'd agreed, which had surprised me and pleased the hell out of the guys.

   "She out?" I asked softly, and Doc nodded. Her eyes were heavy, lidded but still open. He knelt and shined a light into first one then the other.

   "Yep, she ain't gonna remember a fuckin' thing. You just best take care of business and get your ass back here in one piece," he grumbled.

"Copy that." I threw the guys a mock half-assed salute. Trigger gave a wry twist of lips and the middle finger as I backed out the door. I laughed.

I found Reaver and Dray out in the common room. Duracell and Blue were checking over their guns.

"She good?" Reaver asked.

"Yeah, man, thanks for asking." I smiled wide. Data stepped out of his little ops station and laid out several printed pages side by side, their edges matching up to form a map, like from satellite imagery or some shit. I raised my eyebrows.

"So the safe house is this one." Data ringed it in red Sharpie. "You leave the bikes here;" he made an 'X' along what was obviously a road. "You can creep up on 'em this way without even being seen." He used the pen to make an arrow for direction of travel. "There are no windows on this part of the house. Should get right up in it, take them out easy-peasy-lemon-squeezy." He beamed at us.

Four of us gave him blank looks.

"You are such a fucking nerd," Duracell commented dryly.

Dray and I cracked up while Blue smiled big, and Reaver hooked an arm around Data's neck and shook him back and forth.

"How did you find all this out, anyways?" Duracell asked, looking over the images on the table. He took several more sheets out of Data's hands, all pictures of the outside of the house from every different angle.

"You can find anything on the internet, man. It's what I do." The narrow dude shrugged his shoulders and tossed his head back to get some of his lank brown hair out of his eyes.

"Hell if I know how he does it, who cares? I want to finish this and get my woman back home." Dray pulled back the slide on his gun, chambering a round, popped the clip and added another round to the magazine before slamming it back home and tucking the gun into the waistband of his pants, up under his jacket and cut.

My eyes automatically went to Reave, whose woman still thought he was dead. His eyes were as distant and cold as ever, when his monster was let out to play. He said nothing, just shoved off the edge of the table where he'd had his foot propped, tying and tucking the laces of his shoes.

"Good to go?" he asked, all humor whisked away.

"Good to go," I affirmed, after looking at each of the guys. We trooped out the front door and got astride our bikes and rode out.

The house we were headed out to was in the middle of the country, an old, abandoned farm; way out in the far reaches of East County. After our assault on their club, the remaining Suicide Kings had pretty much gone to ground. It was just Bandit, Pipes, and Skid, along with Griz now.

Evening was coming on, the afternoon gloaming starting hard. We pulled off where Data had indicated and parked our bikes at the edge of the road, backing them in a line under a huge old oak.

Reaver used his gloved hands to yank up on one strand of wire while he planted the sole of his sneaker hard on another. We carefully utilized the gap he provided in the humming electric wire fence to duck through to the other side. Duracell repeated the process from the other side for Reave to get through, but smartass that Reave was, he planted a palm on the nearest fence post and vaulted himself neatly over.

Dray snorted a laugh. "No denying it. You're feeling entirely too chipper for what we're about to do."

Reaver's eyes got real wide, showing entirely too much white, and he grinned, nodding his head rapidly.

"I know the feeling, Brother!" Duracell crowed and slapped Reave on the back of his cut.

They started up and across the field, the tall grass swishing against their leathers and jeans. I exchanged a look with Dray, who rolled his eyes. Blue, grinning, shrugged his shoulders and drifted through the tall grass after the two resident psychopaths.

"Gotta love those guys," Dray said ruefully, his head bowed and shoulders shaking with silent laughter. We set off after them, crouching low and staying there when the house came into sight. It was a one-story rambler, the once-dark-blue paint on the clapboards cracked and faded from the elements.

Data was right. On this side, there was only one window, set high, a small narrow thing even a squirrel would have a tough time getting through. The glass was frosted, which told me it was likely a bathroom. To the right was a wide back deck, to the left, the front of the house. We all lined up, crouched low, on our knees in the dirt, waiting for the sun to sink just a little bit more before making our move.

Dray scraped his bottom lip between his teeth and looked to Reaver, who raised an eyebrow. Dray's eyes widened and he shrugged his shoulders. Blue's shoulders shook behind Reave, and Duracell, who was between me and Dray, rolled his eyes and sighed, a quiet but harsh exhalation of breath. I bowed my head and shook it, a grin of my own splitting my face.

Reave snapped his fingers quietly and we all stopped, suddenly alert. He pointed at Blue and Duracell, and to the front of the house. He pointed at me, Dray, and himself, and jabbed a finger at the back. He held a hand up at Duracell and Blue, a classic sign for hold up and then looked pointedly at me and Dray and rolled his hand at the end of his wrist, index and middle finger pointed, indicating we would be the ones to go in through the back and flush anyone inside out the front and into Blue and Cell.

Reaver came around to the left and stilled, his face as serious as I had ever seen it, blue eyes cold, calculating, and totally inhuman. We waited and he gave the signal. We kept low and made for the side of the house, back against the wall, and edged along it. Reave peeked around the corner and drew back.

He gave us the thumbs-up and removed two throwing knives from his tactical vest beneath his cut. Dray rolled his eyes and frowned.

We all had body armor on, but only Reave would bring fucking knives to a gunfight.

I moved from the end of the line, leap-frogged them both, and put my body up front. Reave grinned and bounced his eyebrows, nodding with excitement for me to go ahead. I scowled at him and brought my weapon out from the back of my waistband. I was hot; between the body armor, leather, and adrenaline, I was sweating, and more than ready to finish this and get back to my girl.

I sighed out, counted down from three and, with Reave and Dray at my back, went around the porch, ghosted up the few back steps, raised my weapon, and blew out the rear glass slider. You never follow your own breach. It's a rule. So Reaver went in first, letting fly with one, then the other, of his knives. There was someone, by the glimpse of build I'd say Skid, who stood from the couch in the living room, but he immediately went down. When I got a good look, he had a knife in one shoulder and one in his thigh; not killing blows. Another appeared in the other shoulder when he reached for his gun, but I had mine up and trained on him before he could clear his holster up under his arm.

Dray stepped in behind Reave, who was on his knees in the glass. He'd thrown and then gone down so Dray could fire over his head, which our VP did. Five times, into Bandit's chest, the man jerking and wobbling on his feet like a damned marionette before falling back onto the loveseat.

Pipes went out the front door, the wood panel swinging on its hinges, and we heard a single shot from out front. Blue appeared in the doorway a second later and disappeared down the hall. Cell followed him up.

I held my gun on Skid while Reave went to clear the rest of the house with the other two. Dray turned and had my back so no-one could sneak up on me. Skid looked up from where he knelt on the floor, hands in the air, a resigned look on his face.

"Clear!" The shout came from the back and was echoed a second later, and then echoed again by an unfamiliar voice that must have been Blue's. They returned to the front.

"Where is he?" Dray demanded at my back while Duracell took up position. Blue went back to the front door, looking out.

"Ain't here. Went to handle some business of his, didn't tell us what." Skid was looking me over carefully. "She alive?" he asked.

Reaver went to Skid and pulled out his blades one at a time. Skid groaned and bowed his head, sucking his breath in and out between clenched teeth.

"Who you talkin' about?" Cell called.

"Coon, Dani, she all right?" Skid asked. I crooked a sad smile, my girl's words coming back to me.

"Yeah, she's good," I told him. "Said, outta all of you bastards, she might spare you if it was up to her."

Reaver looked down at Skid and cocked his head to the side. He sighed, shrugged his shoulders, and moved off to stand with his back to the wall, leaning against it.

"What's your problem?" Dray asked.

Reaver fidgeted, and, looking slightly uncomfortable, stated, "He ain't afraid." He scratched his back on the corner of the wall, twisting side-to-side, and shrugged. Dray let off a string of muttered Spanish and Reave grinned.

"Sorry," he said. But by the light in his eyes you could tell he wasn't. Not one damned bit.

Skid sighed and moved, and I trained my gun more solidly on him. Reaver had two knives fisted, one in each hand in the blink of an eye, but all Skid did was chuff a laugh. He pulled a pack of smokes and a lighter from his pockets, the movements causing him obvious pain, his shoulders bleeding freely inside his leather jacket. He shook one part of the way out of the pack and grasped it with his lips.

"It's good she's all right, I worried about her." He lit the smoke and dropped the lighter with a clatter.

"Yeah, she's all right."

"Don't deserve her charitable attitude none. Didn't try to help her near as much as I could have." His cigarette bobbed in his mouth as he spoke, and he sucked on it. The cherry flared orange and he looked up at me plaintively, an eyebrow raised, blowing a plume of smoke out of the side of his mouth.

I saw it then, in his eyes... deep-seated sorrow. Skid had given up a long time ago, and he was totally cool with this being the end of the line.

Resignation took hold of me. I didn't want to put him out of his misery, but all it took to give me the will to do it was the image of Dani, bruised, crying, splayed on her back on the Suicide King's pool table. The pain in her eyes as she'd turned away, the knowing that I'd watched it once, but Skid... Skid had seen a hell of a lot more than that.

"No, you really don't," I agreed, and I leveled my gun and put one right in his face. He toppled over like a felled tree and shuddered, shaking on the ground. I stepped up and leveled my gun once more and blew his head apart in a welter of blood and bone. Tissue and gray matter spattered my boots, blood misted my jeans. I stared down at what I'd done and the only regret I tasted was the regret I had for not getting Dani out sooner.

"Jesus." Dray grunted and crossed himself. I looked at him, then to Reaver. Reaver's eyes met mine and they held a deep sorrow for a flicker of a heartbeat before he nodded. An understanding passed between us and he pushed off the wall. He threw an arm over my shoulders and we headed out front as Cell and Blue dragged Pipe's corpse into the living room and dropped it.

"Do whatever the fuck it is you do," we heard Dray say darkly to the ginger. Blue and Cell policed our brass, meaning they scoured and searched until every shell casing from every round we'd fired was accounted for. I shoved the little sandwich baggie with the spent casings into my pocket when Blue handed it to me.

"Do it," Dray ordered.

"Gotta go back to the bikes," Cell grunted.

We did, and Duracell took back off through the tall swaying grass while we stayed, after he'd fetched something out of his saddle bags. About a-half-hour, maybe forty-five minutes later, he came back.

"We're good," he declared.

Dray snubbed out his fragrant clove cigarette on the sole of his boot and he put the butt in his pocket. None of us were keen on leaving any evidence behind. We climbed on to our bikes, me kick-starting mine, the rest of them flipping their ultramodern ignition switches. I was maybe just a little jealous. My baby could be temperamental to start.

None of us had spoken while we'd waited for Cell to return. None of us spoke now. We just all went back to the club and, like before, shared a stiff shot before parting ways. I looked in on Dani. They were still working on her, her back becoming a riot of color between the flowers and the night sky they were inking in across the top. The tree was a living thing now and she was still as oblivious as I'd left her. So beautiful, her expression so at peace.

I showered and took the bundled clothes I'd been wearing out back, where I met the rest of the guys in the grass beside the garage and Dani's shop. I threw my tee, jeans, shoes, and whatnot into the burn barrel. Blue trudged up in some comfortable sweats from the low outbuilding and waited for my shit to catch and start burning before he added his.

Dray took a pull off a fifth of bourbon and held it out to me. I took it, watching the flames reflected in our VP's black-as-sin irises. Maybe it was just my mood.

"We'll get him," Duracell said with confidence, and stretched.

"We'd better. He's the mind behind all of this. Last thing we need is him putting a new club together somewhere and bringing this war to our table all over again." Dray spit.

We stared into the fire that consumed the evidence of our misdeeds, and not one of us looked happy. Each of us was weighed with our own demons riding our backs. We'd been so fucking close. So goddamned close.

"And then there was one..." Reave muttered cryptically.

"Yeah," Duracell agreed. Blue nodded, his gray eyes distant as he stared, hypnotized, into the flames.

And then there was one...

I turned and left the guys by the burn barrel and went back in to the club. I found myself leaning in the doorway to my room, watching Revelator work. Dani looked tranquil, she was definitely heavily sedated. I pushed off from the door and rounded the massage table. Doc looked up from the thick paperback in his hands before going back to reading. I sat on the floor by Dani's head and buried my fingers in the silken strands of her deep, dark hair, massaging at the base of her skull. Her eyes fluttered open and she turned her head in my direction.

"How you doing, Rocket?" I murmured and her lips smiled faintly but there was a wrinkle between her eyes, a tightness there.

"It hurts," she whispered, "But not too bad..." It was surprisingly coherent and I looked over to Doc.

"What's up?" he asked.

"Think she's coming out of it."

"Almost done back here," Rev stated, his voice a study in concentration. "We'll be able to move her, put her to bed, in just a few more minutes."

I nodded.

"You need something for the pain, baby?" I asked her softly.

"No." She huffed a sigh. "Just promise you'll stay with me."

I gathered her hand up in mine and pressed the knuckles to my lips. It wasn't enough so I leaned forward and pressed a kiss to her forehead. Her eyes drifted shut and, my lips beside her ear, I promised her. I wasn't going anywhere.

Doc pushed something and she closed her eyes. He gave me a look and I nodded my thanks but kept my lips pressed to her hair, breathing her in.

"I love you, Dani."

I did, didn't matter if she heard it, I needed to say it. I was deeply affected by the killing I'd done. While I couldn't, hell, I wouldn't, regret it, taking a man's life had a weight to it. A certain gravity. To not be affected by something like that made you something less than human in my book, even if you found yourself feeling bad for not feeling bad about doing it. I rested my forehead against Dani's hair and continued to massage her neck, a mindless action of affection that was doing more to soothe me than my oblivious girl.

God, how I wanted to leave this part of things far behind... We were almost there. The lot of us. Almost back to being able to go -and stay- completely legit.

And then there was one... Just one... standing all alone. We had to make sure to keep it that way.

26

Dani...

It surprised me. Go through something once, know what to expect, and take all the mystery from it, how easy it is to adapt to it. Bath-time the next morning, after having the color go in, still sucked, but not as bad as the first time, and I didn't find myself spending two days pretty much in bed before getting up and moving around, but rather just the better part of the morning.

Thirteen, after helping me get the rest of the ink off the surface of my skin and anointing the raw areas with thick moisturizing goo, had kissed me and gone back to bed. He wasn't just tired, something weighed on him, and I was betting he had gone somewhere while Revelator, Trigger, and Disney had worked on my back-piece the day before.

I wandered out to my shop, moving slowly, gingerly. It wasn't that it really hurt, I mean, it was uncomfortable but it was more that the skin felt drawn tight, like the skin over a drum. Any time I moved, it pulled, and I loathed the sensation, and so I moved carefully so it wouldn't pull too much. I slipped up onto my stool so I could start sketching at my little drafting table, ideas for new pieces.

Reaver came out at the appointed time to slather my back with more moisturizer. There wasn't a way I could reach it all and I was perfectly content to let my new friends and Thirteen's brothers help me with it. I was surprised at how comfortable I had grown with them in such a short amount of time. Each of them moved around me like I was made of china or might break at too harsh a word or gesture. It hadn't taken me long to realize I was likely not the first lost soul or abused girl to find my way here, a suspicion that'd been confirmed by Trigger one night while we'd all eaten dinner together in the common area. His woman, Sunshine, had come from a bad place, too.

"It's good you're up and moving around the first day after a piece this big. You had more done with the color than you did the last time. Looks like you're getting used to it." Reaver's comments broke me out of my reverie.

"I guess. Maybe I'm just still used to having to adapt quickly," I murmured.

"Aw, yeah. Shit, sorry." He looked sheepish when I glanced over my shoulder.

"It's fine," I shrugged, and winced a bit; right after the lotion went on it always felt better, looser until it absorbed again, which happened rather quickly.

"So you hooked yet?" he asked with a teasing grin.

I rolled my eyes and smiled back faintly. "No. I'm done. This is most definitely the last piece I will ever do. Somehow I think if I wanted any more, Doc would be a whole lot less inclined to drug me into next week to get it done. And honestly, with the way those drugs make me feel..." I made a face, "I don't like being that numbed-out."

"Yeah, well, glad you trust the lot of us enough to let us help you."

He retreated out the door and I nodded. That part had, honestly, been the hardest for me.

Still, it hadn't been lost on me that these men had also taken a leap of faith with me. They'd taken me in, even knowing I would willingly rat-out the Suicide Kings, which just wasn't done in the MC world. No matter how altruistic the intent behind the action may or may not be, good intentions didn't keep you alive in this world.

The Sacred Hearts had taken a big chance on me, letting me live, setting me up here without expecting anything in return.

I scraped my bottom lip between my teeth and sighed, bending carefully back over my drawing. The least I could have done was give them equal measure for equal measure but still, it wasn't lost on me, even with how much my back stung and pulled, that the three brothers of the Sacred Hearts had done me more of a boon than I had for Revelator by making those wedding rings.

I heard the door open again, behind me.

"Forget something?" I asked.

I had grown too confident, it would seem, let a false sense of security settle in over the last several weeks; it was a mistake that I recognized too late, and only when a man's large hand fitted over my mouth. I was dragged back hard into a barrel chest, and the smell of sour alcohol and stale cigarettes stuffed my nose.

"Now what would you be doing here, Coon?" Griz growled in my ear. His breath was beyond fetid, more ashtray-and-booze as it poured over me, the stench of body odor adding to the mix as he hauled my slimmer and much weaker frame off the stool.

The buttons on his denim cut dug painfully into my raw back, but still I twisted and fought and struggled, kicking and screaming muffled cries out from beneath his meaty palm. I tried to bite but couldn't find purchase with my teeth. Griz laughed at me as all I managed to accomplish was slobbering all over the inside of his palm, the tang of metal and grease coating the inside of my mouth.

"Now, where are your new little friends? Huh? I wanna see their faces when I blow your pretty little face off in front of 'em." I froze in his grip as the hard metal barrel of a gun pressed to my temple.

"See, now that's better, bitch. Now walk." He shoved me forward with his body and I stepped as he instructed, his gait awkward as he walked with me and tried not to trip. He turned us to the side and kicked the inside crash-bar to the metal door to the garage. The single door flew wide and bounced off the outside wall.

I tried to breathe calmly, even as my heart raced. He pulled me out into the rich sunlight and I closed my eyes as the warmth touched upon my skin. The Sacred Hearts were outside waiting. I blinked slowly at Thirteen and his brothers, lined up, guns drawn, marching across the grass towards the shop, towards me and Griz.

"Dani!" Thirteen called, "You okay?"

I tried to nod but Griz's grip tightened on my mouth and chin, forcing my head up and back against his chest.

"She look fine to you, boy?" he roared, and swayed on his feet some. I squeezed my eyes shut against the sensation it caused against my back, and tears started in my eyes.

"You just hang in there, chica, we'll get you out of this," Dragon said kindly.

I opened my eyes and blinked at the light, but the only person I was looking at was Thirteen. His expression was cold, shut-down and murderous, as he looked at Griz over my head. Then his eyes fell on my face and something in them softened.

"The fuck you will!" Griz pressed the barrel of the gun into my temple harder and I shuddered. I locked gazes with Thirteen and tried to communicate to him my silent plea.

"Just what the fuck you want, man?" Dray demanded. His dark eyes were burning, a raging inferno, a maelstrom of anger, rage and hatred going on just behind the veil of darkness.

"Justice!" Griz roared. "Justice for m'boy! Retribution, you sons-a-bitches! An eye for a fuckin eye." Griz swayed on his feet again and it was obvious to anyone who had half a mind to put to it that he was drunk, high, or both.

"We told you what would happen," Dragon stated flatly. "He did it anyways. Hurt a girl he had no business hurting."

Griz spat, "A club whore! Weren't no-one's Ol' Lady! Who the fuck cares?"

"I do." Reaver glowered and Dragon put up his hand in the scary man's direction. Reaver stood, nonchalant, idly spinning an open switchblade between his long fingers.

"What you give a fuck for? Weren't nothin' but club pussy! Not worth a man's life, not worth my boy's life! Raised him m'self..." Griz started some nonsensical mumbling and his grip loosened on me marginally. I breathed out and swallowed hard, making eye contact again with Thirteen, pleading with him with my eyes to do what needed to be done regardless of the outcome for me. Griz had lost it. He'd lost it completely and he needed to be stopped.

"Not the point. Girl didn't belong to him, man," Revelator spit on the ground like he had a bitter taste in his mouth.

Griz pressed the muzzle of his gun harder into my temple and I closed my eyes.

I opened them to Thirteen's calm gaze. He stared into my eyes, while his brothers held Griz's drunken attention, and mouthed at me to 'Hold still'. I closed my eyes again and did as my lover asked. I held very, very still as the men argued back and forth. Griz became more agitated.

"Okay, Coon, I'm gonna move my hand, I don't want to hear no bitching or caterwauling, just giving you a chance to tell your man there 'bye before I blow your pretty fucking head off. No screamin', you hear me?" I nodded against his hand and finally he took it from my mouth.

"I love you." I bit my lips together and looked at Thirteen, beseeching him with my eyes before saying out loud, "Shoot him, please, shoot him!" my voice cracking.

"You stupid cunt!" I felt rather than saw Griz's arm draw back to hit me with my back to his front like it was. I closed my eyes and braced for the blow and –

POW!

The gunshot rolled out into the open air, loud and strong, echoing back from the wild blue skies. Something coated my face and globbed in my hair, warm and sticky and wet. I was still tensed and Thirteen was suddenly there.

"Don't open your eyes Dani, don't open your mouth!" His voice was tense and strained and I did what I was told when all I wanted to do was drop in a heap and give over to the panic splitting my chest, cracking me wide and vulnerable. When was it ever going to stop?

27

R ed-XIII...

     I was laying in my bed staring at the ceiling when it went off. A loud buzzer in the common room, loud enough to wake the fucking dead. I bolted from the bed and threw on some jeans and a tee. Tugging on my last boot as I hopped on one foot in the hallway, I watched Ghost and Trig climb up the access ladder to the roof. I caught Reave, who was adjusting the Velcro strapping on his body armor as he went by, by the arm.

"What the fuck is that, man?" I demanded.

"Perimeter breach, someone hopped the fence somewhere. Tripped a motion sensor."

Data called from the fish-bowl ops room of his, "I fucking got it, man! He's going into the garage!"

"Fuck, Dani!"

I moved. Blue fell into step beside me, handing me a gun. I took it, and the rest of the guys fell in with me, as we poured out the back door, but it was too late. He was edging out of the shop's single door, Dani pressed to his body, a gun pressed to my woman's head.

"Keep her calm, man, we gotta wait for an opening for Trig and Ghost to do their thing," Reaver murmured under his breath before we drew near them. I swallowed my heart back into my friggin' chest and, with it pounding, advanced with my brothers across the grass.

Griz stopped short, and did he ever look like fucking hell! His clothes were dirtier than usual and all out of sorts, his hair in a wild halo around his head, coming loose from his ponytail, which was skewed off to the side and hanging over his shoulder. His eyes were so bloodshot you'd swear the whites were pink to begin with and they bounced from one to another of us so erratically – dude had to be on something. There wasn't any way that he was any kind of sober.

He had one massive, dirty paw over my girl's mouth and Dani's cornflower-blue eyes were so wide in her paler-than-usual face it made my heart fucking bleed.

"Dani!" I called out to her, "You okay?"

She tried to nod but Griz tightened his grip, pulling back on her head. Her slender throat worked in a swallow and her eyes squeezed shut before she opened them, leveling her gaze on me. Her expression was beseeching but I knew my girl, my woman...

"She look fine to you, boy?" Griz roared and swayed on his feet, jolting Dani, who swayed limply in front of him. She might as well be a fucking ragdoll and I seethed with anger. Her eyes glimmered wetly with her tears and her expression spoke clearly to me.

Don't worry about me... Kill him, just kill him.

"You just hang in there, chica, we'll get you out of this," Dragon said, his voice low and even.

My eyes, my heart, my very soul was being held against Griz's dirty denim cut, looking at me with wide eyes, frightened but absolutely sure. Purpose glimmered in her gaze where it was locked to mine and I felt my chest rise and fall, hard, a crushing weight making it tough to get enough air as I half-listened to my brothers argue with the fucking shelled-out, drugged-out, crazy-as-fuck man who had a hold on my woman.

"Okay, Coon, I'm gonna move my hand, I don't want to hear no bitching or caterwauling, just giving you a chance to tell your man there 'bye before I blow your pretty fucking head off. No screamin', you hear me?" I focused then, as Dani nodded faintly, a jerky up-and-down against the resistance of his fucking hand on her mouth.

"I love you!" she blurted, and her eyes held such a longing and desolation that I would gladly burn the whole fucking world down. Again with that pleading look. I felt myself shaking my head. No. Not only no, but hell no! I wasn't letting her go, but my woman's lips were moving again. Her perfect fucking lips. And she shouted, "Shoot him! Please, shoot him!" her voice cracking on the plea.

I took a step forward but Reaver grabbed my arm down low, his hand above my wrist. I looked down just as Griz shouted "You stupid cunt!"

He drew back his arm with the gun, intent on clocking my woman in the back of the head. He was going to fucking pistol-whip Dani!

Without thought, with a singular purpose, I lunged just as the bright summer day erupted in a riot of sound and Griz's head exploded. Dani had cringed, knowing, expecting a blow to land, and that her eyes and mouth were squeezed tightly shut is the only thing that saved her from getting them full of the man's blood.

The whole world slowed down; I screamed her name as I covered the distance between us and when I touched her, when I pulled her into my arms, against my chest, it was as if the world let out its collected breath and everything returned to a normal speed.

"Don't open your eyes, Dani, don't open your mouth!" I told her.

Blue grabbed the garden hose and dragged it towards us.

"Cold, baby, this is going to be cold, I'm sorry. I got you, Dani, I got you, I always fucking got you..." I kept talking as she shuddered and shook in my grasp, her hair matted, her face awash in Griz's blood and heavier, wetter things. Dani cried out and I felt the shock myself as Cell turned the crank on the faucet and Blue aimed to get the worst of it off.

My brothers were milling around us, all of them trying to help as the cold water soaked our clothes, soaked our skins and sluiced through Dani's raven-dark hair. The icy water puddled at our feet, running red, then tinged pink as it crept towards the grass.

"Good enough!" Doc declared. "Get her in the house! Hot shower, soap and water. And try not to get it on you!" he ordered. I didn't care; I picked her up, her slender arms wrapped tight around my neck and shoulders, her face cold against my neck. I carried her into the club, Reaver and Blue our vanguard, sweeping out in front of us.

They had the tap going as I set Dani to her feet on the bathroom floor, and then it was a flurry of hands, stripping wet cotton off of the both of us. I didn't care; I wanted him off of her as much as she did. Dani started to shriek, started to scream when the clothes came off, and I couldn't blame her for that either; it was too much, too many people.

I held her fast to me and I wasn't letting go, and I honestly needed the extra hands.

"Dani, baby, it's okay, Shhh, baby it's all right. It's me, it's Chris. Thirteen. I got you, baby, just come on and let us help..." She cried, limp in my arms against my chest as I got both of us into the bath.

Reave poured some of her sweet-smelling shampoo into his palm and Blue appeared from somewhere I hadn't seen him go, with a pitcher.

I held onto Dani while my brothers frantically washed her hair, the shower spray gentler way down here at the bottom of the tub, stopping all together when Blue thrust the pitcher under it to fill. Dani continued to shiver despite the heat from the shower, her face buried in the side of my neck as her slender body shook.

"Head back, baby-doll," Reaver implored and, her eyes still squeezed shut tight, she went with his subtly-urging fingertips and Blue rinsed her hair. She started to calm with every pitcher full of water that sluiced through her hair and across her skin, rinsing her clean, the water going from a faint pink to running crystal clear as it swirled down the drain.

"Dani, baby, look at me," I murmured. She tipped her head up and met my eyes. Hers were still so wide, her damage showing way too prominent, and I couldn't blame her. Every fucking time she thought she was safe for a minute... I sighed. Well, she was safe now. As safe as I could make her, but there wasn't any way I could make her believe it. Not in the state she was in. I tightened my hold on her, rocking her absently, and her eyes slid shut. She tucked her head under my chin and let me take care of her.

Reaver stood up and backed away. "I think we got it all," he said quietly, and, shaking his head, unstrapped his body armor. He muttered something about it being fucking soaked and with a last glance at Dani held tight in my arms, both of us naked in the bottom of the tub, left the bathroom.

"You okay now?" Blue asked Dani softly and I startled. Dude never talked. He was like the Silent fucking Bob to Duracell's Jay. Dani blinked and nodded her head, a bit too rapid. She didn't really have anything to be afraid of, or embarrassed by, the front of her body, hell, even her ass, was hidden from view against my body and my bits were just as hidden by hers. Still, I got her, her discomfort, and I thrust my chin at Blue to get gone over her head.

"Be right back," he murmured and I looked down at Dani; she and Blue had their gazes locked and seemed to be saying something without words.

Blue got up and went out, his jeans and tee clinging wetly to him and he came back with a comb.

He used conditioner in Dani's hair while I held her, and combed it through, making sure that there wasn't anything left. Nothing at all. Dani closed her eyes, her arms tightening around my shoulders as she let Blue do his thing. Something about having her hair combed by the silent brother calmed her, put her at ease, and that in turn calmed me.

A final rinse or two and Blue shut off the tap. Reaver appeared in the doorway in fresh dry clothes and handed Blue some towels. Blue had always struck me as a mellow kind of guy, but this was weird. He closed his eyes and held open the towel, and I asked Dani if she thought she could get up. She nodded and slowly let me go. Standing, she stepped out of the tub and into the offered towel, holding it around herself. I took the one Blue held out to me.

He studiously didn't look at either of us. I wasn't so much worried about that. I could give two fucks. I wrapped the towel around my waist and tucked it in so I could free my hands for my girl. I rubbed over the towel. She was still shivering but I don't think it had fuck all to do with being cold. I drew her to me and gently patted her back dry through the towel.

"Okay?" I asked. She sniffed and nodded, but still hadn't spoken. Instead, she tucked herself into my side and, her arms around me, let me lead her to our room.

"Thanks, Blue." I muttered and, his gray eyes full of worry, he nodded carefully, staying behind in the bathroom as I moved her through the hall. She relaxed marginally when we got into our room; a familiar space. I sat her on the edge of the bed and knelt in front of her. Her dark hair clung wetly to her face and shoulders, dripping on the bed. I dried myself off and did my best to sop the water out of her hair.

"You okay, baby?" I asked, swallowing hard. It was starting to seriously freak me out, her not talking. She nodded her head, her clear blue eyes wounded, and I touched her face. A light touch, grazing her lips with my thumb.

"Did you see?" I asked softly.

She shook her head, too rapidly, and I nodded, sighing.

"I'm sorry..." she whimpered.

I shook my head.

"Oh, baby, no, I just wish you hadn't seen it, is all. For you. Shhh, it's okay..." I pulled her against my shoulder and let her weep.

Some things were just so horrible there wasn't enough brain-bleach in the world to scrub the image out. Some things were just burned in there forever. Trig never missed, and Griz's head had blown apart like a melon. Dani had just been too close, but it was the only shot, the only chance Trig was going to get.

Dani had more than her fair share of mental and emotional scarring, and I vowed right then and there, as she cried it out against my body, that this would be the last reason she would have to cry for anything for a real fucking long time.

28

Dani...

It took a while for me to settle, for the tears to subside as Thirteen held me. He held me sitting on his lap, my face buried in the side of his neck and my hair hiding my face until the strands were nearly dry. He rocked me, and just waited out the storm inside my heart, inside my head. It took a long damned time but he didn't seem to care.

"I love you, Dani," he murmured into the crown of my head, his breath warm. "I love you and this shit is fucking killing me. Seeing you hurting, holding you but not being able to do a damned thing else to fix it."

I'd fallen quiet, exhausted, but his voice, his words gave me strength.

"You are fixing it," I said softly. "Just by being here, by holding me, you are fixing it." I settled against his body, tired, so tired. Mentally, especially emotionally, and even physically to a certain extent. The tattoo on my back having long since dried, the skin was pulling taut and in dire need of attention, but I just couldn't bring myself to leave the shelter of his arms. At least, not yet.

A soft knock at the door had me glancing in that direction. Blue and Cell stood there, Cell covered in dirt and Blue with a pot of moisturizer in his hands. I tried for a smile in their direction but it came out a wan, miserable thing and I gave up the effort rather quickly.

"Dani, you okay to have your back looked at?" Thirteen asked.

"Do you have to let me go?" I asked in return.

Blue shook his head and pointed at himself.

"Nah, babe, not as long as you let Blue have a look, put something on it..."

Duracell leaned against the door and gave me a crooked grin. I nodded against Thirteen's neck and with a little maneuvering we got my back exposed, keeping the towel covering everything else vital to me.

Blue knelt by the side of the bed and I jumped despite how gentle and careful the first touch of his fingers were. The moisturizer he spread thick on my skin was deliciously cool and welcome. My skin was thirsty for it. Once he was done, he capped the pot and set it on the bedside table.

"Church in twenty. You want I should see if you can get a pass?" Duracell asked from the doorway.

"Yeah, man, thanks."

Blue smiled and nodded and the two men left, shutting the door behind them. Thirteen and I were alone again. It was simply he and I.

"'Kay, baby, let's get better settled."

We wound up with Thirteen on his back, my body draped over his, my back laden with the greasy ointment, open to the air and off the sheets. I rested my ear on the center of his chest, which was still marred by discoloration, the skin almost permanently stained where he'd been shot. Thirteen assured me it no longer hurt and seemed quite content with the arrangement of our bodies. One of his hands palmed the back of my head and he pinched the tense muscles at the base of my skull with forefinger and thumb, massaging the tension away. His other hand stroked the outside of my thigh.

I lay with my eyes closed, listening to the steady rhythm of his heart, the ebb and flow of its beat reminding me of a time when I was a girl on a distant shore, holding a shell to my ear at my grandfather's urging, to hear the ocean waves. It had been stormy, and we'd stood in a shop that sold the shells... I had longed to return to the sea on a calm sunny day pretty much ever since.

"Thirteen?" I asked, quietly.

"Yeah, honey?" His hand stroked absently up and down the outside of my leg and I sighed out, relaxing that much further under his touch.

"Dani, what is it, babe?" he asked softly, his voice tinted with concern.

"Do you think we could go? Just get away from here for a day, maybe two?" I asked.

"Where would you want to go, babe? I'd take you anywhere," he said, without hesitation.

"The ocean. I've always wanted to see the ocean again."

"Well, hell, that's an easy enough wish to grant, chica." Thirteen's hands tightened on me but I didn't startle very hard, he'd relaxed me too much for that. I shifted my head enough to peer at the doorway. Dragon's dark and shaggy head poked just past the door.

"Was coming to tell you. Club decision, we leave for Florida end of next week to get the girls. Guys want to leave tomorrow, but we got some things to attend to, if you catch my drift." Dragon gave Thirteen a meaningful look. I shifted my gaze to the man who held me in his arms, his eyes the color of that storm-swept sea from long ago.

"Understood." Thirteen's response was short and clipped. I heard the door thunk softly closed behind Dragon.

"What does he mean?" I asked, confused.

"Disappear that many people in that short amount of time, it's bound to be noticed. We can't go taking off right away as a group. It will look suspicious, baby. Gotta do some communicating down south, move careful."

I pushed myself up off Thirteen's chest just enough to lean forward and press my lips to his. I kissed him, a slow lingering kiss, before I pressed my forehead to his.

"What was that for, baby?" he asked in a hoarse whisper.

"For being what I need."

"Always." The promise slipped from his lips unasked-for and his hand slipped from the back of my neck, withdrew from my hair so that he could graze my cheek with gentle fingertips.

"I got you, babe. I've always got you."

I nodded and kissed him gently again, neither of us really in the mood to take it beyond that.

I lay my head back on his chest as the light from the window crept across the room with the movement of the sun.

When next I woke I was still cradled against Thirteen, just differently than I'd been before. The room was dark and close, Thirteen warm and a comfort at my back where he spooned me carefully.

"You okay, babe?" he asked, sucking in a tremulous breath, his voice thick with sleep. He pressed a gentle kiss to the back of my shoulder and I stopped nodding my head, realizing he couldn't see it.

"Yes," I replied softly. "I'm not sure why I woke up."

"Hmm." He kissed the back of my shoulder again and I relaxed, closing my eyes. He trailed fire with his lips from the outside of my shoulder in, towards my neck, his lips resting gently against my pulse point as he took a moment to breathe me in and - oh God, was that simple action incredibly erotic!

"Back need lotion?" he asked and I rested against him, bringing our nude bodies carefully together, my back to his front.

"After..." I murmured.

"After what, babe?"

"After you make love to me, please?"

"Dani, baby, you ain't never gotta ask for me to do that," he growled into my ear lightly and nipped my ear lobe.

I needed this. I needed him to touch me, to kiss me, to do something just, life-affirming with me after... No. I resolutely pushed the thought from my mind, rolling so that I faced him and so that we could kiss properly. His mouth was hot against mine and his hands gentle as he traced my curves, smoothing gently over my skin in a warm, elegant caress that you just wouldn't expect from Thirteen's rough, daily appearance.

He palmed the outside of my thigh and kept me on my side,

mindful of the fresh tattoo on my back. He kissed me deeply, igniting the blood in my veins with a burning passion that built slowly but evenly between us.

I let my fingers do the walking, touching every inch of his body that I could reach, gliding the tips across his heated flesh, too warm from our recent sleep. Thirteen groaned, his hard length trapped between us, rubbing against my stomach as he rolled his hips in an unconscious thrusting. His mouth claimed mine and he drew my lower body tight against his, one of his hands gripping my ass in that possessive way that spoke louder than any words he'd spoken that I. Was. His.

His to love, his to drive wild, his to protect and to cherish, and I wanted all of those things. With him, with this man, with Thirteen. I communicated these things with every kiss, every touch, nuzzling his neck, nipping him lightly over that spot that drove him to gasping like it did me. I reached a gentle hand between us and stroked his cock. I marveled every time I held him at how he seemingly went on just forever, and this time was no exception.

"God, Dani, baby you're killing me!" Thirteen gasped out. I smiled in the dark of the room and guided him to my wet but still not-quite-ready entrance. He was a tight fit when I was ready for him, after he'd made me come a time or two, but without that prep, he was simply huge. Just this side of absolutely too much. I didn't care. I wanted, needed to be close to him, to have him hold me, to have him inside me.

Thirteen hissed out as he sank into me. He edged his way in, a little at a time, agonizingly slow until he bottomed out inside my body and had me gasping, my forehead dropping to his shoulder, a desperate moan escaping my lips. He felt incredibly good and I needed that, I needed him to be the one to make me feel alive, the way he had been the only one to ever make me fly.

"Mmm God, yes, deeper, a little bit deeper, please?" I begged him and he groaned, and obliged me, oh-so-careful, oh-so-gentle, and I loved that he was. Thirteen, the only man to ever be afraid he might hurt me.

"Baby, you tell me when, you tell me when you need me to stop..."
He held me close, my leg riding high over his hip as he pressed his
hard extreme length into my waiting body. I felt my pussy throb
around him in welcome and listened to his sharp exhale as it did it. I
clenched my muscles around his invading cock and he paused,
gasping.

"Dani, you okay, honey?" he asked me, his breath warm against
my neck.

"Mmm, don't stop!" I gasped and I heard him chuckle.

He captured my lips in the dark and kissed me deeply. He gave a
tiny thrust and I moaned into his mouth. I felt so full, so complete
with him inside me and it was beautiful.

Thirteen broke the kiss and pressed his forehead to mine. "Baby,
you got me, all of me..." My heart melted at the sentiment in his voice
and I begged him to keep going; he chuckled again, low and deep.

"Dani, baby, you aren't hearing me. I've gone as far as I can go.
You've got all of me."

His meaning clicked home and I wiggled my hips a bit. God! He
felt like he was all the way in my stomach! I loved it.

"Good, yes, mmm! Please move," I begged and I could hear him
smile as he did what I asked, withdrawing slowly to surge back in.

I held tightly to him as he moved, gently, firmly, and with
purpose. The sure, calm strokes stoked the fire between us. It wasn't
going to get us there, wasn't going to get us off, but it was going to
build us all the way up to that point and keep us there.

Thirteen had me wrapped around his little finger, if only he
would continue to move. Feral, wanton sounds poured from my
mouth. Great gasps of pleasure with just a hint of my voice to them
crept out into the room as his hands held me fast, as my man cradled
me, safely in the curve of his body, and drove me wild, up and out
among the stars.

I arched at one point as he stroked that deepest, most secret part
of me and he took advantage of the motion, capturing one of my
nipples with his mouth. Heat fizzled along a connected arc between
my breast and my cunt as the feelings Thirteen evoked intensified,

became rich with the added sensation and intensity. I was beyond wet by this point, his cock sliding easily, my body open and inviting to his touch, wanting, craving just that little bit more.

I gazed down my body, into his eyes, dark with desire, fierce with his protective possession of me. I was claimed, and for the first time ever I was glad for it. I wanted it to be that way. I was happy to be Thirteen's girl, his woman, because I had chosen to belong to him. He growled and buried himself as deep as he could go once more and it nearly brought me. I gasped, head thrown back, and rode his body. He nipped the sensitive peak of my breast with his teeth, even as his fingertips grazed the even more sensitive one between my thighs, at the apex of my sex.

He broke his mouth from my tit and growled, "Look at me, baby, I want you to look me in the eye when I make you come. I want to see you come apart for me." I tipped my head downward and gave him what he wanted, the room growing light with the coming dawn as he captured my other nipple between his teeth, teasing the delicate flesh with his tongue. He slicked his fingers in my juices, coating them before teasing my clit with a feather-light touch. I gave a deep, throaty moan and felt myself tighten around him.

It was awkward, the position he held, but he managed to keep the pressure on, his thrusts short but so very deep, thumb on that secret pearl, teeth carefully locked on my breast, and the sensations he wrought building, sending me higher and higher. Finally, with a hard spasm of my cunt around him, I flew apart with a wild devastated cry. My whole body shattered and Thirteen hummed his satisfied approval into my breast, which just set my body to rolling away on another shock of orgasm.

I shuddered in his embrace and he held me to him, waiting for my body to piece itself back together, smiling like the Cheshire Cat the whole time. He kissed my lips, short, chaste little kisses, while my chest heaved against his and I gasped like a landed fish.

"Hang on, baby, I'm not done," he murmured. With a hand on my ass and the other cradling the back of my head, he flexed his hips and thrust, and I swear my eyes rolled back into my head.

"Oh God!" I gasped out and Thirteen smiled even wider, completely in control of himself and his faculties, for which I was slightly jealous.

"Nope, just me, baby, just me," he whispered and kissed me, picking up the pace and intensity of his thrusts.

I held onto him, lovingly, my hands sweeping over his damp skin, following the contours of muscle and bone as he rode me, and I loved it. I loved him so much, so deeply. What he did to me, my body, I lost my breath just as quickly as I'd earned it back and I didn't care. My voice, high and bright, spilled from my lips, punctuating every thrust.

"Oh, yeah, baby, come for me a second time, there you go, yes yes yes yes yes!" I came, my core throbbing unevenly around him, so hard and so soon after my last orgasm that my vision faded for a moment. I was vaguely aware of Thirteen jolting inside me, his cock twitching in counterpoint to my cunt as he came just a moment behind me.

He pulled me tight up against his body and even through his pleasure, was mindful of the tattoo, rolling us so he was on his back and I was draped over his chest and body. He kissed the side of my neck and blew some of my hair up out of his mouth. I languidly gathered the mass and pulled it behind my neck, over my opposite shoulder, so he didn't have it in his face.

"Thanks." He kissed my shoulder to punctuate his statement but I had no voice to offer him in return. He'd stolen it, robbed me of my faculties so completely all I could give him was a long, satisfied sigh. I closed my eyes and lay on him, listening as our uneven breath evened out as we both slowly came back to earth from our trip up into the stratosphere.

"I love you, Dani," he whispered before peppering my shoulder and neck with tiny, satisfied kisses. I cuddled into him tighter and wiggled my hips a bit, biting my lip. He was still inside me and the movement sent off little aftershocks. He sucked in a sharp breath and I smiled good to know I had some sort of effect, too.

"I love you, too," I breathed and kissed him gently.

We lay wrapped up in each other for the longest time, the light strengthening in the room from the high window, chasing back the shadows, the same way with every touch, every kiss and every smile, Thirteen chased back the shadows crowding my heart. I pushed off his chest, and it forced him deeper, which wasn't painful at all, given he was only half-erect. I bit down on my bottom lip and rolled my hips, riding him, and was pleased to see his eyes roll back in his head, his well-formed chest hitching with a surprised intake of breath.

I closed my eyes and just felt him, his palms, warm against my hips, smoothing up my body to cradle the weight of my breasts, his thumbs caressing the nipples, but oh my god, the sensation of being one with him overrode everything else and I never, ever wanted to be parted from these moments. I wanted them, so many more of them... the problem for me was going to be what came attached.

I gazed down at Thirteen as I made love to him and tried very hard not to think about the MC, the complications that being part of such an organization brought, and how my life still lay in ruins around me because of one. I didn't want to deal with any of that right now, but at the same time, there wasn't any ignoring it. Thirteen was who he was, and he was a brother of the Sacred Hearts Motorcycle Club.

I closed my eyes and cried out but still, even at a time like this, that small voice in the back of my mind asked me, *Can you really handle it? After yesterday? After everything? Can you, Dani?*

I didn't have an answer for it. Not one. I didn't know if or when I would. I didn't want to think about it, I didn't know what to do, and so for now I did the only thing I could. I made love to the man who'd saved me. I made love to the man who I'd saved and I tried valiantly to thrust all other thoughts, cares, worries, and anxieties aside so that when I kissed him, it held no taste of regret and it wouldn't taste like goodbye. Because I really didn't want what we had to be over. I just didn't know what to do.

29

R ed-XIII...
　　　Four hours. Dani and I made love for four straight fucking hours *no pun intended* the morning after Griz's head got blown off right next to her. She was amazing, this sultry siren, beautiful and graceful, and I half worried because there were times I would catch a glint in her eyes like she was about to cry and that killed me. I would give anything to make it better, to have the words or the touch to smooth that pain she was harboring away, but I didn't. There was no magic fix for this. Just time, and a very real need to get her to talk, to tell me what she had going on in that pretty little head of hers.

We showered after our marathon sex. It was kind of required after how messy it got, not that I was complaining! Far from it, but I tell you what, both of us were sore and probably wouldn't be going there again for a day or two.

It was after the shower, as I applied the topical ointment to her tat, that I tried to broach the topic with her. "Hey." She looked up at me, her blue eyes focusing; they'd been distant for quite some time as she stared into space, thinking.

"What are you thinking about so hard in there?" I asked softly.

"I..." she swallowed convulsively and I felt my stomach drop. Oh shit, this was serious. Like, really serious. I felt a prickling rush over my skin as I tensed, waiting for it, knowing that I wasn't going to like what I was going to hear. But even delivering bad news, Dani was fearless and honest, and, fuck, she was gorgeous.

"I love you," she stated bluntly.

I set the pot of ointment aside and wiped my hands on one of our discarded bath towels.

"But..?"

She bowed her head and shook it, trying to gather her thoughts. I sat, patient on the outside while I tried like hell not to die on the inside, fearful of what she was going to say... Jesus, was this it? Was she going to quit on me? Her eyes locked on mine and her face crumbled a little.

"The MC, ... I just..." she looked at me, searched my face, which I tried like hell to keep neutral. She'd been through hell in a handbasket and yesterday was no exception to that rule. You come that close to dying and it did some fucked-up things to your head. She didn't need me putting pressure, making any demands, begging like a pussy... She knew what she needed and she was going to tell me or talk to me or whatever. I just had to man up and let her do her thing, even though what I wanted to do was make her stay, to do or say anything to keep her.

"Talk to me, baby, just tell me what you got going on in there." My voice was quiet, I was trying for soothing, no pressure here... *Just please, just fucking talk to me, Dani!* on the inside, but nothing on the outside.

"I don't know what to do, Thirteen. I love you, so much, but I don't know what to do! If I should stay, if I should go... I don't have anywhere to go! I just, ...I just don't know if I can stay, though, be with someone in an MC after everything... I can't go back to that! How do I know I'm safe? I mean, I thought I was safe and then he was here and I wasn't and, and..." I pulled her lightly into my arms.

"Shhh, Dani it's okay. Shhh."

She was panicking, anxiety kicking her full in the teeth, and there wasn't much I could do about that except let her go through it and be here for her. She didn't cry, but her breath wasn't even.

I rocked her gently, and she finally said, miserably, "What do I do? I just don't know what to do... What if the rest of them come? Gordy is still out there, and Pipes and Bandit, what if they come next? Is it ever going to stop?"

Fuck.

This was club business and shit she shouldn't know about. Telling her those fucks were dead was way out of pocket. It would put me and my brothers in danger if she ever turned on us. I stared into her wide, blue eyes, and had a decision to make. My girl, or breaching my club's protocols.

"Dani, baby, do you trust me?" I asked her. She hesitated, but I can't say that was a bad thing. I mean, I wanted her to think about this, *really think about it* which I knew she always did. Aand, there it was. The spark, the dawning of understanding in her true blue eyes; she nodded, sure, no questions asked.

"Yes," she said aloud, for my benefit that we were being crystal clear.

"You don't have to worry about any of them anymore. I swear to you. I promise you. If I'm lying may I be stripped of my fucking cut and put Out Bad. You. Are. Safe."

She swallowed hard and nodded carefully.

"As for the rest, babe, this club has been my life for a real long time, I really don't want to be in a position where I have to choose because it ain't no choice at –"

She pressed both of her small hands over my mouth abruptly and shook her head.

"I won't do that to you. I couldn't do that to you and I really don't want to know. There's been so much pain and so much guilt for so many things... No more. Please, no more," and now her eyes did begin to well.

"Can you give it two weeks?" I asked her, holding her lightly against me.

"Two weeks? What happens in two weeks?" she asked, and I was glad she held me back, her slender arms around me.

"We make the ride to Florida to get the other guy's women. All of us. Just give me two weeks, make the ride with me. Just this one ride, meet the girls, soak up some sun, relearn how to breathe. No decisions until then. If you decide after we get there that you can't do it, I bring you home, help you get set up wherever, doing whatever you want. One day at a time, two weeks, can I have that?" I asked.

She nodded against my chest, "I can do that," she said and she sounded much better, less overwhelmed. Baby steps. One day, one week at a time. One event at a time. Not too much too fast. It was the best I could figure for my smart girl who would take on the world if I let her.

I wasn't giving up my club or my woman. Dani didn't know what I'd been about to say. It really wasn't any choice at all. I would have both. I'd walk through hell in gasoline boots for her and for my club, and there had to be a version of the world where I could and would have both. There had to be.

I helped her dress, and dressed myself, and we went out to the kitchen to find ourselves something to eat, even though she looked like she'd rather hurl than put anything in her stomach. I coaxed her into eating anyways. I knew she was a bundle of nerves, but she was my bundle of nerves and I would take care of her, be there for her, give her some kind of happily-ever-after. She deserved it, she deserved the world, the moon, the stars... hell, everything. I just hoped I could be the man to deliver. I really did.

"What do you want to do, baby?" I asked her when we'd finished eating. She looked at me and heaved a great sigh.

"I know it sounds bad, but I want to go back to bed... to sleep."

I nodded. "Okay."

After everything, and with everything crashing down seemingly all at once, a day in bed sounded like a pretty fine idea and so that's what we did. I'd be a liar if I said I didn't spend that time, all of that time, staring at Dani's sleeping, haggard face; trying to figure out how to keep her, and my club, but most importantly do it in such a way that she would be happy. I'd be a liar if I said I didn't feel a touch of loathing for myself, at what a selfish prick I sounded like inside my own head, but that... that was a problem for another day.

30

D ani...
      The days crept by. I spent a lot of time in my shop, working on things. I spent even more time around the guys and that, some-how, more than anything, made me feel like things really were going to be okay. Thirteen was patient, kind, but even he could tell I was out of joint and so, on the third or fourth day after Griz came after me, he finished putting the Aquaphor on my back for my tattoo and then shoved the pot into one of his saddlebags on the floor by the bedroom door.

"Are we going somewhere?" I asked.

"Figured we'd get you out of here for a day or so, go back up to my cabin," he said.

"A ride?" I perked up at that. The sun and the wind and that sense of freedom was calling my name.

"You really like to ride, don't you?" he asked, grinning.

"By, like, a lot," I was smiling now, probably one of the first full smiles I'd cracked in days.

"You aren't riding like that, better get something better than stretch pants on. I'll be out front." He lifted the saddlebags, which appeared to be packed and ready to go, and left me sitting on the edge of the bed, shirtless and staring after him before my brain caught up to the fact that *I could leave...* I was so used to having to have permission that it hadn't even crossed my mind that I could have left the SHMC compound at any point.

"Jesus, Dani, for as smart as he tells you that you are, you can be dumber than a box of rocks, girl," I muttered to myself as I scrambled to comply, fetching jeans and a shirt and all things suitable to ride in from my wardrobe. My wardrobe, that Thirteen had cunningly spliced into his closet and drawers along with his things, while I'd worked away in my shop.

I went out into the common area. It felt strange to be wearing boots rather than my soft Converse, but for riding, boots were best. They always would be. The jeans were comfortable enough. A favorite pair of mine, the tops of the thighs lighter, discolored from age and wear as opposed to being some fancy designer pair you paid five hundred dollars for. Nope. I came by the threadbare holes that were starting in this pair honestly, although they were designer. I'd found them brand new with the tags still on for twenty bucks at a discount store.

"Ho! Look at you, girl!" Dragon crowed from where he was slouched in a chair. He had work spread in front of him, like old-fashioned ledgers-and-numbers kind of bookkeeping. I smiled and pulled my hair from the collar of my leather jacket. My back itched beneath the weight of the leather and my plain, figure-hugging, black cotton tee, but I would have to get over it. There was nothing I could do for it.

I slipped my bug-eye sunglasses out of my pocket and pulled a cleaning cloth out of the little pocket in the front of the leather meant to hold a cigarette lighter, polishing the plastic lenses as I came more fully into the common room.

"You look good, Rocket," Thirteen said from the door. I smiled for him.

"Thanks," I murmured.

Dragon pushed to his booted feet and came towards us.

"I think this is a good idear, you getting away from here a day or two," he said, and sucked his teeth. I had to smile at the way he said 'idea.' He added an 'r' in there without meaning to, so it came out 'idear' instead of 'idea.' It was such an old-school thing to say, and reminded me of Skid during the few good times. My smile diminished. In my heart of hearts I knew Skid was gone and I kept going back and forth on it; one minute being okay, the next, kind of missing him. I put my sunglasses on in a bid to hide the warring emotions in my eyes and Dragon raised an eyebrow.

"See those?" he asked, holding out a hand. I frowned but took them off and held them out. He promptly gripped them in his big hands and snapped them in two at the nose bridge, rendering them useless. I gaped, taken aback.

He smiled and pulled a case out of his inside pocket.

"Think these might suit you better; they were my wife's." He held out the hard eyeglass case and I blinked.

I knew the story. Dray had been telling me about his woman, Everett, one night while we were all out back sitting around a fire in one of those outdoor copper fire-pit basins, the guys drinking beer, relaxing on these wood lounge chairs that Nox had built with his brother, Rush.

I had been sitting between Thirteen's thighs, back against his chest, his arms around me, cuddling me close, when Dray had just started talking about her, about how she understood him and how he missed her most at times like these. He'd said she got him more than anyone else because of their shared loss of a parent close to the same age. Then all of the guys had started reminiscing about Tilly, Dragon's wife and Dray's mom.

I stared dumbly at the eyeglass case in my hands until Dragon grumbled, "Ain't like I'm giving you the Holy Grail, girl. Go on, open it."

Blinking back tears at the gesture, I opened the case and found a pair of black-framed glasses, the lenses rectangular and a deep lavender, the frames thin and girly.

"Pretty face like yers, no need to be hiding that with big, bug-eyed lenses. Now go on and get out of here." Dragon tapped me on the shoulder, one of those open-handed claps to the upper arm, and I wiped at the moisture in my eyes and sniffed. Sometimes being a girl had its advantages. Like now. I hugged the big, older biker and he barked a bit of a laugh. I slipped the glasses on my face and put the case in my inside pocket.

"Thank you," I murmured.

"You bet, Dani," Dragon said softly, and I reached for and took Thirteen's outstretched hand and let him lead me outside.

The sky was cloudless and as blue as a summer sky could be, and Thirteen's bike idled at the ready just outside the door. I cast a look over towards my tired old Mazda, which hadn't moved since it'd been parked the night I'd brought Thirteen back, and I felt a little rueful. Thirteen handed me my helmet and with a surge of joy I whipped my hair up into a messy knot and, helmet in place, got on behind him.

"You good?" he called over the sound of the engine. I couldn't help but grin. Dragon's small gesture had broken something loose, and the weight of sorrow that I had been carrying since I'd been coated in Griz's blood and brains lifted. I snugged in close against Thirteen's back and squeezed him with my thighs. He bit off a laugh.

"Babe, you're gonna make me hard as fuck, you keep that up!"

"Good! I'll take care of you at the cabin!" I answered, and he barked a laugh.

"You have no idea what riding with a thirteen-inch boner is like. If you did, you'd knock it off," he said. I wrinkled my nose and snuggled a little closer. Thirteen shook his head, put it in gear, and took us down the driveway as the gate rumbled to the side. I held on tight as he turned onto the highway, and let the wind strip the rest of the weight of my sorrow away.

31

R ed XIII...

The ride was great, but Dani had disappeared back inside of herself again. She'd been withdrawn the last few days, quiet and reserved, thoughtful, and borderline secretive. And with every second that ticked by, I felt a distance growing between us. I couldn't read her anymore and that scared me.

Now we were at the cabin, cleaned up and chillin' on the one old wood lounge chair that I'd drug out to the end of the dock. The sun was setting over the lake and I had some beers in a bucket off the side, cooling in the water. We each had one open, Dani peeling the label off her bottle as she stared thoughtfully out over the water. Her blue eyes, bright enough to match the sky earlier, were vacant, almost lost.

"I feel like I'm losing you, baby." The confession was out of my mouth before I even realized I had intent to give it voice. Dani startled and rolled her head back against my shoulder to look up at me. I looked down at her, and I knew my expression was grim.

She frowned, "Why would you say that to me?" she asked and the hurt in her voice was unmistakable. It killed a part of me to hear it, knowing I put it there.

I bowed my head, breaking eye contact.

"Used to be, I could look at you and see your wheels turning and I could just feel what you was thinking." I swallowed hard and took a slug of my beer to wet my mouth, which was suddenly dry. I wasn't used to talking about feelings and shit but this was important. I'd never felt anything like what I felt for Dani Broussard.

She shifted and laid her head against my shoulder, her arms going around me before she spoke.

"A lot has happened and I feel, I don't know... like I've been flung out into space.... Like I'm spinning wildly with nothing to grab on to, and it's confusing." She took a shuddering breath and let it out. "I'm afraid that I'm too needy, that you're going to get bored or that you're going to start hating being my white knight. I'm afraid if I don't get my shit together, you're going to resent me. I'm scared, Thirteen. I've never felt like this about anyone before."

I set my beer down on the dock and I clutched her to my chest, smoothing my fingers through her long hair, gently combing through any tangles. I kissed her forehead, and her eyes drifted shut.

"First, I'm no white knight, baby girl. If anything, I'm just some asshole in aluminum foil." She choked a bitter laugh and I tugged gently on her hair, forcing her to look at me.

"I don't think you get it. I love you just so fucking much, and I don't even know when it happened, baby. I'm fuckin' terrified that you're slipping through my goddamned fingers and it's putting me into a dangerous frame of mind. I don't want to have to let you go. It'd kill me. I'd be less of a man without you by my side, on the back of my bike. You fucking complete me."

She stared up at me, eyes wide, and her mouth dropped open in a little 'o' of surprise. I don't think anyone had ever told her just how much she was worth to them, which was a damned shame all by itself.

"And on another note. You just got out of one seriously fucked-up situation. You've been through the wringer, backwards, forwards, and sideways. Dani, this shit don't heal overnight. Just because it's over don't mean that it ends there. It ain't over 'til it's over. You get what I'm saying?"

Her mouth snapped shut and she swallowed, her blue eyes snapping fire. Her spark was back, that keen intelligence of hers working overtime, her gears whirring and clicking behind those gorgeous fucking eyes of hers.

"I've been really thinking about a lot of things," she admitted, then fell silent.

"Just talk to me, baby, that's all I'm asking." I knew my tone was pleading, but I didn't fucking care.

"We can't live at the club." Her tone was final but I was paying attention. I was paying attention so hard I stopped breathing.

"Okay... what are you saying?" My heart did a barrel roll in my chest.

"I'm saying I want a life with you Thirteen, that if I have to choose a life with you and the MC in it, that I would rather have that than have nothing at all." She wouldn't look at me, her head against my chest, ear resting over my heart.

"I'm not going to make you choose, that would be cruel and incredibly unfair," she said when the silence stretched on for too long. It wasn't that I didn't have anything to say, it's just that... Well fuck me! I didn't have a fucking thing to say! Not in the face of her bravery or generosity, not...

Oh, to fucking hell with it!

I hauled her up my body and claimed her mouth with mine. Her beer dropped from her hand and clacked to the dock, rolling away, leaving a trail of foam in its wake. Her hands were cool against my face where she cupped it as our tongues mingled softly. She tasted bright and crisp and slightly salty, which I realized were her tears a moment later. I broke the kiss and looked at my beautiful girl.

"Dani, you know you ain't got to be afraid, right? You know that me, my brothers, that each and every one of us would protect you until our final dying breath. You get that, right?" I asked her. She stared at me blankly and I realized too fucking late what it was... Dani only had the Suicide Cunts to go by as a measuring stick. As smart as she was, she didn't know how MC's were really supposed to work. How each and every brother was supposed to have your back and, because of that, those of the women and children belonging to you.

"Jesus Christ, I've failed..." I heard myself utter, even as the enormity of what I'd done, or really the lack thereof, hit home.

"What? No! Thirteen, you gave me the courage to get out. You've protected me, cared for me, saved my life in more than one way, how is that a failure?" Her brow creased in worry, concern radiating from her beautiful face.

"Babe, I haven't told you shit. Shit you should probably know. I haven't taught you what it is to be a part of an MC. A real MC. I just kind of dragged you right along with me into my club and didn't give you any cues to go off of, an' expected you to just sort of know how things are really supposed to go. That was setting you up for big-time failure and I am so sorry."

Dani chewed her bottom lip and I suppressed a groan. She had no idea how hot that was but now wasn't the time for any of that. Finally she looked up at me and huffed out a frustrated sigh.

"Okay, you have my attention... Crash course. What do I need to know? What did the Suicide Kings have wrong? What makes the Sacred Hearts different?" She stared at me plaintively and I blinked. I hadn't expected the direct approach and fuck if that didn't make her like a million times hotter in my book.

"Okay, no bullshit. The Suicide Kings were a bunch of misogynistic douchebags, for one. Sacred Hearts has it written in our fucking bylaws. No women and no children, meaning that if or when the shit gets heavy, if we got a beef with a dude or another club or whatever, we keep the women and children out of it. We got respect for the fairer sex. That's just a fact." I trailed gentle fingertips along the side of Dani's face.

"Nothing they did to you would ever happen with any of my brothers. No one gets held against their will, no one does anything they don't want to do... You're a person, baby, not a bargaining chip, not some kind of money-making factory. We protect our own, baby, and you're one of ours now." I pulled her gently so her forehead met mine.

"You're safe, baby girl. That fat, nasty fuck never should have gotten by. He never should have gotten to you. We got cocky. Not a damned one of us ever thought that he would jump the fucking fence and come on to our turf solo like that. I'm so fucking sorry."

She sniffed, nodded, and pressed her lips, which were salty sweet and damp with her tears, to mine. I held her face between my hands and drew back to look her in the eyes.

"I mean it, babe; you're safe, you're free, and - as much as it fucking kills me - if you ever want to go, I'd let you go... I want you to be happy."

She threw her arms around me, buried her face in the crook between my neck and shoulder, and let loose with a few broken sobs.

"Please don't," she sniffed and I smiled and cuddled her close. I knew what she meant but I think I needed to hear it anyways, so I asked her...

"Please don't what?"

"Please, don't ever let me go!" she cried, and I let her have her tears. Didn't ask her to stop, just made soothing noises and let her have a good, strong cry. It was what my mom always used to do for my sister, and my sister always bounced back better than ever, so what did I have to lose?

I held Dani while we soaked in the last of the warmth of the setting sun and continued to hold her as the lightning bugs began their lazy dance in the air around us. Dani's sobs tapered off into the odd sniff, until finally she lay against me, calm and quiet.

"Better?" I asked.

She nodded against my chest. "How did you know?"

"Had a sister."

"Had?"

"My family and me, we don't talk anymore. I'm the black sheep." I smiled in spite of this, and Dani chuckled.

"If only they knew their black sheep was really one serious white knight."

I laughed, how could I not? White Knight? Yeah, not on your life. If only Dani knew the things I'd done, the lives I'd taken and the wrongs I'd committed.

I shook my head. "Asshole, aluminum foil, remember?"

"Thirteen, I'm serious!" she cried and pushed off of me to look at me through the dark, but that's when she saw them, the lightning bugs, swirling and twirling in their lazy dance along the edges of the lake. She gasped, her eyes transfixed, and I smiled. I could watch her watch those little flickering bugs by the light of the moon for hours, if not days.

"It's so beautiful..." she murmured, her voice soft and demure with wonder.

"Not half so beautiful as what I'm looking at," my voice was rough with too much emotion as I stared at her beautiful face, artfully sculpted by God himself. She turned and startled when she realized what I meant.

"Just tell me we're okay, baby girl," I said, and she swallowed hard.

"Of course we are, Chris." I sort of loved that she used my real name, but didn't have time to really soak it in because she wasn't done.

"I love you. I mean, it was crazy how we met, and everything that happened, but you... You're... I don't even have the words. You mean so incredibly much to me. You make me laugh, you make me smile; you hold me when I'm scared, you set my body, heart and mind on fire... You're my friend as much as my lover and I haven't had a friend in so very long. You're so very precious to me." She turned her face into the light touch I laid against it. I couldn't stop touching her if I wanted to. Her words made my heart swell to something like a million times its original size, and I couldn't help but swell elsewhere too.

"God, Dani, the things you do to me," I whispered, and I knew my voice had gone low, husky with a mixture of love and desire. She leaned her whole body against mine and kissed me, and my cock got real uncomfortable in the prison of my jeans.

"Make love to me," she breathed.

I made to pick her up and she looked around. The nearest house was some distance across the water, the light from the windows barely visible through the tall rushes and grass around the lakeshore.

"Here," she murmured, and I paused.

"You sure?" I asked.

"It's secluded enough, isn't it?" Her voice was breathy, a mixture of desire and a little fear.

"Yeah, baby. Yeah, it is... I'd love to love you out here; I just want you to be comfortable." My lips traced hers as I spoke gently against her mouth.

Her arms twined around my neck and she buried her fingers in the back of my hair, dragging my lips the rest of that tiny distance to hers. She was straddling my hips now, and I didn't remember that happening.

My jeans were really pinching now, and with a soft groan, I kept kissing her but let my hands drift off her trim waist to fumble at my button and fly in an effort to relieve some of the pressure. Dani pressed her slender body right up against mine and I got my jeans down off my hips.

Her hands left the back of my hair to gather the back of my shirt. I raised my arms and let her drag it over the top of my head. She spared a glance before dropping it off to the side of the wooden chaise, to the dock, keeping it out of our earlier beer spill.

The slightly damp but still warm summer air slid across my shoulders and back, but Dani kept my chest warm, her body pressing right up against mine the second my shirt was off. She rose up on her knees to either side of my hips to give me room to adjust and as soon as I was set, I let my hands go to her hips.

She'd changed into a short black summer dress when we'd gotten here in an effort to beat back some of the summer heat. Her long, gorgeous hair was an artful tangle held by a hairband at the back of her head, tendrils loose and curling, the beautiful mess made more so by my constant touching and playing with the dark strands.

I loved the feel of her hair. I loved the feel of her skin on mine and right now her panties, delicate lace that they were, were in my fucking way. I gripped them tightly in my fist.

"Gonna rip these," I growled before giving them a rough jerk. I was glad she wore string thongs.

She gasped, her arms tightening around me, which was fine by me. It just shoved my face into her tits. I discarded the scrap of offending fabric and nuzzled between her breasts, kissing and nipping along her skin.

Dani threw her head back and gave a throaty gasp, and my cock throbbed with a very definite need to be inside her. I began to unbutton her dress, the straps holding it up on her shoulders. I needed more skin. I loosed button after button as swiftly as my thick fingers could get them through the holes and trailed my mouth behind them over her silky skin.

She smelled phenomenal, her sex lightly perfuming the air with its musky, sweet scent.

I cried out when she reached down between us and rose up higher to get me inside her. She sank down on me slowly, carefully, and it took everything I had in me not to surge up to meet her downward progress.

"Oh God, fuck, babe, you're killing me," I squeezed out between gritted teeth. I let my hands smooth over all that fine pale skin, left bare by her open dress, and watched them. God–fucking-damnit, there was something extremely erotic about the sight of my work-rough hands on all of that pale perfection. Cupping those gorgeous tits, the pads of my thumbs teasing her pert nipples as she sank ever so slowly, hot and wet and perfect, over my cock.

"Mmm! Chris!" she gasped and gave a little wiggle of her hips. I closed my eyes and turned my head and tried to get it together before I came like some half-assed teenager in the first thirty seconds of his first time ever.

"You good, babe?" I questioned, my voice straining almost as much as my cock.

She looked down at me, her eyes hooded with desire, and rolled her hips in answer. I about fucking died. I grasped her hips, her body framed by the black material of her dress, glowing in the moonlight. She was so fucking beautiful. My very own Lady of the Lake. My personal Goddess, my sorrowful angel.

"God, Dani, I fucking love you," I grated and sucked in a deep breath. A tremulous smile touched her lips and her head tipped back, her hair tumbling loose down her back. I reached up and smoothed the thin dress off of her shoulders and she let it fall.

So. Fucking. Perfect.

"Ride me, baby," I urged her, and that smile was back on her lips, and she did just that, rode me, and I couldn't do anything but lay back and enjoy as I let her take her pleasure, her way.

I was so incredibly grateful that I didn't have to let her go. That she wanted to stay, had agreed to stay...

I teased her clit with my thumb, gently massaging the little kernel of flesh, and didn't bother holding back when she came. I would follow her anywhere, through anything. My brave and perfect girl.

My woman...

32

D ani...

The heat and humidity was oppressive. The long ride had been exhilarating for the first half but had become butt-numbing and wearisome the further south we'd traveled and the hotter it had gotten. I was sweating beneath my jacket and I could see that it wasn't only me. The guys were all just as road-weary as I was. However, they had begun perking up some as soon as we made our way through the little beachside town of Ft. Royal, and even more so now that we were riding down a residential street, a line of houses with the beach beyond them off to our left.

Dragon hung a left into a tree-lined drive and everyone fell in behind him. My heart was suddenly in my throat. This was it: I would be meeting the women who went with some of these men, and I felt my heart rate pick up a little. I was both excited and terribly nervous.

The house was grand, tall and ornate, something straight out of the Victorian era with a very modern front step. Four women stood on the broad, sweeping stone steps.

One of them was very pregnant with fiery red hair in a long, light, summer dress that fit her pregnant form perfectly. She was radiant with how she glowed, and her radiance went up about ten notches as soon as she spotted Revelator backing his big custom chopper into line.

Another woman, the one next to Revelator's 'Red', bounced lightly on her feet in her excitement. She wore cut-off shorts and a tank top, her long, graceful legs tanned to perfection and her wheat-gold hair in a braid over her shoulder. Her hands were clasped together in front of her mouth and it looked like it was taking every ounce of her restraint not to go bounding down the steps and run to whoever she was waiting for.

There was a tiny woman with long, auburn hair, who was smiling and clapping and bouncing just as much as the taller woman beside her, but I knew who she was, I had seen her picture. She was Trigger's Sunshine girl, but I couldn't see her eyes from here to see if the pictures did her eyes any justice, if they were really a true golden hue.

The last woman was as tall as the bouncy one beside Red. Her platinum hair was a short pixie cut, her expression was pinched with impatience, and my heart ached for her. I knew who she was instantly and I knew what had happened to her, what Sparks had done. She was looking for Ghost and when she saw him, her face broke into a smile, but then the smile froze on her face.

Thirteen tapped my hands to jump off, and I did so gladly so he could back the bike in. I stood by and watched as the small woman with the auburn hair launched herself at Trigger. He swept her up and kissed her and held her tight. The bouncy woman went for Dray. Revelator went to his Red and dropped to one knee in front of her, placing a reverent kiss on her swollen belly.

A sharp cry brought my attention back to Sunshine. Trigger set her on her feet and she reached for and went to Reaver, breaking into giant, wracking sobs. Reaver knelt with a sad little smile and took her into his arms in a sweet and careful hug. He laid his cheek on the top of her head while she sobbed into the side of his neck and my heart lightened.

I'd forgotten. The women thought Reaver was dead and gone for these long months. I bit my bottom lip and watched as he passed the small woman back to his best friend and went up to the platinum blonde. Their eyes were a perfect match for each other's, but while Reaver's were somber, Shelly, his cousin's, sparked sapphire flames.

"Hey, Baby Cuz..." he said gently, and Shelly did something unprecedented. She hauled off and belted her cousin, right in the mouth, with her closed fist. Reaver's head snapped to the side and Ghost reached for her.

"Don't touch me!" she snapped and, shaking her man off, stalked for the open door to the house. Reaver touched his face and worked his jaw back and forth while Ghost went after his woman. I was astonished; there was no screaming, there was no violence toward her, just Ghost trotting after her, begging her to stop and talk to him. I was transfixed for a moment, but Sunshine had already moved in and was hugging Reaver around his waist before I could ask if he was okay.

"You okay, babe?" Thirteen asked from beside the bike.

"Yeah, uh... I'm just melting and need to use the bathroom really bad." Which I did.

Revelator called out from where he held his woman in his arms. "Through the front door, all the way straight back. Only door past the stairs, right before the kitchen and dining room."

"Thanks." With a fortifying smile from Thirteen, I handed him my helmet, then I crept through the bedlam of the guys unloading bikes and the like, and went and found the bathroom.

It felt like heaven getting out of the jacket. I was in a light halter top underneath, something nice without being super-flashy, a simple black, held by strings, bathing-suit style, at the neck and around the back with a scooped neckline. The material was a light, fluttery silk. It went well with my jeans and motorcycle boots.

I splashed cold water on my face and dried it, then stepped out into the quiet of the house. When movement caught my eye, I turned my head to look out the sliding glass door and my breath caught in my throat. I was drawn out the back slider, which was open to the breeze, and stopped short at the cement railing of the large stone back patio.

The water was beautiful. Out quite a ways, I could still hear it crashing on the shore. Two people were walking slowly, hand-in-hand, towards the house, one a man, with long brown hair, wearing a cut over his bare chest. The other was a small woman with short dark hair... Reaver's wife. I startled as the man himself stopped next to me. He looked over and down at me.

"Can I leave these with you?" he asked, plucking at the front of his white tee shirt. I nodded mutely. He stripped his cut off and hung it on the railing before pulling his tee over his head. The scars from where he'd been shot were stark and bright pink against his pale skin in the bright sunlight. He put his cut back on, then took off his shoes and socks and left them at the bottom of the rail near my feet. I put my hand on the soft cotton of his tee where he'd slung it over the rail, and he smiled at me after rolling up the cuffs on his jeans.

"Good luck," I said softly, the display with his cousin still fresh in my mind.

He gave me a sad smile.

"First time in a long time I've been scared," he admitted.

I nodded.

"I'm sorry she had such a bad reaction."

"Shelly? Nah. I expected that from her." He gave me a wild, rakish grin, and I laughed, and then he was bounding down the stairs and striding across the sand.

The man saw him first. He stopped cold and a grin spread across his face from ear to ear. The small woman, Hayden, looked up at the man questioningly, and the man had to point for her to take her eyes off him.

The wind carried her short scream to my ears and she startled so hard I thought she was going to fall for a moment. I prayed then, really hard, for Reaver, that this would be a happy reunion, and I couldn't help but smile as the woman, who was crying now, launched herself at him. They crashed into each other and she sobbed into his chest.

He lowered them both into the sand and he held her, rocking her gently while she came apart in his arms, clinging to him with every ounce of strength her small frame possessed. So enraptured was I by their reunion, I missed the other man, who had passed them and was coming up the back step. He stopped beside me and looked down at me and I swallowed hard, making every attempt not to make eye contact with him. Instead, I fixed my gaze on the name flash on his cut.

'Cutter'.

Below that, 'President'.

"And who might you belong to?" he asked, and I let my gaze travel upward by just a bit. He had a neat, trim beard and a full mouth that smiled broadly. His teeth were even and straight, and blindingly white against his very tan skin. I tried not to shake. I opened my mouth to speak when Thirteen saved me again.

"Dani!" He came to me, and wrapped me in comfort and stability from behind.

"Ah... she yours?" Cutter asked, and I looked at him; he was very handsome and his smile made him more so.

"Yes!" I blurted, "I'm Thirteen's."

"Nice to meet you, Dani, was it?" I nodded and quickly shook his offered hand. He cocked his head to the side and his warm brown eyes roved over my face.

"You're okay here, Small Fry," he said, and I made a face.

"Small Fry?"

"Don't like it?" he asked.

"Anything is better than Coon," I mumbled.

His eyebrows went up, amused and he nodded.

"Okay, I'll remember that, pretty girl." He looked to Thirteen. "Nice to meet you, too, man. Welcome to our little slice of paradise." He raised a fist and Thirteen knocked it with his own.

"Thanks, brother. It's good to be here," he said, and he kissed me behind my ear where my hair was up out of the way in its messy bun. I couldn't help myself. I smiled and leaned back against him.

Cutter moved past us into the house and I snuck a look back to Reaver and Hayden, who were kissing passionately now, Reaver's long fingers smoothing away her tears.

"You okay, baby?" Thirteen murmured, his lips barely brushing the shell of my ear. I couldn't help it, the little touch sent shivers down my spine despite the warm temperatures. Thirteen chuckled and kissed the side of my neck. "Later, that's a promise."

I turned in his arms and let him kiss me, and I felt stronger for it. "I'll hold you to that."

"Be disappointed if you didn't. You want to stay out here while I help the rest of the guys, or you want to come back with me?" I gave a sidelong look that was probably full of longing to the sea crashing distant on the shore.

"Say no more, baby. Relax, enjoy the ocean. Be back before you know it." He pressed a kiss to my shoulder and nipped it lightly, which made me giggle, before he retreated back into the house.

Hayden had gone quiet, and Reaver simply held her, rocking her slightly to the ebb and flow of the sea, an unconscious gesture. Watching them together, more than anything else, told me just how much they loved one another and I couldn't imagine... I didn't want to imagine what the last six months had been like for either of them.

A cool, light touch on the back of my shoulder made me jump. I turned, and Revelator's woman was beaming at me.

"That's my man's work, isn't it?" she asked. I nodded dumbly.

"It's beautiful. I wish I could draw like him." Her voice was wistful and she held out a glass of iced tea towards me.

"Thank you." I took it and tentatively took a sip. It was crisp and sweet and the perfect thing after such a long ride.

"My name is Mandy, what's yours?" she asked.

"Dani, I'm Dani Broussard." She smiled much bigger.

"That's a beautiful name."

"Have you decided on a name yet? I mean, do you know what you're having?" I asked, and prayed I sounded normal. Mandy seemed sweet. She radiated gentility and calm.

She smoothed her hands over her stomach.

"We don't know, we decided to keep it a surprise." She gave a gusty sigh. "Zander really likes some of the old works, Dante's Inferno, Milton's Paradise Lost, that sort of thing. I'm okay with our son being named Dante, I really am, but if we have a girl he wants to name her Beatrice." She made a face and crossed her eyes, and I burst out laughing.

"You can't come up with anything else that he likes?" I asked.

"I tried! I really did, I suggested Trinity and he sort of kind of liked it but he really wants it to fall in line with either Dante or Milton and I can't find anything else." She sighed again and bounced a little on her feet, her face twisting into a bit of a grimace.

"Honestly it's probably a moot point, this child is all Zander's and a little slugger. With as much as it punches and kicks, it has to be a boy."

I cocked my head to the side and considered Mandy. "What about Eden?" I asked.

"Eden?" she echoed.

"Yeah, as in the Garden of Eden from Paradise Lost."

"I could be on board with that."

We both turned at the same time. Revelator was leaning in the sliding glass doorway.

"Eden. I actually really like that."

Mandy's face broke into a beatific smile and she went to her man, leaning against him and twining her arms around his broad shoulders, the white gold ring I'd fashioned for her winking on her finger, sparkling in the sun. That made me smile more than anything.

"See you've met Dani, sugar." He kissed Mandy's cheek and she nodded.

"Yep, Zander told me you made our rings. I wanted to say thank you but, silly me, I got sidetracked."

"It was nothing, really. I like making things and it was more than a fair trade."

"You're all probably starving..."

Mandy was a kind and gentle soul. She took me under her wing immediately and I could tell she would make a fine mother.

The reunion between the club and the Ol' Ladies was a happy one. Cutter and some of his men built a bonfire on the beach and fired up the large grill on the back patio.

Meat was grilled, beers were cracked, and a feast commenced, with laughing and some singing.

Disney was reunited with the love of his life, Aaron, and the two were very openly affectionate. What struck me about it though, was that none of the Sacred Hearts men were the slightest bit fazed by it and the few men of the Kraken who were uncomfortable were quickly put in their place by their President, Cutter.

The whole experience was eye-opening to say the least, and now most of the couples were gathered on blankets in the sand around the roaring flames, using rocks and washed up logs as backrests. I sat between Thirteen's legs, my back resting against his bare chest, and relished the skin-on-skin contact.

One of the men of the Kraken was clearly drunk and rambling, and all of us were stifling our laughter at the outlandish and strange things he was saying.

"Man... I wonder what anal sex is like. I've never done it," he said.

Duracell, who was chilling next to Blue, an arm slung haphazardly over the other man's shoulders in brotherly affection, barked out a laugh.

"I'd imagine it feels like having a dick in your ass," he said dryly, and the whole fireside erupted into laughter. Even Disney and Aaron laughed.

"No, no, no, no, man!" The Kraken member protested and tried to backpedal.

My laughter was slightly silenced by a slight nip to the side of my neck. I turned, Thirteen's eyes were aglow with more than just firelight. I smiled slightly and he lolled his head in Cutter's direction, who sat next to Reaver and Hayden. Hayden was curled tightly in Reaver's lap and he held her as if he would never let her go again, which made me smile.

"Thanks for having us here," he said quietly, and Cutter nodded.

"No worries, man. We were glad to help," but Cutter's eyes were distant as he stared into the firelight. His words, while meaningful, were hollow and if I had to guess, the reason why was curled tightly in Reaver's arms. Cutter's eyes snapped from the flames to mine and I smiled a bit sadly. He gave me a secret smile in return and we shared a silent moment while the festivities continued around us.

"Getting tired?" Thirteen asked. I nodded.

Cutter looked us both up and down.

"Space inside is limited but it's supposed to be clear and nice tonight. Why don't you two take the hammock over there?" He gestured with his beer bottle.

"Yeah?" Thirteen asked.

"Sure? Why not? Think Dani likes the idea." I could hear rather than see his crooked grin. My gaze was out on the vague glimmer of white as the waves rolled onto the shore.

"Sound good to you, baby?" Thirteen asked, low and careful.

"Sounds perfect."

33

R ed-XII...
     We lay swinging gently in the wide, deep-blue canvas
hammock. The party had definitely died out but I could tell Dani
wasn't asleep yet. She lay snug against my side, staring sightless at the
rolling surf, a lot on her mind.

"Talk to me, babe. What's going on in that head of yours?" I asked,
low and quiet, pressing a kiss to her forehead.

"I like it," she said, and she sounded surprised.

"You like what?" I asked, hoping she would expand on the
statement.

"The club, being here with you... it's so different in so many good
ways. The girls are amazing and so loved. Your whole club is based in
love and respect and brotherhood. Is this what it was supposed
to be?"

I couldn't stop the grin from overtaking my face if I tried.

"Yeah, babe. Yeah it is. This is what it's supposed to be like.
Through the bad, through the good, this is it. We protect what's ours."
...and you're mine. I kept the last part silent, for fear it'd be too much.

"I wish Jared had found your club instead," she whispered finally.

"Me, too," and it was only half a lie. I would give anything to spare

Dani the pain and sorrow she'd been through but I couldn't, wouldn't, wish for any fate that didn't put her square in my arms like we were now.

"What are you thinking about so hard?" Her soft voice interrupted my brooding.

Uh-oh, busted.

"You. I am so fucking lucky to have you here, like this."

"You think so?"

"Fuck, baby, I know so... What are you doing?"

"It's quiet, no one else is out here anymore." Her hands worked deftly at the button and fly on my cargo shorts.

"Here? Now? You sure?" I double-checked with her; I knew she was shy about people watching after what happened. We'd been clear for whatever we'd wanted to do at the lake, my dock was shrouded from all the other nearby houses by tall cattails and reeds.

"Yes, now shush and kiss me."

Well, fuck me! I wasn't about to argue with a command like that. I kissed her, my hands twining in the silken strands, holding them away from her face as her warm fingers wrapped around me. Oh God, that was nice! I groaned into her mouth, past her lips, and it was met with a sultry whimper from her own soul.

I palmed the outside of her thigh and ran my hand up to knead her perfect, tight little ass and she smiled against my mouth. Someday I'd like to take her there, but not now, not tonight.

She'd changed in the house into one of my tees and a pair of her boy-short panties before coming out to lay under the stars with me. There was way too much fabric to just tear off her body, so I shifted to get between her thighs to pull them off.

Big mistake.

Hammocks were made for lounging in. Not for sex. The damned thing tipped violently, Dani shrieked, and I put my arms around her and turned with the momentum of the swinging canvas. I landed, hard, on my back in the sand, Dani on top of me. The wind was knocked clean out of me; I tried to pull in a breath but it wasn't happening for a minute or two. Dani pushed off of me and knelt in the sand by my hip. My shorts were down around my thighs, my cock rapidly deflating and waving in the breeze. She blinked at the sour expression on my face.

"Are you okay?" she cried.

I wasn't able to speak just yet so instead I waved her down, trying to signal with my hand that I just had the wind knocked out of me when it happened.

She laughed, the purest, sweetest, most infectious sound, just as I was able to draw breath again, and she kept laughing. She laughed high and wild and free until the tears seeped from the corners of her eyes and she clutched her sides and damn it if it wasn't so fucking ridiculous and funny that I couldn't keep from joining in.

So we sat there, sand getting into the crack of my ass, and laughed until she couldn't breathe and I couldn't breathe again. The amorous mood was destroyed but had been replaced with something much better in its wake.

Damn, it was good to hear my girl laugh.

34

Dani...
   I looked out the kitchen window above the sink, out over the stone patio, out over the fine white sand, to the hammock swaying gently back and forth in the light morning breeze. We'd managed to find our way back into it and had resumed lying in each other's arms, talking softly late into the night until we fell asleep soundly in one another's arms. There were no more sexual escapades resulting in disastrous spills. I still couldn't keep from smiling, a broad dopey grin; every time I thought about it.

   "What's so funny?" Everett asked. I startled.

   "You... um, ...you really had to be there..." I hedged. She grinned and laughed lightly and handed me two cups of coffee. I added the requisite amount of cream and sugar to both mine and Thirteen's liking, and smiled back.

   "Okay, I'll take your word for it." Everett winked at me, and Ashton and Mandy grinned. I had woken with the dawn and left Thirteen sleeping, coming back into the house to shower and dress for the day. I was surprised that the rest of the women were up too, by the time I got out of my shower.

   Apparently the plans for the day involved relaxing, and enjoying the sun and the water. I didn't have a swimsuit, but between Ashton and Hayden, they had me covered. Well, Ashton did. Hayden was still secluded with Reaver in the room she shared with Ashton. Ashton and Trigger had stayed on the couch the night before. The big man still slept on in the big living room on the couch that wrapped around and could easily seat a dozen people.

I wore a bikini, the first time I had ever worn one in my life. It was white and held up by strings and I felt truly blessed that it fit me well enough. Ashton even went so far as to lend me a wrap for the bottom so I wouldn't feel ridiculously exposed. The wrap was bright, large white flowers with yellow centers on a backdrop of bright green leaves and what could be palm fronds.

The outfit was cute, and with the rest of the girls dressed similarly and completely at ease, I felt comfortable enough. I was still nervous about the men of the Kraken and how they might behave, but for the first time that I could remember, I felt safe.

I had some things I wanted to give to show my appreciation and belief in the men of the Sacred Hearts who had spent so much time, effort, and care in looking out for me. I put my hand on the Crown Royal bag hanging out of the waistband of my swimsuit and wrap, and smiled.

"Time to go wake up Sleeping Beauty," I said, and Mandy laughed. I picked up the two cups of coffee and she held open the slider for me. It was already getting warm outside and promised to be a scorcher.

"Wait!" I turned, and Ashton dashed out onto the back patio. "Put those down really quick and step over here."

I set the two mugs of coffee down on the glass tabletop, a big square thing that, like the living-room couch, would easily seat a dozen. It was shaded from the morning sun by a canopy. I went over to the small woman. I mean, I was five-foot-five, the same as Thirteen, but Ashton was almost a half a foot shorter than me and so fine-boned that she resembled a small child. I didn't know how her and Trigger matching up was even humanly possible.

She brought out a can of sunscreen from behind her back and

grinned impishly. I smiled and held my arms out and, laughing and giggling, she sprayed me down thoroughly.

"Hold out your hands," she ordered, and I did and she sprayed the palms liberally.

"Do your face."

I scrubbed my palms over my face; she nodded and, beaming, handed me the can. I tucked it in the crook of my arm, thanked her, picked up the coffee cups, and went back down to where Thirteen still slept in the shade of the two palms the hammock was strung between. I knelt in the sand and tucked the can of sunscreen and the two mugs into it so they wouldn't spill.

He was beautiful to me, in sleep, awake, it didn't matter. His face was devoid of its cool assessment and calculation in sleep. The lines of his strong and handsome features were slack and relaxed, at peace. Still. Even so, the lines of his body told a different story. Strong and corded with muscle, his hands scarred and calloused, even in sleep Thirteen looked like a dangerous man.

I slipped the black cord over my head and undid the loop I'd made around the ring. I held my breath unconsciously. I wasn't like my grandfather. He could look at a person's fingers and instantly know their size. I worried my bottom lip between my teeth and tried Thirteen's index finger, so very carefully. I didn't want to wake him.

No luck, so I tried his middle finger; again, the ring was too small.

I groaned a bit inwardly because it looked like it would fit... the ring finger of his left hand. Which wasn't my intent.

He chuckled and I startled. I looked up into his sea-green eyes, his lips curled in a smile that made my heart melt.

"What are you doing?" he asked.

"I made this for you; I'm just really bad at guessing sizes. I hope you don't mind. I just really wanted to surprise you." I sat back on my haunches and felt myself blush at the hungry, heated look he gave me, his eyes traveling slowly up and down my body. His smile grew.

"I'm really liking what I'm seeing, baby girl." His voice was husky, soft, and the look in his eyes was filled with such a love and lust. I blushed faintly.

"Um, thank you, but what do you think about the ring?" I asked, suddenly nervous. I hoped that he didn't hate it.

He lifted his hand, putting it in front of his face, but I could see the effort it took him to tear his eyes off of me. The effort must have been worth it though, because he did a double-take at the ring.

It wasn't fancy, just a simple white gold band set with thirteen rubies around its circumference. I'd used the reddest rubies I could muster out of my collection of stones, cutting some of the larger ones smaller just to get them all sized the same. Thirteen twisted the band around his finger and I could see he was counting. His lips spread into one of the most winning smiles I'd ever seen on him.

"You did this for me?" he asked.

I nodded, mute, and tried to hand him one of the coffees. He took it from me and set it back into the sand.

"Dani, it's beautiful. You're beautiful." He captured my face between his hands and leaned forward precariously to kiss me long and slow.

"Hey! What's going on out here?" Reaver was striding across the sand, his wife leaning into his side, her arm around his waist. Her eyes were so very green and glowed fiercely with a happiness and relief I could only begin to imagine. I'm pretty sure I'd felt some of the very same the night Thirteen had been shot, when he'd touched my hair and proven that he was very much alive and I could believe that he really was okay.

"I think Dani just asked me to marry her." Thirteen held up his hand and I felt myself blush furiously.

Reaver's wife, Hayden, laughed.

"Did you say yes?" she asked.

The silence behind me lasted a hair's-breadth too long; I whipped around when he didn't deny it. Thirteen was considering my face very carefully, his eyes gleaming with mischief and, underlying that, a grave seriousness.

"I think, if she really wanted, that I would let her make an honest man out of me."

My butt planted into the sand as we held eye contact for what felt like forever. I thought about it, I mean *really* thought about it.

"Are you playing with me?" I asked softly.

"Serious as a fucking heart attack, baby girl. Think about it, I'll leave it up to you."

"I don't have to." I blurted. This was crazy, this was insane, *Did Thirteen just agree to marry me?*

"Good, it's settled then. We'll work out the details later." Reaver stretched luxuriously, Hayden taking the opportunity to lean into him harder.

Reaver stretched luxuriously, Hayden taking the opportunity to lean into him harder. "We were sent down to fetch you for breakfast," she said and she winked at me as I sat in the warm sand, stunned.

"You okay, Rocket?" Reaver asked.

I nodded mutely, not trusting my voice, and glanced back at Thirteen, who was smiling, an amused look on his face as his gaze roved over me from head to toe.

"You should keep that suit," Hayden said judiciously. "It looks better on you than it does me."

"I'm sorry?" I said.

Reaver laughed. "Okay, you two. Breakfast. Club only, on the back patio. Ashton's gonna have a fit if the food gets cold, so let's move it."

Thirteen picked up his cup of coffee and downed it in three large swallows. He hoisted himself out of the hammock and reached down to help me to my feet. I let him heave me up and retrieved the sunscreen and my cup of coffee.

"I have something for you," I said to Reaver. "If it's okay?" I checked with Hayden with a look and she smiled at me broadly and nodded.

I slipped Reaver's switchblade from the Crown Royal bag at my hip and held it out to him.

"I don't think I need this anymore, and since it was your favorite..." I swallowed nervously and he beamed a smile at me.

"You sure?"

I glanced at Thirteen and smiled. "I'm sure."

Reaver plucked the knife from my fingers and in a blink, simply made it disappear. He winked one of his bright blue eyes at me and his wife smiled up at him adoringly.

"Seriously, Ashton is a sweetheart, and I don't want her all butt-hurt that we let breakfast get cold. Let's get a move on, people." Reaver steered his wife around and back toward the house.

Thirteen curved his arms around my shoulders.

"You doing alright, baby girl?" he asked me, low, so the two in front of us wouldn't hear.

"Do you really mean it?" I asked.

"I don't say things I don't mean, Dani. I don't ever want to let you go. It's a weird as fuck way to get engaged and I feel kind of like a jackass for not doing it right –" I stopped and pressed gentle fingertips to his lips.

"You're really sure?" I asked, and he smiled beneath the pads of my fingers, his blue-green eyes dancing with laughter and light, and he nodded. I slipped my arms around his neck and hugged myself to him, his hard, strong arms going around my back he held me back.

"I love you," I murmured, and he kissed my shoulder lightly.

"Hey! Food *now,* you two!" Revelator yelled from the patio, and with a slight laugh I pulled back from Thirteen.

"Shut the fuck up, man! I just got engaged!" Thirteen hollered back, and all movement on the back patio ceased.

I smiled, my heart taking flight when Ghost yelled down, "No shit?" Shelly elbowed him in the ribs, and the shouts and the cheering started. I laughed and Thirteen picked me up and swung me around.

Holy shit. I accidentally got engaged and it felt amazing!

"Really, forever?" I checked one last time.

"And ever," he promised and we kissed.

We joined the rest of the MC for breakfast and I handed out the rest of my tokens of appreciation for all that they'd done.

For Dragon, I'd made a hair clasp of silver made into his name-sake that was fashioned to hold his thick horsetail of hair. The eyes were a rich garnet, a tourmaline in a rich amber color was grasped in its jaws to give the appearance of breathing fire.

I'd made a tail holder for Trigger too; his was a silver disc with raised crosshairs like you would see through a sniper's scope. Ghost had let me look through one. At the center of the disc, a perfectly round ruby. I'd made a heavy white gold ring for Ghost with the same motif at the center, a thank-you for saving my life using their particular skill-set.

For Revelator, there was a silver band fashioned with ivy vines around its circumference. Dray I had made a heavy silver ring, a rose in full bloom, a deep red garnet at its center to match his bike. For Rush and Nox, I'd made two tags, one etched with each brother's name. I gave them to the opposite brother.

Duracell, I gave a wide black leather bracelet with an old-fashioned silver key plate bolted to it. I gave the key, on a black leather cord to Blue. Both of them traded looks and smiled at me, Duracell wickedly so, before hooking me around the back of my neck and kissing my forehead unexpectedly. I'd startled and he'd let me go as quickly as he'd grabbed me, and I smiled. I was safe here, and I felt it keenly in that moment.

I gave Doc a wide leather bracelet as well, only I'd fashioned a caduceus to his. He hugged me and let me go with a murmured thanks.

Finally I stopped in front of Archer, who was watching me curiously. I picked up his hand and dropped the hair tie into it and curled his fingers around the gold.

"Why?" he asked.

I smiled. "Because you're family. I understand it now," I murmured. He cocked his head to the side and opened his hand and looked down at it and his face collapsed into near-tears. It was a gold disc, set with a tiger's-eye stone. Simple. Rush and Nox had told me it was their brother Grinder's favorite stone and had told me about how close he and Archer were growing up. It felt right. Fitting.

"I don't understand," he said, and tried to hand it back. I pushed his hand back towards him.

"Because you were there, too, when Griz tried to take me. You were standing there, side by side, ready to fight, to do whatever it was you needed to do to get me back for Thirteen and you did it without a second thought. Even though you don't like me that much." I gave a brave little smile. Truthfully, Archer still intimidated and scared the ever living hell out of me with how intense he could be.

He nodded and looked thoughtfully out to sea and that was okay. I moved on to Disney and smiled.

"Me, too?" he said, smiling.

I gave him a pin, a simple silver bar set with seven stones. Seven round cut stones. Ruby, yellow topaz, citrine, emerald, blue topaz, sapphire, and finally amethyst. He blinked and smiled and took the delicate but strong pin in his long fingers and turned to his boyfriend.

"Pin this on me?" he asked. Aaron smiled warmly and pinned the rainbow pin to Disney's cut, over his heart, just below his name flash. I smiled and hugged the slender man.

"Thank you."

"Any time, Dani," he said and pressed a kiss to the top of my head.

"Thank all of you, for what you did for me. For what you did for Thirteen, for us, so that there could be an 'us'." I sniffed and went to Thirteen, who was seated at the table, and dropped into his lap. He put his arms around me and kissed my shoulder.

"Darlin', you know you didn't have to do any of this for any of us right?" Trig asked gently. "You're supposed to be rebuilding a life for yourself out of these bits of metal and pretty rocks."

"I have more," I said softly and smiled. Ashton was braiding her man's hair and she smiled softly to herself as she bound the end with my gift. Her face was alight with pride and love.

"I think what the Big Man is trying to say is: we 'preciate it, and thanks." Dragon said with an affable grin. I smiled broadly.

Thirteen cuddled me close and the rest of the women were similarly close to their men. Reaver slid the ring with a bright blue topaz, the match for his eyes, around and around on his thumb. Hayden smiled at her husband and raised the palm of his hand to her lips to press a kiss at its center. Reaver's eyes closed and it was the most at peace I had ever seen the man, like whatever demon resided inside him was kept at bay simply by his woman's touch.

Thirteen gave me a gentle squeeze and I looked down at him and smiled.

"I love you, Baby Girl."

"I love you, too."

Safe. Loved. Family.

Never in a million years did I dream I would live to see the day, but I had, and it was here, and I vowed to be a smart girl and seize it. I kissed Thirteen under the bright, Florida summer sky and felt a little less damaged, a little more together, and with a whole bright future in front of me.

EPILOGUE

C utter...

"You doin' all right, Captain?"

I blinked and looked up from where I'd been staring off into space, my gaze drifting downwards to Hannah Hossler, crouched at my feet, her hands pressed to my knee. I smoothed fingers through her long blonde hair, an affectionate touch, and pursed my lips. She gave a sigh that was somewhere in between exasperated and pained.

"I can't believe her. You carry her ass for six fucking months, then he shows up and she's right back to him like you never existed."

"Hossler..." I growled, warning in my voice.

"No, it was a bitch thing to –' The crack of my hand silenced her quick. The back of my hand stung. She brought her head back around and glared up at me.

"I warned you." I told her, and gave her a pointed look. She lightly tongued the spot of blood forming at the corner of her mouth and nodded.

"That you did. Doesn't stop you from being a real son of a bitch." She pushed herself to her feet and stalked out of the back room of my bar and out to the front.

"Don'tcha think that was a bit harsh, Cap'?" I looked over at my best buddy and Road Captain of my club. Pyro put up his hands and leaned back in his chair, cocking one knee out further to give his bitch some more room to work his cock. "Just sayin', Hoss is worried about you. Hell, we all are. You ain't been the same since Li'l Bit left town with her man. Shit, we all knew you had it bad for her since the minute you laid eyes on her..."

"It doesn't matter." I grated, and it was true. It didn't. I liked Reave. Bonded with him pretty fast and pretty fierce, he was just that kind of a guy. He'd asked me to take care of his woman. I knew he was alive but I couldn't tell her and it killed a part of me watching her spiral down, diminishing more and more each day with her grief. I had promised Reaver I would take care of her and I did. I just hadn't counted on falling in love with her myself in the process. I didn't envy them their pain, but I sure as fuck couldn't keep myself from envying their happiness.

I stared out the porthole set in the wall and took another pull off my beer. I was brooding and I knew it but fuck all... I missed her and I was probably going to keep missing her until a suitable distraction came through the front door. Which was likely to happen about, oh, the time it started fucking snowing outside.

"You're a cruel son of a bitch, you know that?" I muttered at God, Fate, the Universe or whatever the fuck it was.

I sat on my throne in my tiny little castle in my kingdom by the sea, and wallowed in the deep, tearing ache of my loneliness.

"Man, you should've fucked her rather than hit her. Now the bitch is going to put a snake in your underwear drawer."

I scoffed, "Might just fuck her yet, now shut up and get your dick sucked."

"Aye, aye, Captain." Pyro saluted me with his drink and settled into a more comfortable position. The bar was closed to the public so there was no concern there. I sighed and returned to my brooding and staring off into space... haunted by a pair of emerald-green eyes and the loss of a woman who was never mine to begin with.

ALSO BY A.J. DOWNEY

2. His Cold Blue Command

3. A Low Blue Flame

4. His Wild Blue Rose

Paranormal Romance (with Ryan Kells)

1. I Am The Alpha

2. Omega's Run

3. Hunter's End

ABOUT THE AUTHOR

A.J. Downey is the internationally bestselling author of The Sacred Hearts Motorcycle Club romance series. She is a born and raised Seattle, WA Native. She finds inspiration from her surroundings, through the people she meets, and likely as a byproduct of way too much caffeine.

She has lived many places and done many things, though mostly through her own imagination...An avid reader all of her life, it's now her turn to try and give back a little, entertaining as she has been entertained.

Stalker Information:
www.ajdowney.com